GWTHIO FE DDAW

# The

# *Archivist*

## of Duntisbourne Hall

✌

www.fast-print.net/store.php

## The Archivist

ISBN: 978-178035-381-4

First published 2012 by
Fast-Print Publishing
Peterborough
England

*To Chris*

# - 1 -

BS Moreton was feeling rattled. He had planned to spend the morning in the office in case Radio Shropshire rang. He had floated a programme idea past a researcher there a few days ago and was hoping she would get back to him. Twenty minutes after he had settled down at his desk, however, Rosemary brought a memo up from the estate office. On first reading he had puffed at it and dropped it on to the top of his hot file, but after a few moments' thought, he retrieved it and read it again with a rising sense of irritation.

> *To: BS Moreton, Archivist to the Earl of Duntisbourne*
> *From: Simon Keane, Chief Executive*
> *Re: The Dywenydd Collection*
> *In order to incentivise the forward planning for the new season, Sam Westbrook from Interpretative Exhibition Design has been appointed Exhibition Manager. The trustees are confident a new exhibition will drive footfall to the Hall, but recognise that in order not to wrongside the demographic, professional expertise is essential. Please ensure this information is cascaded down to all concerned.*

'Oh, blow!' BS said as he flung the memo aside.

An exhibition of the Dywenydd Collection? It was an absurd idea and one which he had successfully stalled for five years, ever since Keane, that land agent from Chatsworth, had arrived. BS was the archivist here at Duntisbourne; if anyone was going to create an exhibition it was him, but he had good reasons for not wanting the spotlight to fall on this particular collection. For scholars it was fascinating, but the general public wouldn't see it that way. Would they be interested in the craftsmen who created the objects, the historical figures who had used and enjoyed them? Of course not. They would come in their tittering hordes because the collection dealt with the erotic, which was why it had been locked away upstairs from public view in 1838, and in the opinion of BS Moreton, that was exactly where it should stay.

He creaked back into his chair and stared out of the window across the empty courtyard. He would much prefer to spend the morning waiting for Susie from Radio Shropshire to call because she had an attractive voice when he spoke to her on the phone, and he was hoping to fix a date to meet her in person. He sighed heavily. Perhaps he was going to have to face the inevitable, that Westbrook would arrive and the exhibition would go ahead, but he wasn't going to make it easy for him.

'Blow me down to the ruddy ground,' he muttered and reluctantly began to pack the memo and a few essentials into his rucksack before setting off through the empty Hall to make his way upstairs. The archivist was feeling his age. His knee was aching, and he had that old hot pulse deep in the left-hand side of his lower back.

During the winter, Duntisbourne Hall was run by a skeleton staff of cleaners and conservationists, but today BS met no one. He made his way along the minstrels' gallery to a small oak door studded in metal and pierced with woodworm. Struggling with the keys at his hip, he chose one and unlocked the door. Opening it towards him, he stood at the foot of a spiral staircase to get his breath before starting the steep ascent. The stone of the treads was buffed and dipped in the centre from centuries of traffic, each step only large enough to take his feet if he tucked them sideways into the outer edge. He supported himself on the central column with one hand, and navigated with his stick on the outer.

He was a tall man, heavily built, and could only proceed if he stooped. As the years passed he found the staircase increasingly claustrophobic, and this morning in particular he felt as if he was trapped in a tube of stone, a drop spinning away behind him, the ceiling inches from his head. He could never remember how many turns he had to make and today it seemed as if he would never reach the top. Eventually he stretched up his hand and heard the rattle of a brass doorknob in the darkness. He turned it and entered the room known as the sealed chamber even though the seal had been broken eighteen years earlier by his own hand on the instructions of the earl.

As the central light flicked on, the first thing to greet him was a portrait of a fleshy-faced man dressed in a sable cloak with three rows of black ermine tails on the collar. The sitter was corpulent, and his stomach protruded from beneath the brocade waistcoat, bulging over spindly legs clad in royal blue velvet pantaloons. His mottled face looked out from under the powdered wig with an expression of fat-lipped lechery. BS didn't imagine the ninth earl had been particularly pleased with this portrait, but considering the 'wicked earl' had been a philanderer, a pornographer, an opium addict and a heavy drinker, it may have been the best Thomas Lawrence could do. The painting had been hung as a temporary measure on a row of stout Victorian coat hooks which ran along the left-hand wall because BS had been worried that he might put a foot through the canvas if it remained at floor level. That had been sixteen years ago.

The room was dusty, but not damp. Situated above the great hall and underneath the rafters, any residual heat from below rose to keep the sealed chamber a few degrees warmer than the rest of the

Hall. It still smelt of bats, a scent that BS liked because it reminded him of the den he had created as a child in the roof space of the miner's cottage where he grew up. He was sad when he realised the colony had left the Hall at some time during the nineties when essential repairs to the guttering on the north side were undertaken.

The collection in the sealed chamber was in disarray, but it was housed in the mahogany furniture which had been installed in Victorian times by the tenth earl. The walls on either side were fitted with deep drawers below and shelves above. Artefacts that were too large for the drawers had been boxed and put on the shelves, and those too large for either stood behind a screen which stretched across the left-hand corner of the room. To the right of the screen was a plain desk, chair and lamp, provided more recently so that scholars had somewhere to work when examining the collection. They were not allowed to take anything from the room, and had to be supervised. BS had spent many days alternately reading and snoozing on a threadbare chaise longue in the other corner while a visitor studied.

BS Moreton was a man of habit, and before he began his task he liked to arrange his desk. He burrowed into his rucksack and found his foolscap notepad ruled in blue with the crest of the Earl of Duntisbourne at the top. Many years ago one of the shop managers had put in an order for these and added one zero too many, so instead of two hundred they had received two thousand, shortly before the foolscap size was replaced universally with A4. Although BS could never find a ring binder that fitted the pages, he felt more at home with foolscap paper. He didn't like the squat A4 size – it was too modern for his taste.

When he was working he followed the tradition of the British

Library, always using pencils in case he accidentally marked one of the books. He bent to pull the waste bin towards him and began to sharpen half a dozen HBs using an ancient but efficient pencil sharpener. As he completed and inspected each pencil, he laid it down next to its companion. Finally he retrieved from the rucksack his large, green artist's rubber, the smell of which always transported him back to his schoolroom days.

Thus organised, it was time for his coffee. This was brewed for him each morning by his wife, who warmed the thermos with boiling water before filling it. BS had been told by his doctor that he should cut down on the caffeine, but he couldn't see the point. If he was slowing up a bit, surely the best thing for him was a belt of strong coffee every few hours. Besides, he didn't take a lot of notice of medical advice because it was always changing. Take alcohol consumption, for example. After years of feeling guilty that he had a drink every night, lo and behold it turns out you live longer if you have a drink every night. In another few years the doctors would be telling him that he should make sure he had at least four cups of strong coffee a day because there was good evidence that people who drank strong coffee lived seven years longer than people who drank green tea, or some such nonsense.

'Decaffeinated, darling?' his wife would ask each morning as she reached for the ground coffee.

'No, Patricia my love, give me a belter,' BS replied. Decaffeinated could wait until the weather improved.

Warmed by his coffee, BS reached into his rucksack and drew out the memo. As he reread it, the fury he had felt earlier that morning returned. Why this man was unable to use plain English baffled and exasperated him in equal proportion. When did visitors become foot fall? He laid the memo down on the desk and shook his head at it. Keane was unable to write or even speak without resorting to business jargon and often, instead of making a point clearer, it rendered the meaning impenetrable. For example, the first time BS heard the CEO talking about pushing the envelope, he thought it was a euphemism for something smutty. The recollection brought a smile to his face and lightened his mood, galvanising him into action.

He made his way over to a shelf of books which ran along the back wall. Somewhere in here, hidden in plain view, was an inventory of the Dywenydd Collection and he wanted to go through it before Westbrook arrived. He ran his fingers along the spines and eventually drew it out. There was no blocking on the spine to tell the casual observer the contents of the book, but to BS each spine was as distinctive as the features on a person's face, and although he could never recognise an actor when they played a different role on television, he had an uncanny ability to pick a book out of a shelf of hundreds of volumes.

He needed both hands to lift the tome down. It was heavy and the leather binding had softened from use into a texture which was more like suede, stained with age to the colour of dark tobacco. BS carried the volume across to the desk and opened it. The spine creaked and popped and a rich smell of age rose up from the pages, the mustiness sweetened by a trace of vanilla like a corked wine. The ledger had been filled out by a number of different hands over the centuries, but during the last couple of decades BS was confident the only eyes to read the material had been his and he doubted anyone else now living had read the words in this volume.

BS had several reasons for keeping the book to himself. It not only itemised the erotic accoutrements but specified their uses, and it was this aspect of the tome that BS wished to conceal. He was a devout Catholic and believed that holy purity was impossible to obtain if the act of human union was not accompanied by love – the love between a man and his wife. Throughout his life he had maintained his own guard against impurity but he knew that when people faced temptation, it was often hard to resist. When scholars came to study items in the collection he trusted their motives were erudite, but he suspected that if they were able to read the vivid descriptions of these objects in use, it might put evil thoughts into their minds, and he did not want the responsibility of corrupting another man's soul. The knowledge could lead them away from the historical importance of the object and encourage them to lose interest in the craftsmanship involved. He preferred to speculate with them through discussion as to the use of the items, which had the added advantage of allowing him to appear to have an uncanny breadth of learning and deduction.

He sat down in front of the book and began to turn the pages. He should decide now which pieces were suitable for an exhibition and could be handed over to Westbrook when he arrived, and which were not. Pulling his notepad towards him, he began his task. He drew a line down the centre to create two column; the left-hand one he entitled 'Exhibition' and the right-hand one 'Muniments Room'. He would repack any particularly salacious pieces and ferry them downstairs to the undercroft while the exhibition was being created, leaving no one any the wiser.

He made a note of the Thomas Lawrence painting of the ninth earl in the left-hand margin and looked around deciding what to do next. Should he start opening cases, pulling out artefacts and making notes? Or should he work systematically through the inventory locating each item in the correct order? He couldn't decide, so he dragged the library steps over to the first shelf, climbed up to the fourth step, and lifted a dust sheet covering a group of boxes to see if anyone had written the contents on the outside. No one had.

'Well,' he said, 'let's start with you,' and he flipped the dust sheet aside and with care brought the box down from the shelf. He placed it on the floor by the desk and scraped away at the string with his penknife. Opening it, he reached in and worked his fingers through the sawdust. It reminded him of searching the bran tub as a child, trying to identify a wrapped toy before committing to drawing it out and claiming it. His fingers felt the edge of a plate which he drew up and into the light.

To the ignorant eye it would have looked like an exquisite antique dish, but BS immediately recognised the work of Fabergé, the great Russian jeweller, and knew that this was the pudenda display tray of Peter the Great who was said to have had a particularly fine set of pudenda. He brushed the sawdust away with the cuff of his shirt and placed the tray next to the open inventory. His memory had not let him down – the description confirmed that it was one of the Russian trays. It didn't take him long to locate the next item on the inventory, a glass tray with a raised coloured pattern thought to have belonged to Catherine the Great because of its different shape. He sat back in his chair and pondered the pieces before noting them down in the left-hand column. Without an accurate description of their use, these fine pieces could certainly grace the exhibition.

According to the inventory, there were at least two more display trays somewhere in the collection, but the next item that BS drew out of the sawdust looked more like two cream jugs fused together but without handles or spouts. Although heavily tarnished, he could see the object was made of solid silver and must have weighed a good six pounds. Moving across the room so that he was standing under the central light he turned it over in his hands until he found the hallmark. He was right, RG – Robert Garrard of London, beginning of the eighteenth century. And on the bulbous base, he could make out the earl's coat of arms with the motto, *Dywenydd o Flaen Anrhydedd*, Pleasure Before Honour, which had been adopted by the wicked earl to obfuscate the contents of the erotic collection and swiftly changed back to *Gwthio fe ddaw* by his bookish son, the tenth earl, after his death. BS chuckled to himself. It was difficult to translate this original motto without it sounding salacious. The College of Arms maintained the closest Welsh translation was Push, It Will Come, but he intended to devote time at some point researching this original family motto and arriving at a more worthy interpretation. Placing the silver item on the desk, BS ran a finger down the inventory until he located the silver testicle cooler, noting it in the left-hand column. It was a lovely piece of craftsmanship, and without the description it could indeed be a type of jug. There was nothing in the design to suggest it was used to chill the testicles before sex in order to increase the chances of conception.

As the morning wore on, BS relaxed into his task. When he first took up his post he had looked through most of the boxes of artefacts, but that was many years ago. He had revisited some of his favourites periodically over the years, and every time he did, he was struck anew by the beauty of many of them.

He congratulated himself on the number of items he had approved for the exhibition. He was keeping an open mind about the situation. However, he continued to feel troubled by the thought of prurient eyes peering at them. During his days as headmaster at the Cathedral School he had taken a group of classics scholars to Italy, and had been appalled at their behaviour when they visited the Gabinetto Segreto in the Naples museum. These bright, intelligent creatures had dissolved into snorting idiots when confronted by ancient interpretations of the act of love. BS feared that the modern holidaymaker would be unable to separate eroticism from pornography.

Judged on tummy-time, BS felt the morning was nearing an end. He had achieved a fair amount, and was working his way through the contents of one of the drawers which had several objects in it that were proving difficult to find on the inventory. He could remember some of the tasks performed by groups of items: the silver scissors, for example, the blades of which formed the shape of a pair of women's legs, went with the sharpened silver straw used to inflate the testicles after nicking a small hole in the scrotum. The resulting orgasm, the ledger explained, was a great deal stronger. He identified the foreskin crimpers and a set of scrimshaw stiffeners, but he could not fathom an object the size of a large walnut which was evidently made of gold. Taking a watchmaker's eyeglass from the drawer of the desk, he squeezed it out of its velvet pouch and wedged it under his brow, bending low over the desk to bring the object into the pool of light thrown by the lamp. The work was intricate in the extreme, the design oriental – he could make out the snarling mouth of a Chinese dragon. As he ran his fingers over it, it sprang open into two halves, and immediately BS guessed what it was – a glans helmet to enlarge the head of the penis, the clever spring holding it in place however active the wearer became.

'What a beautiful object,' a voice behind him said, and swinging round BS found himself looking into the eyes of a handsome woman who stood a few paces behind him. Beyond her the door into the sealed chamber was open. Smiling, she held out her hand, palm up, and added, 'May I see?'

BS clapped the helmet shut and hid it behind his back. 'I'm sorry, my dear. You really shouldn't be up here. This part of the Hall is off-limits, particularly for women.'

She lowered her hand and smiled at him, but there was something in her eyes that made him think she could be mocking him. To his shame, he felt a glow of heat rising up his neck.

'Oh, Mr Moreton, this part of the Hall is very much on-limits for me,' and she raised her hand again, this time to introduce herself. 'Sam Westbrook, from Interpretative Exhibition Design. They told me I would find you up here. I'm glad to see you've already made a start.'

## - 2 -

The previous night had been a filthy one for driving and Sam Westbrook had left London later than she intended, which meant she hit the rush hour. The rain began as she was inching her way around the North Circular, and by the time she broke free of solid traffic and hit the M1 it was dark and the rain was coming down in stair rods. She had calculated the journey would take her about three and a half hours, but after four she had only reached the outskirts of Birmingham and was navigating her way with difficulty through and out on to the M6. Lorries rose up ahead of her like wraiths, a pall of mist billowing across from their wheels. At Wolverhampton she pulled off at the motorway services to fill up, went inside for a coffee and a sandwich, and rang the number she had been given for a Mr Pugh who was meeting her at Duntisbourne Hall to show her the flat.

'Where are you now?' he asked.

'I'm near Wolverhampton.'

'Oh dear,' he said, and she heard him sigh before continuing, 'well, you've broken the back of it. It's less than an hour from there, I would say.' There was a pause.

'Can you leave a key for me?' she asked.

'You'll never find it on your own. No, stick to the original plan. Come to Dolley Green Gate. I'll wait up, and I can take you over and let you in. Don't worry, I never turn in much before midnight.'

'I hope I'll be there before then.'

His laugh had the crackle of a heavy smoker. 'I'm sure you will. Drive safely. Remember, it's better to be a bit late in this world than too early in the next.' Nice man, Sam thought as she gathered up the box with the half-eaten egg sandwich and headed back out into the rain.

She did make it before midnight, but not by very much because she got lost in the town and had to stop at an all-night garage to ask directions to the Hall. The girl behind the glass looked astonished that she didn't know. Eventually her headlights panned across a gateway. Pugh must have been looking out for her because without her having to get out of her car, he appeared in a lighted doorway. She saw him pulling on a coat and patting the head of an overweight Labrador as if apologising to the dog that a walk was not in the offing. Then he came down the path of the gatehouse, hunched against the rain, raised a hand to beckon to her to follow, and climbed into a four-by-four which was parked on the verge.

He drove slowly in front of her. It was so dark she could only see his red tail-lights ahead, her own lights picking up nothing on either side, until the car in front slowed and his headlights illuminated a deep stone archway into which they both drove. He stopped and got out of his car. She rolled down her window.

'Mrs Westbrook? I'm Pugh. Nice to meet you. Shame it's such a filthy evening. Why not leave your car here for tonight? Save getting wet when you unload,' he said.

'How will you get out?' She seemed to be blocking him in.

'I can get out in front of you. The road goes round and back through the park. But you'll have to move it in the morning when you've unpacked. You can put it in the staff car park – it's just through there.' He pointed up ahead and into the blackness.

She had just stepped out of the car, her footsteps echoing in the cavern of stone, when the scream of a human voice on the very edge of hysteria exploded out of the air a few yards from the tunnel making her shoot her hand out and grab hold of Pugh's arm, shaking the torch beam vigorously up and down.

'Who the hell ...?' Sam breathed.

Pugh patted her hand and chuckled. 'Foxes, my dear. Just old Mr Fox. There's a den out there, down through the woods this side of the lake. Not a country girl then?'

'Absolutely not.'

There was another screech, this time further away, and Sam tightened her grip on Pugh's arm. 'That's another one, or else we frightened him off and he's on his way home. Don't worry, he won't hurt you. Come on, better get you upstairs and inside.'

Reluctantly releasing the waxed sleeve, she followed Pugh into a recess which she had not seen even though her car was parked next to it. He clicked a switch up and down a few times and cursed, then shone the torch beam up a flight of stone steps. 'We're up here,' he said. 'I'll have a word with Maintenance and try and get that light fixed. Do you have a torch?'

'A torch? No.'

'Oh dear. You'll need one. I'll leave you with mine for tonight.'

He took a couple of steps up and Sam went to follow him, but he turned back to her and said, 'On second thoughts, let me take some of your luggage up. Seems daft to make a wasted journey.'

Carrying as much as they could manage, they began to ascend, Sam treading carefully. The steps were damp and green with moss near the wall and she thought they might be slippery. At the landing Pugh shone his light up another flight and they continued to the top. Eventually they reached a door which he opened and they entered the flat.

'At least you're all right for power up here,' he said, flicking on the switch. The room was large and cold. 'We laid the fire,' he

pointed over to an open grate, 'but there's probably no point lighting it this late. It takes a bit of time to warm the room, and I expect
you'll be turning in soon.'

'I expect so,' Sam said.

Pugh carried her suitcase through a large opening to the right
and put it on a blanket chest at the foot of a double bed. 'This is
the bedroom,' he said, 'as you may have guessed. Housekeeping
should have put a hot-water bottle in for you,' and he plunged his
hand under the sheets and felt around. 'Yes, it's there. Not piping
hot, but it will have taken a bit of damp out of the bed. Awful
thing, damp. You should never get into a damp bed – leads to all
sorts of problems. Through here,' he opened the door on the left
of the bed but didn't go in, 'is the bathroom. And over here,' he
came back past Sam and walked across the sitting room to another
door and pointed, 'is the kitchen. I asked Housekeeping to put a
few essentials in there for you – milk, tea bags, that sort of thing.
Let's close these for you,' and he drew a set of curtains across a
large arched window that looked out into darkness. 'You get a
lovely view from this room in the daytime. I'll put your keys on
the dining table here, which you can use as a desk, I expect. And
...' He cast his eyes around and finished, 'I think that's about it. So,
how long are you here for?'

'Just a few weeks, I expect – maybe a month.'

'Here to give Mr Moreton a hand?'

Sam smiled. 'Yes, I suppose that's one way of looking at it. Anyway, I mustn't keep you. It's late and ...' she opened her bag to find
a tip, '... thank you so much for all your help.'

'Don't bother about that,' he said, raising a hand. 'We're not
a hotel.' He paused for a moment before adding, 'I'd better get
going then. Keep the torch. See you around tomorrow, I expect.'

'Thank you so much,' she said again as she closed the door behind him. She heard his first few footsteps recede down the stone steps – he was treading cautiously in the dark.

Sam went into the bedroom to close the curtains, but before she did she looked out of the window. As she watched, a fast-moving light appeared out in the dark and she guessed this was Pugh on his way back to the gatehouse. She drew the curtains. The fabric was heavy and ornate, the lining had yellowed and perished from years of sunlight. Turning back into the room she opened her case and began to unpack. There was a linen press against one wall and when she looked inside, she saw that the upper part had been converted into hanging space with an eclectic assortment of coat hangers pushed to one end of the rail. The drawers beneath were stiff, and the linen press rocked as she struggled to open them. She proceeded with more care, watching all the time to make sure it wasn't starting to topple over.

Next she went through to the kitchen. The strip light buzzed for a moment, then flashed a few times before filling the room with unforgiving brilliance. It reminded her of the kitchen in her parents' house when she was a child – red formica worktops, a huge fridge from the fifties, so ancient the style was making a comeback. The handle was large enough for a commercial meat safe and had a keyhole in the side to lock the food away from the staff. She opened the door and its cooling system came on with a shudder and a purr. There was no milk in there. She took the tops off a couple of storage jars near the electric kettle. She found a ginger biscuit in the base of one, soft with age; the other jar smelt of coffee but was empty. There were no tea bags.

She went back into the sitting room and stared at the fireplace, suddenly feeling profoundly lonely. Balls of newspaper lay scrunched up at the bottom of the grate, a handful of kindling and a few lumps of coal piled on top. She toyed with the idea of lighting the fire to bring a bit of cheer to the room, but at that moment her stomach let out a long extended grumble of hunger and she realised she was ravenous. With a feeling of despair, she sank down on the sofa. It was covered with a fringed shawl, and she knew that if she looked underneath, it would be hiding sprouts of horsehair and stains. She thought about giving Claire a ring; it would be seven in the morning in New York, but when she looked at her phone, there was no signal.

She wished she was in her flat in Chelsea. She had had a few lonely times there too, but she was always comfortable. She had bought it ten years earlier when the family home was sold after the divorce. The first night she slept there, an extraordinary thought struck her: it was the only time in her life she had lived entirely on her own – after she left home she had shared flats with girlfriends, then she had married, and when her husband left she had her daughter for company. Claire eventually left too and she was surprised to find solitude brought with it a sense of peace. She decorated her flat the way she pleased and filled it with the things she loved. She had compromised all her life, first for her parents, then her husband, then her child. This was the first time she had enjoyed true independence and freedom.

A year later Claire moved back in. It was only going to be a temporary arrangement, and they enjoyed one another's company, but as the months passed and Claire's applications for work in the States failed one after the other, Sam began to wish she had her space back to herself. She couldn't stop that old sense of maternal duty from splicing right back into place. She began to feel guilty if she wanted to stay on late at the museum; if she arranged a trip to the theatre with a friend, she felt she should ask Claire along. Within a few weeks she was picking up after Claire again, washing Claire's clothes again, cooking Claire's meals again, pulling a twenty-pound note out of her wallet and saying, 'Take a taxi. On me.' It wasn't Claire's fault, she knew that, but what daughter would fight against behaviour that was comforting and familiar? Her role of confidante and counsellor clicked right back into place too, and she paused her favourite television programmes whenever Claire wanted to dissect and reconstruct her husband's motives for staying out in the States. She comforted her daughter: Jake had more opportunities in New York. But he can get work back here, Claire would counter. Not for the money they offer him on Broadway. Jake was a dancer. At first Sam had assumed he was a gay friend – that Claire was his beard, his cover, his hold on a conventional life, but Claire married him. A lavender marriage? Of course not, Claire responded, angrily. They had a great sex life ... and Sam had called a truce. She believed her. All Claire needed was the right job in a law firm in New York and everything would be fine.

Eventually everything was fine. Claire found the right job and left for the States. Sam came home the evening she had gone and walked from room to room like a dog looking for a lost pup. She found a T-shirt under the bed which smelt of her daughter, and suddenly missed her with such an ache she fantasised about selling the flat in Chelsea and buying a run-down farm house where Claire and Jake and the children that were yet to come would live. She would have a barn converted just across the way where they couldn't see one another's front door, but would be close. New York seemed a long way away. Although Sam missed her daughter, she had her flat back. She ran the washing machine once a week again, washed the dishes by hand and watched what she wanted to on television in the evening, padding into the kitchen when she felt like it to fix herself a sandwich.

Sandwich ... She had forgotten the half-eaten sandwich in the glove compartment of her car. Springing up and snatching the keys from the table, she opened the door and staggered back. Beyond the small pool of light thrown out from the room there was a wall of darkness so deep it was as if someone had flopped a blackout curtain of thick velvet around the stairwell. For a moment her resolve weakened and she wondered if she could make do with the flaccid ginger biscuit, but she remembered Pugh's torch, and taking it from the table, she propped the door open to guide her back and stepped out into the darkness.

The descent of the first flight of stairs wasn't too bad. Her eyes began to adapt to the dark and the light from the open door above penetrated the gloom further now that she was surrounded by blackness, but when she turned and looked down the next flight, Pugh's torch wasn't strong enough to light it right to the bottom. She was amazed at the dark. She had never lived in an environment without artificial lighting before, and felt foolish at her own astonishment. She had never thought of herself as frightened of the dark, but now she teetered on the edge of the abyss with her heart in her mouth.

'Get a grip,' she said aloud. Her voice in this deathly quiet vitalised her, and she hurried down the steps, her heels echoing on the stone, and pressed the key fob. The car tweeted and turned on its internal light, and she dived into the passenger seat, scrabbled around in the glove compartment for the boxed sandwich, slammed the door and locked it, and was halfway up the stairs again when the car turned off its internal light and she paused, distracted for a split-second by the return of darkness at the foot of the stairs. The fox screamed out across the estate, a quavering start, a rising crescendo and again that edge of hysteria as if provoked by profound fear like a prisoner at the moment he realises his determination not to talk has been broken.

Sam fled up the stairs, rounded the landing and pounded up the second flight and through the door, slamming it shut and locking it with shaking fingers. She looked down at the sandwich in the box, the crusts curled, the yolk darkened and solidified, and flinging it on to the table with her keys she went through to the bedroom.

# - 3 -

'Well, Mr Black,' the consultant said looking down at the notes, 'there's really very little more we can do for you.'

'You mean I'm going to die?'

Dr Usher raised his eyes above the rim of his spectacles and frowned at Max. 'Of course I don't mean that.' He rapped the notes with his knuckles and went on. 'But you are already on every drug we can find to lower your blood pressure, and unless you make some dramatic changes to your lifestyle, you won't be making old bones.'

Max didn't warm to Dr Usher. When he had started to feel ill the previous autumn, he was seen by a younger doctor whom he much preferred.

'Retired stockbroker, eh?' he had said. 'Got any hot tips?'

'Never put your money in the stock market,' Max had replied.

The young doctor laughed heartily, but his smile began to fade as the cuff around Max's biceps slackened and he read the dial. He pumped the cuff again, and a third time, then went to fetch Dr Usher. The consultant had peered over the top of his spectacles and watched the readings twice before turning to the young registrar and saying, 'This man must not leave the hospital.'

Now, whenever Dr Usher peered over his spectacles, Max felt control slipping away from underneath him as if he was about to lose the contents of his lower bowel. In his mind, Dr Usher had taken on the appearance of the grim reaper, the tattered black cape now a crisp white coat, the scythe replaced by a scalpel, the hour-glass by a blood-pressure monitor. The night he checked out of hospital and arrived home with a carrier bag of drugs, Max knew with certainty that he would come and get him. It was too late to collect Monty from the neighbour, the house was empty and cold, and Max sat bolt upright in a chair in the sitting room, staring into blackness. His hands felt as if tiny spaceships were buzzing around just under the surface of his skin, and he could see his own blood rushing in streams before his eyes. He wanted to get out of the chair and ring his daughter in Bristol to make sure she knew that he loved her before he died, but he was paralysed with fear.

After about an hour he got bored waiting to die and went and traded online instead, which calmed him.

Max gawped across the table at Dr Usher. 'Make dramatic changes? Whatever can you mean?'

'I want you to see the nutritionist again. We have discussed the detrimental effect of salt, but these results make me suspect that you haven't cut down on your salt intake at all.'

'I love salt.'

The consultant glared at Max before returning to the notes. 'And, as I tell you every single time I see you, you have got to give up smoking.'

'I've cut down,' Max lied. The pale eyes flicked up again.

'And get yourself a job.'

'It was the job that put me here in the first place.'

'I doubt it.'

'The marriage then.'

'You need structure back in your life, a routine.'

'At fifty-four?'

Dr Usher dropped the notes on to the desk with a thump which made Max start. 'It's up to you,' he said. 'I haven't prescribed all these drugs so that you can continue with a lifestyle that put you in hospital in the first place. We have caught you just in time, you have a second chance, but if you decide to carry on exactly the way you have been, you'll be on dialysis within the next couple of years. Do I make myself clear?'

'Crystal,' Max replied.

Up until last autumn, Max had enjoyed excellent health. He smoked sixty cigarettes a day and never got a cough, he ate junk food and never put on weight, and he swallowed two packets of painkillers a day to stop himself getting headaches. Looking back now, he wasn't sure why he took so many painkillers. It had started when he was still married, and he ascribed his headaches to the constant stress of having Sadie as a wife. She went off him the day after the wedding, or that was the way he remembered it, and it was only because of Charlotte that he stuck it out for ten dreadful years. Eventually he surprised his wife by giving her what she had been asking for for ten years – a divorce, and within a few months of sharing custody of Charlotte, the little girl said she wanted to live with her dad because her mum was always out. That was the year he effectively took early retirement, selling his share of Black and Hamilton to his partner Malcolm for a sum sufficiently large that he didn't need to top it up for several years – at which point he was able to make an income with a bit of online trading. It meant he was at home for Charlotte most of the time, a place he loved to be now that his wife had gone.

He began to feel ill shortly after Charlotte left for university. It coincided with him reading the information sheet that came with the painkillers and seeing that one of the side effects was headaches, so he stopped taking them that night. Then he started to feel ill, then he lost his appetite, then he started throwing up in the evenings, and sometimes in the mornings too. He told all this to Dr Usher, suggesting to the consultant that all his problems stemmed from giving up the painkillers, but he also mentioned that his daughter had recently left to go to university, that he finally had the house to himself, but felt rudderless. Dr Usher insisted he see a counsellor after he was discharged from hospital, and this irritating woman had some crazy notion that Charlotte leaving home had triggered his illness.

'Women do not find the empty nest syndrome easy,' she had said.

'I'm not a woman,' Max had pointed out.

'I was merely making the point that it is not an unusual reaction – particularly as you have had sole responsibility for your daughter for many years – to feel a crippling sense of loss now that she has left, even panic at the thought of being on your own again, without the company or need to care for someone else.'

Max wanted the session to end, so didn't give her the satisfaction of telling her that she was right, that he was panicking, that he woke up each morning with a sense of impending catastrophe hanging over him. For the first time in his life he experienced a horrible feeling that he wasn't going to get out of this alive. Like Woody Allen, he wasn't afraid of death, he just didn't want to be there when it happened, and the experience of handing control over to a band of white-coated doctors and well-meaning nurses was terrifying. If there was something really wrong with him he didn't want to know, but everywhere he looked he found portents of doom. He stopped buying a daily paper because every article seemed to be about 'High Blood Pressure – the Silent Killer' or 'Heavy Smokers More Likely to Die of Bladder Cancer than Lung Cancer' or 'Living Alone Shortens Life by Ten Years'.

One evening early in March, a few weeks after his appointment with Dr Usher, Max was outside the Chinese takeaway having a cigarette while he waited for his order. Monty was sniffing the dirt at the base of the outside step before raising his leg and peeing on it, and as he watched the dog Max thought, Monty never worries about the answer to the ultimate question of life, the universe and everything. He never lies awake in his basket wondering if the ache in his side is sinister. Max was not a religious man, but a thought struck him. Was that what had happened in the Garden of Eden? The fruit from the tree of knowledge was a bad idea because it gave humans insight? Monty had immortality, at least as far as he was concerned. At some point in his later years he might think to himself, I feel really rotten, but the moment he slipped off the plate, he wouldn't be able to think any more, so he wouldn't know he had died. Max however ... and then he spotted a poster held in place against the window with soiled blu-tack, advertising the start of the new season at Duntisbourne Hall.

Max was fond of Duntisbourne Hall. Before he went to boarding school in Hampshire he had spent many happy summers exploring the estate and fishing on the lake with his friend Roger Everett, and the thought of those carefree summers blew away his morbid thoughts. He should go back and have a look around the estate again. It was only fifteen minutes up the road from his house, but since his return to the area, he hadn't driven in through the gates once in nearly fifteen years. He didn't imagine much would have changed.

'I should take you for a walk there, Monty,' he said. 'That would be a change in lifestyle for us.'

Monty looked up at him and tilted his head to one side, certain he had caught the word 'walk'. Max bent down and rubbed the little dog's rough coat, and from this new lower level, he spotted a line at the bottom of the poster: 'Staff wanted for the start of the new season. Vacancies in all aspects of Visitor Services at Duntisbourne Hall.' Max was particularly encouraged to see the words 'No previous experience required.'

# - 4 -

BS Moreton raised his eyebrows and released the watchmaker's eyeglass which he had pressed into his eye socket minutes before. It fell to the floor with a click and rolled a few inches before coming to rest against his shoe. This provided him with the diversion he needed, and after bending down to pick it up, he turned his back to Sam and took the opportunity of closing the inventory on the desk and pulling the notepad over the top of it before dropping the gold glans helmet into the drawer along with the eyeglass. When he turned towards her again, he pressed the drawer shut with his buttock and leant back on the desk hoping to achieve a relaxed posture. He wanted her out of here – he needed her out of the sealed chamber, and he had no intention whatsoever of showing her any of the collection.

'My goodness me,' he said, 'you certainly gave me a turn. I wasn't expecting you today at all, in fact. I got the memo about you only this morning from the CEO.'

'Really? We had our final meeting with the trustees just after the New Year.'

A rich chuckle rose from deep in his frame and he looked towards her with an inclusive expression of exasperation. 'That's Duntisbourne for you,' he said. He pushed himself away from the edge of the desk and looked around for his stick. 'You know what,' he went on, 'I was about to set off and find myself a bit of bait. My wife has me on short commons at the moment,' patting his belly and nodding at her, 'and I would love an excuse to abandon that wrinkled apple and pot of cottage cheese she tucked into my rucksack this morning.'

'That does sound grim,' Sam said.

'And it's a cold, damp day outside. And the canteen isn't open at this time of year. What say you we take a trip into town for lunch? The Blue Acorn does a serviceable pie and mash, a different pie for each day of the week.'

Sam scanned the room and the shelves of boxes, then turned a brilliant smile on him. 'So what's Thursday's?' she said.

'Thursday's? Oh, I see.' BS puzzled for a moment then said, 'Beef and ale, I fancy.'

'Sounds terrific,' she replied and he followed her out of the door of the chamber, pausing to lock up again behind him as she made her way carefully back down the spiral staircase.

Once he had moved her away from the chamber, his spirits began to lift. He accepted Sam's offer to drive because he very much felt like having a glass of red wine with his meal, and he was doubly pleased with this decision when, as they walked across the gravel towards a sporty green Mazda soft-top, the back lights blinked a welcome to them as the central locking released.

'My!' BS said. 'This is very nice,' and he was rewarded with another glowing smile from Sam.

'Thank you,' she said. 'I gave up estate cars once my daughter left home. I know it may be a bit ludicrous at my age ...'

'Not at all,' BS said. 'What a shame the weather's so poor. It must be fun driving with the top down.' BS was well known in the village and liked the idea of being spotted in the passenger seat of a sporty green car driven by a blonde. Within a few moment, however, he had another reason to wish he was climbing into the car with the top down.

Sam had sprung into the driver's seat, pitched her handbag on to the shelf behind, and started the engine to give the windscreen a blow-over while BS organised himself. He posted his stick into the footwell first and, holding on to the edge of the roof for support, placed his right leg in the car, hopping on the other leg as he tried to find an equilibrium before folding himself in. Unfortunately, he wasn't flexible enough to bend his head below the level of the roof and almost lost his balance. With a great deal of huffing and puffing he repositioned himself for a different trajectory. He started to back towards the car, folding his body as far as he could as he pushed himself deeper in, clinging on to the edge of the door frame like grim death. He was concerned that he was presenting Sam with an unflattering view of his posterior when, with a final groan, he dropped precipitously on to the seat, knocking his head on the roof before manhandling his legs in, one after the other. Puffed and panting he smiled triumphantly over at Sam and said, 'My, this is smart. Oh blow, I can't quite reach far enough to close the ...' but Sam was out of her seat and round to his side to save him any more effort.

As they spun through the country lanes, BS glanced across at his companion. Her careful grooming and style of dress had fooled him into thinking she was a young woman, but glancing down at the hand that reached periodically for the gear lever and back to the steering wheel, he guessed that she was probably somewhere in her forties, although he was notoriously poor at guessing people's ages.

'So you have a daughter?' he said.

'Yes, she lives in New York now. She's a lawyer.'

'Goodness,' he said. 'You don't look old enough.'

Momentarily he wondered if he had produced this compliment a little early in their relationship, but Sam answered graciously,

'You're very kind.'

Buoyed by this success he said, 'I have to tell you something rather amusing.'

'What was that?'

'I assumed you were a man.'

'From the way I dress?' A wave of anxiety gripped BS. Had he offended her? He looked sharply across at her and was relieved to see she was teasing him.

'No, no,' he said. 'I read the memo from the CEO and imagined that Sam was a man's name. It never crossed my mind that you were going to be a Samantha.'

'Do you have a problem with that?'

'Not at all. In fact, it may surprise you to know that I have spent most of my working life in the company of women. That is, working with women. First of all when I was teaching in Manchester, and then here. No, I'm extremely comfortable in the company of women. Actually, if I'm completely honest, I prefer the company of women to the company of men.'

Once they had parked in the village, BS co-opted the help of a doughty passing tourist to extricate himself from the car and they made their way across the road to The Blue Acorn. BS liked The Blue Acorn. It had an old-world quality he admired and it smelt of woodsmoke and cooking, which reassured him that the food was home-made, not heated up in a microwave. It was good, honest food and there was plenty of it. He had been right about the day too – it was a beef and ale pie day, and he had a bowl of chips on the side which he dusted liberally with salt. This was a great deal better than an apple and cottage cheese for lunch. He resolved to compensate that evening by eating very little. Raising his glass of Shiraz to Sam, he took a sip.

'Yum,' he said. 'That certainly spanks the palate.' He scanned the pub, taking in the other diners. An elderly gentleman lunching with his wife had been appraising Sam but looked away when he caught BS's eye, and BS turned back to Sam feeling a swell of pride that he was lunching with an attractive companion and that it had been noticed.

'So, Sam Westbrook,' he said as they ate, 'what brings you out to our neck of the woods?'

'Probably the success of the Warren Cup exhibition at the British Museum,' she said.

'The Warren Cup eh? Fascinating piece of ...' He hesitated for a moment, then added 'heritage,' and as he rattled on about the artefacts found at Sutton Hoo (which was about all he could remember at the British Museum) he wondered what on earth the Warren Cup was, what it had to do with Duntisbourne Hall, and what Sam Westbrook had to do with the British Museum. He couldn't remember any mention of it in the memo from the CEO, and he worried that if he asked her to explain, it would show his ignorance and might suggest to her that he was out of touch or didn't have the ear of the trustees – which, of course, he didn't. He was the earl's man, and the earl distrusted the CEO. The earl disliked change every bit as much as BS.

'Did you see the exhibition at the British Museum?' Sam said.

'I haven't been up to London for a long time,' he replied, 'but I love the British Museum.'

Recognising that Sam was leading him away from a light lunchtime conversation and back on to the subject of that wretched memo, he used her earlier reference to having a daughter in New York to steer the conversation away by relating an amusing tale of the time he had to accompany a valuable tapestry all the way over to America for an exhibition at the Met and the hilarious stopover he had to make in Amsterdam much to the consternation of Patricia, his wife.

'Anyway,' Sam said, 'the Warren Cup exhibition turned out to be blockbuster of a success. I worked closely with Aled Lewis, and as the British Museum successfully explored attitudes to sexuality' – BS swallowed down heavily on his final chip – 'your trustees thought we could present the Dywenydd Collection from a similar point of view and show your artefacts in the context of the times they were created, as opposed to when they were banned in Victorian times with the rise of the concept of pornography.'

BS creaked back into the leather banquette and mopped around his mouth and nostrils with his napkin. 'Pudding?' he said brightly, but seeing mild surprise in his companion's face, he frowned and added, 'Perhaps not. Let's have a couple of coffees – they come with truffles. I'll order it at the bar on my way to the little boys' room,' and he struggled to his feet.

He took as long as was decent in the gents to allow a natural change of conversation on his return. As he washed his hands in the sink, he looked up at himself in the mirror to check that none of his lunch was stuck in his beard. Without his reading glasses on, he thought he was ageing rather well. His hair and beard had gone white years before their time so he never associated this with old age, and by keeping his beard neatly trimmed in a style not dissimilar to that of George V, he thought it made him look younger. A few years ago he had been persuaded by one of his sons to shave it off before they went on holiday, and to his horror its removal revealed deep wrinkles running between his nose and mouth, and a large volume of spare skin under his chin. Where could that have come from? he mused. Had it been gathered up under his hairline all these years ready to work its way down and pool under his chin? His beard had grown back to a smoothing stubble before his return to work, and he vowed never to repeat the exercise. He was also lucky to have retained a good head of hair, so much so that he was able to cultivate a decent flop of white fringe across his forehead which obscured two other deep wrinkles which similarly baffled him. They ran from his temples down to the middle of his eyebrows, and however many different faces he pulled in the mirror, he could not work out how they could possibly have developed.

Smoothing his hair to one side with a damp hand, he unhooked his stick from his arm and ambled out into the pub again. He could see Sam in the far corner with her back to him. She was bent forward, probably clicking away at one of those wretched telephones they all have.

'My son has been urging me to get one of those,' he said, lowering himself on to the banquette once more, 'but I say to him, 'Technology reached its peak with the quill pen.'' Sam looked up at him and frowned. 'Anyway, have you worked for the British Museum for a long time?'

Sam put her iPhone away in her bag and said, 'I don't work for them. I've been a freelance curator for ... oh, over ten years now.'

'A free lance.' BS separated the two words. 'I love that concept. A knight riding through the countryside ready to fight any cause he chooses, free to use his lance against any foe he likes. It's interesting how many of those heraldic sayings have fallen into common parlance. Like the coat of arms, for example. You see,' he continued, sprinkling a tube of demerara sugar into his coffee and stirring it in, 'armour was exceptionally hot to wear, particularly in the sun, and so they covered the metal with a coat – a coat of arms, and if this coat was slashed and cut, it showed they had seen combat. If you look at the earl's coat of arms ('accomplishment' is the correct word, of course, but you probably know that) you will see the swirling cuts and slashes in the mantling around the helm which shows that in the past the earl's ancestors have seen real combat.' He popped the spoon into his mouth and dried it between his tongue and upper lip before dropping it on to the saucer.

'This is all very interesting,' Sam said, 'but I think it's diverting us from the job in hand.'

BS looked up at her with a benign smile of interest but the gaze she returned had an intensity that left him in no doubt that her patience was running out. He leant forward and rested his elbows on the table with an expression of deep attention and said, 'Of course, my dear. Where would you like to start?' Before Sam could reply he continued, 'I was thinking this afternoon I could take you for a whistle-stop tour of the Hall which will give you a good grounding in background material, vital for understanding the collection itself. I am, as you know, completely at your disposal.'

## - 5 -

As he approached the final roundabout before the main gate into Duntisbourne Hall, Max Black resolved he would drive three hundred and sixty degrees around it and make his way back home. What on earth was he doing squeezed into a suit which fifteen years ago looked sharp, on the way to his first interview in a quarter of a century? It was madness. He was perfectly happy with his lot, apart from this wretched health business.

He was already on the roundabout now, and he felt the pale eyes of Dr Usher peering at him over the trees where he could just make out the brick chimney stacks of the Hall. He knew that if he ever wanted a life without Dr Usher, he was going to have to make those changes. He was not a stupid man, he knew he wasn't living a healthy life, and if he didn't want to face up to it himself, he had his daughter bleating at him every time she came back home.

'Your house stinks.'

'You never complained when you lived here.'

'I know, Dad, but when I come back, I really notice it. I wish you'd give up smoking.'

'And I wish you'd start eating meat.'

He pulled up at the gatekeeper's box at the top of the drive. 'I've got an interview with Rosemary Welsh,' he said to the gateman.

'Have you now, sir?' Pugh replied. Max caught the strong smell of rolling tobacco on his breath and warmed to him. 'I'll radio up to the Hall and let her know you're here. Just you hang on a tick.' He pressed a button on the two-way radio. 'Gate to Rosemary, there's a gentleman here to see you about a job interview ... ' Pugh nodded and winked at Max as he listened to the reply. He then roared with gravelly laughter and signed off. 'Now sir, park your car up by the Hall, to the left of the courtyard, and Miss Welsh will come down and find you.'

The wind raced across the courtyard and caught the handful of visitors by their waterproofs, shaking them vigorously and sending them rattling for shelter. It hit Max the moment he opened his car door and cut through him like a knife, momentarily taking his breath away. He tugged his waistcoat down over his waistband to cover up the top button of his trousers which wouldn't quite do up. Weaving her way between the topiaried trees, a woman was approaching him across the gravel, her head lowered against the wind, a green puffa jacket held tightly together at her throat. She didn't look up until she was nearly upon him and then she extended a frozen hand and shook his firmly.

'Hello, Mr Black – or is it all right to call you Max?'

'That's fine.'

'I'm Rosemary Welsh, Head of Ops. Come on through and I'll show you where we can get a cup of coffee.'

The tearooms smelt of old biscuit tins and boiled cabbage. Rosemary negotiated the serving areas with ease until she had gathered two cups of coffee, a handful of milk sachets, a few tubes of white sugar and a couple of teaspoons and signed them out in the staff book, all with the other arm pinning a bunch of files to her side.

'Right,' she said a little breathlessly as she settled herself down. 'There has been quite a lot going on here at Duntisbourne Hall, hence the recruiting drive. The trustees have been coming up with all sorts of initiatives to get a few more visitors in through the gates and last year they brought in a team of business consultants from outside which has shaken everything up a bit. It seems rather common to keep talking about making money, but I suppose that's the way ahead, and the place needs a huge amount of work done to it. Anyway, they seem to be expecting a great many more visitors this year, so I've been told to get a few extra people on board, and that's what this is all about. So when you've finished your coffee, I'll ask you to give your address and everything to the office and they'll send you a parking sticker for your car. When can you start?'

'I've got the job?' he said.

'Of course. Do you have any questions?'

'What exactly is it that I'll be doing?'

'Oh, sorry! Guiding, of course.'

This is hopeless, Max thought. He hated public speaking – in fact he was terrified of public speaking – and his grasp of history was negligible.

'I didn't realise I'd be guiding,' he said. 'I thought visitor services was taking money for tickets, that sort of thing.'

'We leave all that to the young ones, the students. You don't want to be outside in all weathers at your age, do you? Anyway, looking at your CV, you're perfect: public school educated, nicely spoken, smart. I don't suppose you were ever in the army?'

'Heavens no!'

'Naval man?'

'More of a legs man myself.'

Rosemary frowned. 'It's not important,' she said, 'just that the earl likes men who have been in the services. You'll soon pick things up – just follow a few of the team around and learn the blurb, and off you go. It's ever so easy.' Max wasn't sure it would be all that easy.

'History has never been my strong point,' he said.

'It's not that difficult, and besides, most of the people coming here know a great deal less than you, so it really doesn't matter what you say at all.'

'And is there a dress code?'

'Well, just wear the sort of things you'd usually wear in a earl's house,' she replied, beaming.

'Right.'

'Now, come along, I'm going to hand you over to Bunty Buchanan. She's our head guide and it would be much better for her to show you round than me. I know how to get a difficult window open but for the history side, Bunty really is your girl.'

Max stood up, gulping down the last few mouthfuls of coffee. Rosemary was already at the door of the canteen and moving fast. He bounded up the stairs behind her, missing half of what she was saying to him over her shoulder. 'This is the staff staircase. Awfully small treads, I'm afraid, but I suppose the maids had terribly little feet in those days. Probably all those potatoes and no protein. Ah! Here's Bunty.'

Coming down the passage through the gloom was a woman in her late sixties. Max noticed that her tights were laddered.

'Good morning, Rosemary. Is this my new recruit?'

'Yes,' said Rosemary. 'This is Max Black. He will be joining us ...?' She left the sentence hanging in the air as she surveyed his face expectantly.

'Oh, well,' stuttered Max, 'I'm free from Monday.'

'Excellent,' said Bunty. 'I need you to follow a few of the guides around. Don't just learn the spiel – it's meant to be a guideline. I'm sure you'll develop your own style soon, just mug up on the parts of history that interest you. We'll soon have you licked into shape,

Mr Black – or shall I call you Max?'

'Yes, yes. That's fine.'

'Right. Now, let's start where the tours start. It'll make more sense that way. Come along. Here we are in the great hall. '

Max looked up at the high barrelled roof which bore the faint traces of painted motifs. In front of him a wide staircase led from the centre of the hall to a smaller left and right rise of stairs up into the minstrels' gallery which ran around three sides of the hall. This magnificent structure had been made from fine oaks hundreds of years ago and had darkened to a sepia-black over the centuries. The staircase was embellished with hefty carvings of medieval fish, trading vessels in full sail, gauntleted hands holding dishes and chalices, ghastly gargoyles, naked maidens, faces of saints and angels, pomegranates and Tudor roses. The deep red carpet that should have accentuated its sweep and turn was stained and worn bare all the way up its centre. Portraits of earls and countesses from the past peered down through the gloom at him. Everything in the great hall was faded and threadbare – even the earl's banner above the door was meshed with broken threads and a few pieces of the ancient appliqué twisted in the draught like loose autumn leaves. Beneath the banner was an ancient man pacing up and down and talking to himself.

'Hello, Claude,' Bunty hailed. 'This is Max Black, a new boy.' Claude Hipkiss stopped pacing, spun round on a heel and looked Max straight in the eye, astonished by the interruption. Bunty bustled on past him and Max let his proffered hand of introduction sink back to his side, unclasped by Hipkiss.

'Claude,' she said to Max, 'has been with us for a great many years. He's very interested in the Bomford Collection.'

'Bomford Collection?'

'Oh dear, you really didn't do a lot of homework, did you?' she chuckled. 'Well, never mind. I'll give you lots of reading material before you go. No, the Bomford Collection goes back to the 1920s and is housed in the Egyptian Folly.'

Max watched Claude Hipkiss as he paced and muttered. He was lofty, decrepit and whippet thin. His tweed jacket caught across his shoulders as if the coat hanger was still inside it. Underneath he wore a thick Viyella shirt with a knitted tie knotted loosely around the collar from which his neck emerged like that of an ancient tortoise. His trousers were hiked high up above his waistline and his brogues shone brightly against the rest of his dishevelled wardrobe. Above his high forehead his comb-over had been dislodged by the wind which whipped through the great hall and hung down sparsely on one side, brushing his collar. Occasionally he batted it away from his face with a pat of irritation. Max thought he bore a remarkable resemblance to the mummy of Ramesses II.

'Lots of lovely carving here,' Bunty said, wafting a hand above her head. 'Always a good idea to mention that. And up there's the minstrels' gallery. Sometimes,' she added confidentially, 'when there's a function on down here in the great hall, the earl creeps out of the private apartments and glares down at the revellers. A number of the more well-oiled diners swear they've seen the ghost of Duntisbourne Hall. He really hates the general public, you know.'

A group of tourists ambled along the far side of the great hall, followed by one of the guides who was deep in conversation with a visitor. 'Laurence!' Bunty shouted, making Max jump. 'Control your group from the front.' Laurence peered across the open space and cupped his hand around his ear. 'The front!' Bunty bellowed.

'Get to the front of your group.' Laurence pushed forward in a state of some panic and ushered his group away and out of sight.

'Right,' Bunty continued. 'Let's go on down the corridor to the lower hall. You won't need to know the names of all these statues, but it's a good idea to have a bit of a working knowledge just in case you get some clever clogs who thinks he knows everything about sculpture and tries to catch you out. I like to have a little put-down line up my sleeve, something to stop them dead in their tracks, such as 'The sculptor was a sodomite.' I find that's the best way to handle them. '

'Was he?' Max said.

'No idea.'

They steamed on through a series of grand rooms, and as Bunty dispensed information left and right, Max began to feel baffled and confused. Would he ever be able to remember any of this? Would a day ever come when he would be able to throw handfuls of information at the visitors with the same confidence and relish as her?

By the time they reached the state dining room his attention was waning, but as they rounded the corner, ahead of him he saw something that piqued his interest immediately so that he found himself concentrating hard, but not on Bunty. Coming across the dining room towards him were two people deep in conversation – an elderly man who leaned heavily on his stick every other step, and a woman. The flutter of interest that he felt was quickly over-ridden by the thought that she could be in her thirties, not much older than his daughter, because her blonde hair and figure gave an impression of youthfulness. He admonished himself at the same time as feeling a bleat of disappointment. Her companion stopped at the head of the table and pointed to a golden hand which was suspended on chains above the chair of the earl.

'Good morning, BS,' Bunty said.

The old archivist hobbled towards them. 'Good morning Bunty.' He gestured towards his companion and added, 'this is Sam Westbrook. She's going to create a new exhibition for us here this season but I thought I would give her a general tour of the Hall as background. I was telling Sam about the golden hand.'

Max had been dawdling on the periphery of the conversation admiring Sam when BS spotted him and said, 'I do apologise, I thought you were a visitor.'

'I'm showing him around too,' Bunty said. 'He's joining the guiding team.'

'Max Black,' Max said, holding out his hand. 'I'd love to know about the golden hand. I may have to tell someone about it on Monday.'

'You certainly will,' BS said. 'It is probably one of the most important things to the family. This isn't the original, of course. The original was made by Cellini. It was solid gold with natural pearls at the wrist and mother-of-pearl fingernails harvested from the South Seas – very valuable. So valuable in fact that one of the earls –' here he paused and turned briefly to Sam '– probably the ninth earl in fact,' and continued, 'sold it off. However, this replica, commissioned by the eleventh earl in 1899, is still pretty valuable. It's giltware, solid silver, dipped in gold – if you look carefully you can see that the fingernails were protected in some way and left silver.' Max wasn't looking at the golden hand, he was looking at Sam as she gazed up at the treasure, and as he studied her, his ungallant observation pleased him. She was not in her thirties at all – the softness of the skin around her eyes and along the line of her jaw indicated she was not a great many years younger than himself. As if she sensed his observation she turned towards him and smiled. He felt a ripple underneath his ribcage, nodded and looked back up at the golden hand.

'The hand symbol is in the coat of arms,' Bunty said. 'You probably spotted it. It dates right back to the Crusades. Some people like to call it the Golden Hand of Jerusalem. There's an ancient legend that one of the knights saw it in a dream and knew he was called. I've never quite worked out what it has to do with the family, but I'm not that hot on heraldry.'

'Give Bluemantle a call,' BS suggested. 'The College of Arms are always extremely helpful. Or I may have some more information about it in the files upstairs. I'll dig it out for you.'

'Thank you, BS. But we mustn't keep you. Come along, Max. Let's go on through to the lower dining room.'

Let's not, he thought, but he was swept reluctantly away and on and on through the house, past Lelys and Holbeins and Slaughters and Reynolds.

## - 6 -

Maureen Hindle sat on a chair at the end of the indigo library looking through the state rooms to the dining room. She was on security. To her left she heard the click of the door at the far end of the room – the door up to BS Moreton's office. She felt her pulse begin to knock at the base of her throat and turned away before he emerged. She could hear the murmur of his voice; she was aware that he was walking up the library towards her, and he was talking to someone. She glanced up. It was that new woman, the one who had come to make the exhibition of those disgusting objects that were locked away above the minstrels' gallery, which was exactly where they should stay. She didn't acknowledge the couple but kept her gaze fixed on the dining room until they passed, and BS didn't acknowledge her. Of course he didn't. He had another handmaiden now. It was embarrassing seeing the old fool preening and fussing around her, showing off. He just couldn't resist. And why did he have to wear his tie flopped out over the top of his V-neck jumper? He was like some ancient baboon displaying.

She watched them recede down the corridor, silhouetted against the light flooding up from the dining room, BS leaning and swinging on his stick, his large head bent towards his companion who was only a few years younger than Maureen, but slim and well-dressed. Maureen could see she was a shallow woman. No one who spent that amount of time on grooming could be anything but shallow. Maureen felt a bat-squeak of hypocrisy at this thought because she spent quite a long time at the mirror in the morning backcombing her hair and dragging on her eyeliner, but Sam Westbrook looked glossy and understated and irritating, and Maureen hated to see BS Moreton schmoozing around her. It disgusted her. She saw them stop in the dining room. She saw Bunty coming over to speak to them accompanied by that man she'd heard was coming in today – a new guide who was starting this season. She could tell he was looking at Sam Westbrook in an admiring way. At their age! It was revolting.

And then a memory rose up before her: Michael looking across the congregation at her in just that way thirty years ago. She felt her eyes stinging, tears from what? Nostalgia? Regret? They had met through their church. As a student in Nottingham she had joined the Young Christians chiefly out of loneliness. She had hoped that college would salve the feelings of isolation which had dogged her throughout her adolescence, but it had only exacerbated them. She had always felt big. Not so much fat but large, the tallest girl in the class with the deepest voice and big feet and hands and teeth. She had big eyes too, but these did nothing to outweigh the rest of her physical appearance. She remained outside the circle of bright young things, her seriousness and lack of self-esteem keeping her on the perimeter looking in, and as the months passed she found herself sickened by their shallowness. Instead she struck up a friendship with another girl whom she recognised as her equal – another outsider. She was German, larger than Maureen, and had the livid red skin of an acne sufferer. When Monika asked if she would like to come to her rooms for coffee one evening, she accepted.

Monika's rooms were in another block, away from the main campus, and when Maureen arrived she was surprised but also relieved that other students were already there. These were the Young Christians of the college. They were friendly and welcoming, drinking coffee together and talking. Some nights one of them would bring a guitar and they would sing – 'Michael Row the Boat Ashore', 'The Rivers of Babylon',' The Streets of London'. Maureen soon began to attend their church meetings and although she had never thought of herself as a religious person, she found comfort among a group of people who accepted her and were eager to see her. She started to feel that she was on a higher spiritual plane than the rest of the students on campus and enjoyed criticising their behaviour with her new friends.

Her secret struggle in this new religious life was with an overpowering sense of guilt. She had had her first sexual experience at the age of fourteen when she was riding a rickety bike down a long hill towards the hockey pitch at her exclusive girls' boarding school. She had left the rest of the group some way behind and was freewheeling with the hem of her brown culottes flapping around her knees. About halfway down the hill the road had been recently resurfaced and, as the bike hit the loose gravel and began to judder beneath her, she felt an extraordinary sensation. She did not know what it was, but she was certain she did not want it to stop. The bike went faster and faster. Maureen rested her feet on the singing pedals and gasped at the rising sensation in the base of her abdomen. She heard the others shout from behind to warn her she was going too fast, she could see the end of the road ahead where it petered out into a rutted farm track beside the hockey pitch, but she was impelled to keep going, to let the feeling build, and as the bicycle hit the hardened ruts of the track a huge feeling of release swept through her lower body. The bike rattled past the sports pavilion as her throat released a loud wail which poured from her mouth until the bike hit the barley field at the end of the track and she tottered and fell full length into the crop.

She had never spoken about this encounter to anyone, but now she knew God knew, and however hard she tried to suppress it, He probably knew she had been hoping to repeat the sensation. It thrilled and disgusted her in equal measure, but she wanted different things for her life now: she wanted to walk with Jesus, she wanted to find salvation, she wanted to help others and, to her shame, she wanted Michael.

Michael was a lay preacher who came to their church on alternate Sundays. Their courtship had been serious but simple, their wedding night an intensely embarrassing experience and nothing like riding a bike down a hill. She sensed Michael's unease, but gradually they developed a deep fondness for one another which brought her through her shame and disappointment, and in her mind she gave thanks to her God for this good man. They produced two sons, and their lives settled down to a routine packed with responsibility. For the first two decades, her decision to educate the children at home overwhelmed her waking hours; then she had the responsibility of trying to police their daily lives once they had left home, which both boys desperately wanted to do the moment they reached eighteen; and just when she should have had some time to do what she wanted to do, the needs of Michael's elderly parents slipped into the vacuum and stole away her freedom and happiness.

Now the menopause had struck and she remembered how she and Monika had laughed that the German word for a nipple was a chest wart, the German for pubic hair was shame hair. All these years later, she inadvertently caught sight of herself in the bathroom mirror, and that was what she saw – two warts on her chest and a thin straggle of shame hair. She hated her body even more than she had done as a young adult. Her life had passed and she had wasted it waiting for something better. Some days she felt strong and belligerent: life wasn't fair – she had worked hard, she had prayed, she had sacrificed her youth and her freedom. Other days she faced the sickening truth that she had never deserved anything better – she was plain and she was lumpy. Even her grown children did not seem to want her company and her parents-in-law criticised and complained no matter how hard she worked for their comfort.

The only person is this sorry mess who seemed to be on her side was Michael, and Michael never touched her, and she didn't blame him because she was sweaty and wrinkled. She was sickened when she saw couples embracing in television dramas, she looked away as they munched at each other's lips.

She had taken the job at the Hall to get out of the house, and she was a good guide. She admired BS Moreton. When she saw him taking a group of visitors around, she would position herself carefully so that she could hear what he was saying. She admired his knowledge and his gravitas, and wished she could emulate his manner, passing on history as if he was chatting over a dinner table. She always felt she was lecturing to visitors. He had been so kind to her when she had her accident, even though he hardly knew of her existence before. It was horrible at the time, but good things can come out of bad, and that winter, when she was fully recovered, BS asked if she fancied doing some extra hours when the Hall was closed, to help him in his office with some tasks. She knew he needed her help – he was hopeless at organisation.

BS's office was tucked away in one of the maids' rooms above the music room at the end of the indigo library above, the mighty Wurlitzer organ which had been rescued from the Odeon cinema in Cardigan Bay days before it was demolished. It was a low-ceilinged room with two circular windows, one looking out across the courtyard, the other under the main portico into the great hall. Along one wall stood a heavy table piled high with towers of papers, between which the scratched and worn leather top was visible. Behind the table was a large and equally worn nineteenth-century leather chair, a few tufts of horsehair peeping out from the front of the armrests. This was BS Moreton's desk. Beside the table stood a magnificent mahogany filing cabinet with tarnished brass name plaques on each drawer, empty of any annotation. Every surface was piled high with papers and ancient leather books in various stages of dilapidation. Along the adjacent wall was a smart computer, black and silent and covered with a thick film of dust. BS hadn't had the help of an assistant for some time. He had his 'hot file', a pile of unanswered memos and letters and notes scrawled on the backs of envelopes, and Maureen knew she could sort all that out for him, set up a proper filing system and protect him from making a fool of himself.

'Rosemary tells me you're a whizz with computers,' BS said.

She felt flattered. 'I can use most office programmes, word processing, emailing, that sort of thing.'

BS brightened and said, 'Management keep sending me emails, and I get Rosemary to print them up for me so that I can read them.'

'I can sort that out for you. What's that computer over there used for?'

'I haven't dared turn it on in case I banjax the whole thing,' he had replied. So Maureen connected the computer and the printer, and the IT man came in to get them on to the internet, and BS was full of wonder and admiration for her skills, and Maureen felt good about herself.

She had never set foot in the Hall during the closed season, and being one of the skeleton staff that winter made her feel special. She wasn't just one of a crowd of guides any more – she was recognised by the managers and they said 'good morning' to her, and 'how are you?' BS started lending her the pass key 'to save my legs,' he told her, and when she ran an errand for him she had access to parts of the Hall that no other guides visited. She found a suite of locked cloakrooms which was only opened for functions – three spotlessly clean loos, a pile of hand towels next to the sinks, Molton Brown soaps and hand creams and a bank of mirrors. Maureen began to visit these cloakrooms regularly, washing her hands with the expensive soap and rubbing on the hand cream afterwards.

BS loved to waste time and he particularly loved to waste time chatting. Maureen thought it wasn't a bad way to earn seven pounds an hour, sitting with her hands nursing a cup of coffee and listening to his stories. He was indiscreet and passed on far more about the earl and his wayward children than he should have. When the earl was away BS took her over to the private apartments on the pretext that he wanted to update his information files on the prints and paintings over on the private side. She felt like a naughty schoolgirl under the protection of the head boy as they peered into the rooms where the earl's guests stayed. BS swayed over to the window of one of the rooms and beckoned to her. His height and stature made her feel small, almost petite, when she stood beside him. 'Imagine waking up to that view,' he said, and he leaned over towards her and they laughed.

He showed her the rooms where the Victorian maids had slept, let her climb up the ladder to the roof while he waited down below gazing up as she ascended. From there she looked out across four acres of tiled roofs. The countryside was brown with winter, the margin of the lake edged with ice muting the colour of the water which glowed red from the clay soil, the River Lugg shining like mercury between the trees.

They went for drives around the estate and he showed her where the third earl had been buried, the one who was killed at the Battle of Preston in 1648 and brought home by his warring sons. He showed her the plaque on the huge oak at the end of the river walk which was dedicated to the twelfth earl who died during the Second World War when the Backslider's Club in Pall Mall took a direct hit. She came with him when he gave his talk 'The Ladies of Duntisbourne Hall' to the Women's Institute and although she thought some of his stories verged on the salacious, when the ladies gathered around him afterwards she was awed by his easy, urbane charm with them and she felt special because she had the privilege of enjoying his company every working day. He asked her to look up his lottery numbers each week on the internet; she showed him how he could browse the catalogue of the British Library online; he sat close to her and watched over her shoulder, so close she could smell shaving soap on his neck; she caught him looking at her knee which peeked out from the wraparound panel of her skirt.

Then she told him about her idea for the library project and he embraced it with enthusiasm. She began to work more than the few days a week that had been originally suggested. BS explained that there wasn't enough money in his budget to pay her for extra days and she said she didn't mind. She knew he needed her, she was on fire with this new project, and he said she was wonderful. When she prayed at night, she thanked God for letting her have this opportunity, and she asked God to bless BS Moreton because he was a good man. Looking back on that winter, she had an image of BS which looked completely different from the man she saw now. During that winter she was drawn to him, she had grown an attachment to him. He didn't seem as old to her as when she had first started working for him. She looked forward to coming in to work. She loved the atmosphere of the little office above the library – the fresh coffee and the ozone smell of outdoors that came in with him, on him, as he swung through the tiny room and dropped into his chair and said, 'Make mine a belter, Mo.'

Two weeks before the Hall opened for that season, Michael took her up to their holiday lodge in Scotland, leaving the ancient parents in the care of his sister. She took long walks around the bay when Michael was in town doing the shopping, and she thought about BS. She missed him. She sent him a postcard, a picture of a pale-coloured Highland with a jaunty note that the bull's hairstyle reminded her of him, but without the horns (exclamation mark). She wondered how many days he would need her when the season started, how the CEO had reacted to her library scheme. She even imagined not going back to guiding but writing more material for handbooks on other collections in the Hall – the watercolours, for example. The skin on the outsides of her index fingers was now white patches of shining scar tissue. She couldn't remember the last time she had left them alone long enough for them to heal.

For the first week of that following season she thought BS was away. She had heard his radio broadcast over the weekend, Radio Shropshire's version of *Desert Island Discs*, and she was looking forward to telling him how well he had come across, how glad she was that he had included one of her favourite pieces of music in his list, '*E lucevan le stelle*', the aria from *Tosca*, but he didn't appear down in the Hall.

The following Monday she saw him in the distance across the courtyard, heading for the staff car park and he was with the buxom northern guide, Donna Falkender and Maureen felt such a jolt at seeing them walking out into the crisp spring sunshine that she turned away from the front door, feeling nauseous. She made her way back to the state dining room where she sat and chewed at the outer edge of her index finger. When the left-hand one became too painful she began to work her teeth along the edge of the right-hand finger, nibbling and tearing at it like a piranha. It soothed her, but then she felt ashamed and pulled her hands up inside the sleeves of her jumper to hide them.

BS came to speak to her at the end of the week when he saw her sitting on security at the end of the indigo library. When she sensed him approaching she began to tremble. It was late in the afternoon and the library was empty of visitors. He started by asking her if she had had an enjoyable break in Scotland, thanking her for all her excellent work over the winter. He then went on to explain that he wouldn't need to take up any more of her valuable time because Donna Falkender was going to be helping him over the next few months. She spoke French and German and could translate some of the documents he was working on at the present time. Maureen listened and nodded, but knew he was lying. She wanted to say 'I know why you want that woman up there in the office with you,' but instead she tried a light dig at him and said, 'So you've got a new handmaiden now, have you? I suppose it was time to move on to a younger model?'

BS glanced away and removed his reading glasses, studied the lenses for a moment and looked down at Maureen with such contempt it pressed her back into the chair.

He drew himself up to his full height, towering over her because she had left it too late to get to her feet. 'How dare you speak to me in that manner,' he said quietly, but she could hear his breathing quicken. 'What makes you think you have the right to make such an insinuation? The appointments I make are based purely on ability, and you are completely out of order to suggest that I would appoint someone for anything other than the most honourable motives. The work you have done for me over the winter does not qualify you in any way whatsoever to speak to me with such familiarity. If you ever speak to me like that again, I will see to it personally that you leave Duntisbourne Hall immediately, and let me tell you, my influence is such that no other stately home in England will employ you,' and he turned his back on her and walked away down the library, the ferrule of his stick smiting the oak boards.

She stared up the state rooms, watching Laurence with his tour moving along the rooms towards her. She was not allowed to leave until he reached the library. When he arrived she handed him the radio without a word and made her way towards the staff cloakroom. It was untidy because there was no paper towel dispenser on the wall and opened packets spilled their contents over the shelf beneath the mirror, not like the cloakroom she had used in the winter. Maureen stared at the image in front of her. She hated it – the sallow skin, the hint of a jowl along her jawline, the lumpy outline of her upper arms underneath her navy cardigan. She turned away and went through the inner door where she could lock herself in. She put the mahogany cover down to make a seat before sitting, then she rolled up the sleeve of her left arm.

The skin underneath was marked with brown lines, old scars from her fingernails. She bent her arm and dug her nails deliberately into the skin just below the elbow which was paler and had fewer scars on it. It hardly hurt at all and as she pulled her nails through the skin and saw the livid red lines oozing, she began to feel a little calmer again.

She heard the outer door open and someone turned the handle on the other side of her locked door. 'Sorry!' a voice said and Bunty left the cloakroom. But it was too late – Maureen knew Bunty would be waiting somewhere in the corridor outside for her to finish, and she was going to have to leave. She pulled her sleeve down, stood up and flushed the toilet. The wounds on her arm were beginning to smart, and the agitation and distress that had begun to abate rose again in her chest even more powerfully, fuelled this time by a crushing sense of guilt and shame.

## - 7 -

Over the next few days Max turned up at the Hall for a few hours and tacked himself on to the small groups of visitors shivering their way through the state rooms. He began to get to know the other guides: Claude Hipkiss he had met on his first day, but he wasn't confident Claude had any idea who he was; he also recognised Laurence Cooke, a beautifully dressed resting actor, the man Bunty had bellowed at across the Hall. Maureen Hindle seemed a little more senior to the rest of the guides, which may have explained her aloofness; then there was Noel Canterbury, a beady-eyed man with a good sense of humour and an enthusiastic admirer of the opposite sex even though Max doubted he would ever see sixty again, and Major Frodsham, splendid in tweed plus-twos with a matching jacket and waistcoat taut over his enormous stomach. The Major's eyebrows intrigued Max. They were the same squirrel-red hue as his magnificent moustache, but the left eyebrow curled like a horned beast up towards his temples while the right eyebrow brushed down towards his cheek giving his face a mischievous asymmetry. Max noticed that the Major never quite managed to do a tour, preferring to slumber quietly at the end of the indigo library, his almost completed *Times* crossword slipping from his lap. There was one guide to whom Max took an instant dislike, not because of her appearance as would be expected (she had the body of an ancient anorexic, her large lollipop head accentuated by a solid mane of peroxide yellow hair) but because the first time she spoke to him it was to dress him down loudly for standing in the statue corridor instead of going up to the guides' room and having a cup of tea. Her name was Edwina Lemon, although she preferred to be called by her nickname, Weenie. She also insisted that for centuries her surname had been pronounced *Limon* because she was descended from an ancient family of French landed gentry. Despite the solid mask of make-up that she wore over her parchment-thin skin, and her vulgar dress sense, she was under the illusion that visitors mistook her for the countess, a sophisticated and elegant woman who oozed money and breeding in as full a measure as Weenie spilled gaucheness. She seemed to have some sort of understanding with Roger Hogg-Smythe, a guide about the same age as Max who made a great fuss about the rota whenever he was called 'to the bench'. At first Max wondered why a High Court judge would take a job as a guide, but he soon realised that Roger was nothing more than a JP.

Max found the diary system bewildering. On his application form he had agreed to work three days a week, Mondays, Wednesdays and Fridays. During his second week he turned up to work on Friday to a rather frosty reception from Bunty.

'What happened to you yesterday?' she asked.

'In what sense?'

'You were down to do an early tour,' Bunty said.

'But I don't work on a Thursday,' Max said.

'No,' Bunty said. 'I don't think you have quite understood how important it is to check with the diary before you plan your week. We were short of guides yesterday, and you had been put down to work. It's quite clear,' and she opened the dog-eared handwritten diary and pointed. 'Here you are, beside this tour which came in before the Hall opened.'

Max stared down at the page which was covered in handwriting and a great deal of correcting fluid. 'I'm sorry, but I can't see where

I am at all,' he said.

'Here, here next to the Probus tour. MB. That's you, isn't it?' Max peered and sure enough the initials MB were written next to the tour in faint pencil.

'I had no idea,' he said apologetically. 'I don't work on a Thursday.'

'You have to check the diary,' and Bunty snapped it shut and disappeared up to the guides' room.

Noel Canterbury wandered over to Max. He was chuckling.'The diary rules,' he said, 'and Maureen has her favourites.'

'Maureen?'

'You know Maureen Hindle, the weird big one, looks a bit like a tranny. You must have noticed her, she wears the same thing all the time, huge baggy clothes, always black or navy. She does the rota for the diary. Don't get on the wrong wide of that woman or you'll find yourself dropped when you want to work, and slithered in when you least expect it.'

'Surely if you're put down on a day you don't usually work, someone should ring you?'

'That's not how it works. Check it at every opportunity or you'll be caught out and made to feel a complete heel. That's if you can find the damned diary – quite often Maureen disappears with it. She hugs it to her matronly bosom like a talisman, her precious. She draws her power from it. If you're on the last tour, you don't need to come in until eleven, and if you come in at 10.30 by a mistake, not having noticed that you're on the last tour, she'll make you sit up in the guides' room and have a coffee so you don't get paid for that extra half hour. And remember,' Noel continued, 'what's written in the guides' diary often has no bearing whatsoever on the main Hall diary.'

'The main Hall diary?'

'Oh yes. The office takes bookings for tours and writes it in a different diary, that diary is then photocopied at the end of each day and a copy goes down to the gate so that Mr Pugh knows which tours are expected – and then of course there's BS's diary.'

Max smiled broadly at Noel. 'Go on then, tell me about BS's diary.'

'BS has a diary where he books in tours which have a vaguely educational theme to them, and then he and Bunty get together once a week and allocate specific guides to take them. However, quite often they forget to tell the main office, and sometimes guides get allocated in BS's diary but no one gets round to writing them in the guides' diary.'

'So basically, however many times I check the diary, I'll still get it wrong.'

'Oh you will get it wrong. Maureen likes to catch you out. She gets vicarious pleasure from other people's mistakes. It makes her feel better about herself.'

Despite this, after a lifetime of being his own boss Max found it relaxing to spend a whole day without having to make a decision. Bunty told him when to do a tour, when to stand in the saloon on security, when to go and have a cup of tea and when to go up to the guides' room and have his lunch.

The guides' room was housed in the old servants' quarters above the statue corridor, a large low room with filthy windows which looked out on to an enclosed courtyard full of the detritus of the kitchens three floors below. The carpet was held together with pieces of parcel tape, the furniture was drab. There was one chair that had been patched and mended a number of times and rendered comfortable purely by the laxness of the springs and the rest of the seating consisted of damaged upright chairs abandoned by the caterers. The sink in the corner had no running hot water, and Max was warned not to drink water from the cold tap because it came straight from the lake. Instead the kettle was filled from a water cooler, provided someone had remembered to replenish it, and the milk had to be fetched from the kitchens in the morning. Maureen brought her own coffee in a thermos, so when she filled in for Bunty, there was never any milk because she forgot to send a guide down to collect it. Max once made the mistake of popping down himself as the doors to the Hall opened only to be roundly admonished on his return for using his initiative. As a punishment (or so it seemed), the rest of the guiding team were obliged to drink black tea for the rest of the day. Maureen held the hurt of his disloyalty to her for months until he came to dread entering the guides' room and finding her nursing a cup of coffee and staring broodingly into space.

On one of his breaks he found Noel and the Major upstairs. 'Have either of you ever been head guide?' he asked. Noel threw his head back and roared.

'Don't be unkind, Noel,' the Major said. 'No, Max, I wasn't head guide, but I was senior guide for a few months when Bunty went off to have some small op.'

'Best fun we've had,' said Noel. 'You made an absolute pig's breakfast of things, didn't you old chap?'

'My approach may have been unorthodox, but it wasn't a complete disaster. That recruitment thing settled down fairly well.'

'You mean the Troika?' Noel said. 'Or did we decided to call them the Hydra?' His voice trailed off into a high-pitched squawk as another wave of laughter overwhelmed him. 'Right Max, let me explain. Unfortunately, during the week the Major was 'in charge', four characters turned up for interview, and he persuaded Rosemary to employ the lot of them: a decent enough chap who was stone deaf, a charming diabetic who had lost a foot, a Russian student who didn't speak much English, and a delightful fellow who was recovering from a stroke and had no short-term memory.'

'Or long-term either, as it turned out,' the Major said.

'Quite. Anyway, Max, the Major's solution to the problem was 'the sum of the parts are greater than the whole'. He tucked the lovely Svetlana Strapnakova off to BS Moreton's office from whence she swiftly fled back to the wasted Russian steppes in preference to BS Moreton's over-burgeoning admiration of her polyester slacks, and the Major amalgamated the three remaining new guides into a team. The one with no short-term memory pushed the cripple in a wheelchair, who in turn fielded questions on behalf of the deaf one who was doing the tour. Capital!'

'Oh really Noel, you do exaggerate.'

'Anyway,' said Noel, 'I'd better get downstairs before Maureen berates me for being up here for too long. Guarantee she's timing me. Toodle pip!'

'Must trot too, old chap,' said the Major and followed hard on Noel's heels.

As he supped his coffee, Max decided that Duntisbourne Hall was perhaps after all his kind of place. There was enough to amuse and interest him, and Sam, in particular, interested him a great deal. The new order the job had brought to his life was making him feel calmer, and the lack of opportunity to smoke had forced him to cut down dramatically, so all in all he felt Dr Usher would approve.

By the time the freezing winds of March had mellowed, Max was feeling good about himself. He had bravely faced his first solo guided tour a number of weeks ago, and the small, disparate group of visitors he had been unleashed on had surprised him by their concentration and nodding approval. By his third tour he had begun to throw in a few lighter comments that had gone down so well that he warmed to his theme and had them rocking with mirth by the time they reached the indigo library. He was beginning to feel invincible, but then he had several groups of leaden French exchange students who were unruly and more interested in snogging than in anything amusing he had to say, and a little of his confidence waned. Now he began to appreciate the coachloads of older visitors, particularly the enthusiastic Women's Institute. Once he had learned not to stride ahead too quickly – he had once made it all the way through the statue corridor when he realised that none of the Zimmer frames were able to move as fast as him, and he had to scurry back to retrieve them – he began to look forward to that sea of blue-rinsed heads.

He had spotted Sam a number of times, but an unusual and inexplicable shyness seemed to grip him whenever an opportunity arose to strike up a little conversation with her. He was sufficiently smitten to mention her to his daughter when she rang about taxing her car.

'Daddy, my daddy,' Charlotte began, as she always did ever since she had spotted her father dabbing a tear from his eye one Christmas when they were watching *The Railway Children* together.

'Hello, sweetie. How are things?'

'Big problem with the car, I'm afraid. It failed the MOT – apparently I need a complete new set of tyres, and the tax disc runs out at the end of the month.'

'How much?' Max wasn't a pushover, but he found it hard to deny Charlotte. His mother and father had been consistently generous with him and he knew no other way of parenting. He worried that Charlotte would never learn to stand on her own two feet if he kept bailing her out, but consoled himself with the thought that even if she never returned his generosity in kind, she would treat her own children in the same way. Besides, if he could afford to help, he would; if he hadn't been able to afford it, he probably still would. Whichever way, he seldom resented putting his hand into his pocket for his child and Charlotte was tactful enough to show surprise when he did.

'Are you sure, Dad? You don't have to. Honestly.'

'Let me.'

'OK then. Thanks. You're the best dad in the world.'

'Best dad for you.'

'Now you've got that new job you must be rolling in money.'

Max laughed loudly. 'Yes, three days' work at Duntisbourne Hall is going to make all the difference,' and to his surprise he found himself telling Charlotte some of the silly things that happened during his working day and then all about Sam.

'Is she a hottie?'

'Honestly, Charlotte, you do say the most extraordinary things. I don't even know what that means - and I don't want to know what that means.'

'Have you asked her out?'

'No. Heaven's above, I'm not sixteen, you know. Besides, she a lot more important than me, and it's all very feudal at the Hall. She's working on a new exhibition that they're building at the moment, but the whole thing is shrouded in mystery. She drives a really nice little green sports car. I always feel rather cheerful in the morning if I see it parked there, but she's not always at the Hall. Sometimes she's up in London.'

He had seen the car this morning and was leaning back on a large marble table at the side of the saloon, hands stretched out and flat, absorbing the comforting coolness of the marble and thinking about what he would say to her the next time she glided past him, the next time he had the pleasure of seeing the National Treasure, the name he had given to her gloriously shaped rear view. And as if his thoughts had magically conjured her up, there she was. She had just entered the other end of the saloon and was studying something above the doorway. He felt a wave of excitement rise in him: this time he was definitely going to say something. He chuckled to himself at the thought of nonchalantly wandering across the saloon and coming right out with it: 'Hello, Sam. I suppose a shag's out of the question ...' when suddenly, in front of him, stood the earl.

'What the hell do you think you're doing, man?' The earl towered over him, red in the face. Max jumped to attention and resisted the urge to wipe away the beads of spittle that had flown from the earl's mouth and struck him on the cheek. 'What the bloody hell are you doing lounging around on my furniture? And who the hell are you? I don't employ people like you to lounge around with their hands all over my furniture, staring into space! Haven't you got anything better to do?'

Max was speechless. He was aware that a group of visitors close by had stopped peering into their guide books and were now gripped by the scene developing behind them. He also sensed that Sam had turned and was watching his humiliation.

'Smarten yourself up, man!' the earl barked. Max blinked impotently and the thought flashed through his mind that he was a great deal better dressed than the earl who was sporting a rather revolting pastel cashmere that resembled a Battenberg cake. 'We have standards to maintain and you, boy ' – he spat this last word out like an expletive – 'are quite clearly below standard. And what's that on your name badge? Nerys Tingley? Nerys ruddy Tingley? Is that your idea of joke?'

It had seemed quite funny that morning. Max had left his own name badge at home and over his first cup of coffee in the guides' room he had amused the gathered company by rifling through the spare badges. 'Who shall I be today?' he asked. 'Shall I be Claude? He's not here today. Do I look like a Claude? And what about old Frodders? Is the Major in later today? Or Roger Hogg-Smythe? I think I'm man enough to carry that name off.'

'Can't see you on the bench, old chap,' Noel said, laughing.

'Maybe not. Ah, this is it. Today I'm going to be ... Nerys Tingley!'

'Your chin's certainly whiskery enough,' Noel remarked.

The joke didn't seem so funny now. The earl raved on: 'This is my house, this is my furniture, and I will have you drummed off the premises in a heartbeat unless you damned well shape up.'

Max felt his blood rise but as he opened his mouth to voice a rejoinder, the earl turned on his heels and clicked away down the lower dining room.

Silence filled the saloon, a silence so profound that Max felt it drumming on his ears. It was broken by a visitor who had crept up beside him.

'Was that the earl?' the visitor asked, his face aglow with pleasure and eager interest.

'Oh yes, sir,' Max managed to say. 'That certainly was the earl.'

The visitor returned to his group and they clustered around him smiling and nodding. One of them tried to catch a picture of the receding aristocrat with his digital camera, but Weenie (who had thoroughly enjoyed seeing Max's mortification) fell on the visitor like an ocean and reminded the trembling tourist that he would have his camera taken away from him and wiped of pictures if she so much as saw him handling it again.

Max turned his back on them and stared out of the windows across the park to hide his expression of impotent fury. He had never been spoken to like that, and the worst thing was that he hadn't managed to say a thing. He was going to walk out right now, drive away and never come back ... but then he felt a gentle hand on his shoulder and turning he caught a hint of warm scent. It was Sam.

'Who's been a naughty boy then?' she said softly in his ear, so close that he could feel the warmth of her lips flutter across his skin. Then she was gone.

'Max!' Bunty was calling him. 'Max! Come along. Your group's waiting.'

'What group?' Max groaned.

'Mr Pugh has just radioed up to say they're making their way to the front door – the Co-op South-East Counties Veterans' Association.'

With a heavy step Max made his way back through the great hall to the front door.

'Dear me, old chap' Noel Canterbury said, 'you look dreadful. Are you all right?'

'Just had an altercation with His Lordship.'

'Huh!' snorted Noel. 'Bloody man. I would choke rather than call him His Lordship. Nothing lordly about him, he's the most graceless son of a bitch you could ever meet. And what has he ever done anyway except get born?'

Max was a little taken aback. He knew that Noel's son stood as a conservative candidate somewhere on the south coast and he hadn't expected a left-wing outburst from him.

'The second earl,' Noel carried on, 'now that's a different matter. At least he had the phlegm to bed good Queen Bess. He deserved every title she gave him in my opinion.' Noel twinkled mischievously at Max. 'And the fifth earl, he was a pretty brave chap, he deserved his title ... but eight generations on, and we've got this idiot. He's uncultured, thick as sump oil from the inbreeding, unpleasant to look at with those revolting bloodhound eyes, makes me shudder, and on top of all that, the man's a crashing bore. He treats us all like dirt and one day it'll come back and slap him in the face if there's any justice in the world.' Noel nodded to himself a few times to emphasise his point of view.

'It's good to hear I'm not alone,' said Max.

'Good God no. You talk to anyone – take Pugh, for example. Last year his son worked on the gate for a few months after university. Lord Montague arrives at the gate and tells the lad to hand over fifty quid from the takings – the little git's short of cash. What's the lad supposed to do? He tries to say no, but he's the earl's son and heir, for God's sake. What option has he got? So he hands over the cash – never sees it again, of course – and the management take it out of the lad's wages! We're all on minimum wage here as it is, and him a student too. That sort of treatment hardly encourages loyalty.' Noel looked around the Hall and then leaned a little nearer and said conspiratorially. 'You know what, Max, when it's quiet one of my favourite games is planning how to give the old bastard his comeuppance. It would be richly deserved.'

'What sort of thing?' Max asked.

'Well … oh blast, here's your group. Chat later,' and Noel tapped the side of his nose with a forefinger and gave Max an amused, knowing look.

Noel had lifted Max's spirits considerably, and by the time the Co-op South-East Counties Veterans' Association were struggling slowly up the steps to the front door like the walking dead, grunting and groaning and leaning on one another for support, his good humour was almost up to its normal levels. It was restored in full when one of the veterans fired off a stentorian fart which, despite echoing around the beams above the great hall, seemed to go unheard by the ancient gentleman who had delivered it.

# - 8 -

BS woke at four o'clock the following morning. He lay staring at the lightening window because he couldn't rid his mind of a frustrating series of worries. Eventually he swung his legs heavily over the side of the bed and felt around in the half dark with his toes until he located his slippers. Patricia rolled over in the bed beside him and placed a hand in the small of his back. 'Are you all right, dear?' she asked, her voice thick with sleep.

'Yes, my love, just wide awake. You go back to sleep.' He made his way through to the bathroom, his first few steps the stiffest and slowest, and stood staring at his reflection in the mirror as he waited to pee.

Recently he had successfully filled up Sam's time with background work, but he knew he couldn't spend the next month ferrying her around the estate and taking her out for long lunches, enjoyable though her company was. Then a thought struck him. He wondered how much of this scheme had been discussed directly with the earl. Very little, he imagined. The earl was old school, old family, congenitally wealthy, the class of person who didn't have to buy his own furniture. Earning money was anathema to him. His father had opened the doors of Duntisbourne back in the fifties purely as a tax dodge, inheritance tax not being levied on the parts of the estate that had public access. Making money from the visitors had not been the primary objective – Duntisbourne Hall was not a company and the earl was not a businessman. He abhorred the visitors, seeing them as a necessary evil, and BS doubted that he wanted more of them to pour in through the doors and snigger over the antics of his own ancestors. Of course the earl was the person to whom he should appeal. The earl would put a stop to this.

His Lordship had returned yesterday – he had been abroad for the winter – and done his usual walk-through of the Hall to check that nothing had gone awry during his absence, but BS had missed seeing him. He resolved to ring Dean the butler first thing and arrange to lay his concerns before the earl himself, show him that this was the top of a greasy pole down which the Hall might slide. What could that lead to? The earl's son, heir to the title, appearing on reality TV? The earl would never allow this kind of media rot to begin and BS was the earl's man.

BS recognised that the earl didn't really know how to categorise him. He was better educated than the earl, clearly more intelligent, but His Lordship was well connected and intensely well bred, so it was hard to define which of them had the upper hand. BS thought the earl probably regarded him in much the same way he did the local vicar. However, he had been his advisor for years, his speech writer, his supporter, Thomas Cromwell to his Henry VIII, and he was confident the earl had no hand in pushing this ridiculous exhibition.

Buoyed by his decision, he made his way downstairs. The kitchen clock said six, but the Aga kept the kitchen cosy. BS poured himself a bowl of cornflakes. He spied a pot of cream which Patricia had tucked away at the back of the fridge, and glancing over his shoulder to check he was alone, he splashed a generous tablespoonful on to his cereals, then topped the pot up with milk so that she wouldn't notice and scold him about his weight. After eating, he poured himself a cup of tea and took it back upstairs. He had an hour and a half to kill before he could ring Dean, and thought it could be usefully spent on making himself spick and span to create a good impression on the earl.

After showering, he braved the magnifying side of the shaving mirror, lathering the upper part of his cheeks and carefully shaving down towards the edge of his beard. He couldn't abide men who let their beards straggle up towards their eyes, thin and bitty, blurring their faces as if they were out of focus, or allowed them to creep down over their throats, making them look unwashed. He liked to keep his topiaried, proof that it was not the idleness of old age that made him sport his magnificent Verdi beard. Carefully checking to make sure that all errant whiskers had been snipped off his cheeks, he then trimmed his beard into the sink with scissors and patted pungent cologne on to his skin. He smeared a little vaseline on his fingers and ran them along his eyebrows to flatten the tougher hairs, took a brush in each hand and pushed them one after another over his hair, checked to make sure no cereal adhered to his teeth following his breakfast and finally scrubbed his fingernails and pushed the cuticles back. He made his way through to the spare bedroom which he now used as a dressing room, pulled on a crisp handmade shirt and took his smartest double-breasted suit out of the cupboard, sweeping the cashmere fabric on the shoulders with a stiff brush before laying the jacket to one side until he had finished dressing. He took the greatest pleasure from being able to afford these luxuries in his latter years. He sat down on the end of the bed to tie the laces on a pair of Ducker shoes which Patricia had polished to a glass-like finish, then he picked out a silk tie and fastened it with a Windsor knot. He put the jacket on and admired himself in the full-length mirror, arranged a triangle of handkerchief in his top pocket, chose his smartest walking stick and went slowly downstairs. He found his wife in the kitchen.

'Goodness me, BS,' she said, looking up from her *Daily Mail* and peering at him over the top of her reading glasses. 'You look as smooth as a rat with a gold tooth.'

'Thank you, my love,' he answered. 'Good enough to talk His Lordship out of going ahead with this ridiculous exhibition, do you think?'

'Dressed like that, you already look the victor.'


Dean said the earl could see him at nine. The morning was bright and dewy and as BS drove along the familiar road towards the Hall, his confidence was high. By the time he reached the gates the atmosphere of the morning had changed, fog had crept up from the Red Lake and lay still and low across the estate.

'Snow this evening,' Pugh called out when he saw BS in the courtyard heading over towards the private apartments. 'Hope you've got your snow chains.' BS raised a hand and smiled. He knew Pugh's cheerful portents of doom too well to take much notice. He pulled the handle at the side of the wooden door and heard a bell ring deep in the undercroft. Several moments later he saw Dean through the glass of the door stooping to turn the key in the lock.

'Good morning, BS' the butler said. 'Come in.' BS slipped past and descended the stone steps. He waited at the bottom until Dean had secured the door. 'The earl is expecting you,' he said.

'Is he in a good humour this morning?' BS asked. The butler looked back over his shoulder and pulled a face.

As they passed through the double doors into the back of the undercroft, BS smelt the remnants of a cooked breakfast mixed with the scent of gun oil, and passing under the vast bell boards they made their way up the steps and into the butler's pantry. 'You'd better wait here,' Dean said. A Labrador stirred from a pile of old blankets underneath the pantry table and clicked across the wooden floor towards him. BS leant forward to pet her as he waited for the butler to return. The dog flopped on to the floor at his feet and exposed her stomach, but BS straightened up and sniffed the tips of his fingers, then pulled a handkerchief from his pocket and wiped his hand.

'Dirty girl,' he muttered. The dog's tail thumped the floor.

After a few minutes Dean beckoned to him, and he followed along the thick carpet until they reached the smoking room.

'Mr Moreton, Your Lordship.' Dean stood to one side then departed, closing the door soundlessly behind him.

The earl was sprawled in his favourite corduroy armchair in the smoking room, a tray of coffee at his elbow and a newspaper spread across his lap. He didn't look up when BS came into the room. BS stood in the centre of the Savonnerie carpet, swaying slightly on his stick, as he waited patiently for the earl to finish the article he was reading. After a minute or so the earl put the paper aside, took off his reading glasses and reached for a packet of Dunhill Internationals. He placed one between his lips, lit it with a heavy silver lighter and blew a plume of smoke into the air as he turned to face BS.

'What do you want, Moreton? I hope you've dug up something a bit more bloody interesting than another laundry list from 1820,' he drawled. 'I'm rather busy this morning, and frankly I may not be able to summon up a great deal of interest in how many hand towels the ninth countess embroidered in the summer of 1818.' He flashed a sarcastic smile at BS and took another long drag on his cigarette.

BS, nettled by his insolence, ignored the lack of an invitation to be seated and limped over to a chair in front of the earl. He sat down heavily and said, 'I've come to acquaint you with the facts surrounding a new exhibition which has been instigated by your CEO, Simon Keane.' The earl studied the old man from beneath his hooded lids. Tucking the still smoking Dunhill between his lips, he narrowed his eyes against the smoke and reached forward to pour himself another cup of coffee. BS ploughed on. 'Keane wants me to help an outside curator to set up a public exhibition of the Dywenydd Collection, and as I know that the very idea would appal Your Lordship, I thought it expedient to lay the proposition before you in order for you to prevent any more valuable money being spent on this futile enterprise. I know that people like Keane put the pursuit of money above everything else. Apparently he even intends giving women access to the exhibition when it's complete. I also know that he acts on a need-to-know basis and imagine that he did not think there was a need for you to know about this scheme.'

The earl brought his hand back to his cigarette, he drew on it deeply, then turned to flick the sagging column of ash into a leather bin at his feet. It fell instead on to the carpet. 'For God's sake, Moreton, of course I know about it. I suggested the damned thing.'

'You?' BS said, adding hastily, 'Your Lordship?'

'Bloody unmannerly of you to think I didn't know, Moreton.'

BS was thrown off balance. He had never meant to show the earl a lack of courtesy, but the revelation rendered him momentarily speechless. The earl continued in a tone that added to BS's feeling of discomfort. 'In fact, bloody impertinent of you. This is my house. What on earth made you think anything happens here without my knowledge? You're getting above yourself man.'

'But ...' BS floundered for a reply and chose his words badly, '... this is bastardising the memory of your ancestors to make money.'

'What?' The earl ground his cigarette down into the ashtray, smoke snorting from his nostrils, before he looked across at BS with ill-concealed irritation. 'On your feet when you speak to me, man!' BS heaved himself up out of the chair. 'Do you mean to lecture me on the memory of my ancestors?'

'I certainly do not, My Lord.'

'Really?' The earl got to his feet and took a step towards BS. 'Or on the need to keep this place solvent then?'

'No.'

'Good. Then let me explain once again. This exhibition will go ahead, and you will do what I pay you to do. I don't care about your feeble Catholic principles. You either shape up or you ship out.'

They stood facing one another for a few moments until the chiming of the quarter hour from the ormolu clock on the chimneypiece broke the stand-off and the earl barked out, 'Dean?' The butler must have been within earshot of this altercation as he slipped around the door within seconds. 'Moreton's leaving,' the earl said before returning to his chair and retrieving his newspaper with a histrionic snap and rustle.

Dean led BS back through the butler's pantry to save him having to use the stairs again and let him out into the morning room of the main Hall. He didn't comment on the shortness of the meeting and BS was thankful – he felt humiliated enough as it was. He passed Rosemary bustling along from the offices. 'You look smart,' she said. 'Got an audience with His Lordship?' BS grunted and continued through the state rooms towards the library, desperate to get up into his office before he had to engage in conversation with anyone else.

He was glad to have the office to himself for the rest of the morning. He knew Bunty would be coming up to see him in the afternoon to discuss the allocation of guides for his special tours, and he hoped his ill humour would have evaporated by then. This tradition had been established so long ago that no one queried BS's involvement in the rota except for Maureen Hindle.

'She probably thinks we sit up here and gossip,' said Bunty.

'Which we do,' BS said, 'but as my dear mother, God rest her soul, used to say, "Show me someone who doesn't gossip, and I will show you someone who isn't interested in people."'

That afternoon the first thing Bunty said was, 'Are you ill, BS?'

'No, I think I'm ageing,' he said with a sigh. 'I'm at my wits' end, Bunty.'

'We'd better have a cup of tea then,' she said. 'And a chocolate biscuit, I fancy.' She went over to a cabinet near the window where a kettle, a caddy and a handful of milk pots from the canteen stood on a tray. She clicked the kettle on and rooted around in the cabinet below to retrieve two mugs and a spoon. 'Come along, BS,' she rallied over the clatter and pop of the kettle. 'Get the biscuits organised while I do this.' Pushing down on the arms of his leather chair which creaked under his weight, he rose to his feet. He manoeuvred around Bunty.

'Just lean forward a bit,' he said, opening a cupboard by her shoulder and drawing out a tin of Cadbury's Chocolate Biscuit Collection which he put on the desk before negotiating his way back.

He landed heavily in the leather chair behind his desk. 'Oh dear, let me get my breath back, I'm a bit puffed today. I'll just rest for a moment,' he said, shutting his eyes and folding his pudgy hands across his belly. He heard Bunty clinking the cups before placing them on the desk, then her rustling around in the biscuit tin. After a few moments he felt revived and heaved himself forward.

BS liked Bunty. She had the round, cheerful face of a country-woman, her cheeks brilliant red from the thousands of tiny veins under the skin which had broken through years of strong sun and biting winds. She wore flat, comfortable moccasins which were scuffed and muddy, a pleated tartan skirt down to her calves, and a knitted jumper frayed at the cuff. Bunty was well into her sixties, but still ran her livery stables for polo ponies. Her husband was many years older than her, ex-army, and BS knew they were wealthy. He recognised breeding when he saw it. A woman couldn't get away with so little grooming unless she was rich and well connected.

'Oh, Bunty,' he said, 'I'm feeling very much under siege at the moment.'

'The exhibition?'

'Of course the exhibition. I'm fed up to the back teeth with the whole business – molars awash. I've just had a distressing meeting with the earl. He's always supported me, but although it beggars belief, he says the exhibition was his idea.'

'Doubt it,' said Bunty. 'Probably likes to think it was though.'

'I imagined he knew nothing about it. I couldn't believe he would let an outsider come in and stir around in those licentious artefacts, and to add insult to injury, I'm supposed to help.'

'It's a bit late in the day now, isn't it? Everything's under way. You should have spoken out earlier if you were this uncomfortable about it. And besides, you wouldn't have wanted it handed over to an outsider without being involved, would you?'

BS sighed again. 'Oh, I don't know, Bunty. Perhaps you're right.

But you've seen who they've sent to work with me? A woman! I simply can't credit it.'

'You embarrassed, BS?'

'Embarrassed? Of course not.' He crunched down mournfully on a digestive and brushed the crumbs from the summit of his stomach. 'Well, it does make it rather awkward, I suppose. I mean, there are things in that collection I wouldn't even want you to see.'

'You're being oversensitive BS, and it's because you're too much of a gentleman.'

'Really?' he said, flattered by her observation.

'Of course. A charmer and a gentleman.'

'Why, thank you, Bunty.'

'But times have changed, people move on. Sam Westbrook isn't some blushing girl on work experience – she's from London, she must have dealt with this sort of stuff before or they wouldn't have sent her.' She bit down on her biscuit and then a thought seemed to strike her and she added between chews, 'Come to think of it, Noel was talking about the Warren Cup – he went and saw the exhibition at the British Museum. It's buggery, you know.'

'What is?'

'The theme of the cup.'

'Buggery? How on earth can a cup have anything to do with buggery?'

'The images are male lovers.'

'Well, blow me down to the ruddy ground!'

Bunty stopped crunching her biscuit and laid it down next to her mug. 'If this whole thing really is too difficult for you BS, ask Noel to deputise for you. This sort of thing doesn't bother him in the least.'

'Are you suggesting I'm some kind of a prude?'

'No. Maybe a bit.'

'I'm a man of principle.'

'Of course you are. So why don't you get Noel to steer Sam Westbrook through the collection?'

'Because I'm the archivist,' he answered.

'You can't have it both ways, BS. You either suppress your sensitive side and work with this woman, or you swallow your pride and let Noel handle it. Either way it's going ahead, and there's precious little you can do to stop it.'

BS stared out across the courtyard. A deep gloom seemed to fill the park as if the evening was coming early. 'It's all very tiresome,' he said.

After Bunty had gone, he thought over her scheme and came to the conclusion that it had a number of advantages. The first was obvious: it saved him the embarrassment of sifting through these objects with a woman, although he was reluctant to let Noel enjoy Sam's company, but that couldn't be helped. The second advantage was that if the exhibition was a flop, he would be above reproach. He could say that unfortunately his deputy was not as fully acquainted with the collection as him, but that his enormous workload had prevented his full involvement. And the third advantage was that as Noel had never seen the inventory, there was no chance of being caught out by a slip of the tongue about a piece of the collection that might have been misplaced. He was free to squirrel away as many of the more contentious objects as he liked and no one would be any the wiser.

He did, however, need to move the inventory. At the moment it was still sitting up in the sealed chamber, throbbing underneath the foolscap notepad like a piece of deadly kryptonite. He couldn't risk putting it back on the shelf if Noel and Sam were going to be poking around there without him. He must put it somewhere safe, and where safer than the muniments room down in the undercroft? He checked his watch – it was a quarter to five. If he waited another fifteen minutes most of the staff would have left and he could fetch it and stow it before he went home for the evening.

## - 9 -

Maureen was getting ready for the day. The mirror over the desk she used as a dressing table had been picked up at an antiques fair and was heavily foxed. She liked the foxing – it gave the mirror charm and she preferred the image of herself blurred by the misted silvering on the ancient glass. She saw the image of her husband in reverse coming out of the bathroom. He was holding something white in his hand. She couldn't see it clearly unless she turned round, and she was afraid to turn round.

'How did this happen?' Michael was holding one of Maureen's blouses in his hand, he must have taken it out of the laundry basket.

'What are you doing with my washing?' she said. He never did her washing.

'I hadn't got enough for a full load of whites so I thought I'd put some of yours in.'

She laid her lipstick down on the dressing table and turned to face him. He came over towards her thrusting the stain on the sleeve up and pushing it near her face. 'Look,' he said. 'There's blood.'

'It's ... you know ...' she looked away from him and down, implying that this was a woman's private business. She knew he wouldn't believe her. She heard him sigh, heard him fling the blouse on to the floor, heard him walking over to the window. She knew he was getting himself under control. Perhaps he was even saying a prayer, asking God to help him overcome his feelings of disgust. Within a few minutes she heard him pulling a bedroom chair over and setting it near her. He sat down on it, reached out into her lap and pulled her folded hands over towards him.

'Look at me, Maureen,' he said. She couldn't. Her insides were writhing and coiling and pulling her chin further and further down towards her chest. 'Look at me,' he said again, and when she didn't, he turned one of her hands as if he was about to read her palm and moved the sleeve of her dressing gown up her arm, and she heard him inhale. 'Oh Maureen,' he said. 'What have you done to yourself?'

She snatched her arm away and stood up, pulling her sleeve back down and pushing past him. She went around the other side of the bed before looking back at him. He was still sitting on the bedroom chair, slumped forward, his elbows resting on his knees. He was watching her with an expression of contrived sympathy, but his eyes were filled with abhorrence and she knew her behaviour was repugnant to him. He got to his feet and came towards her again but the bed was between them. 'Please,' he said, 'please come and sit down again. I'm here to help.'

'I disgust you,' she said.

'No,' he said. 'I just have ... ' he paused and looked away, casting around to find the right words. 'I have trouble understanding how doing this to yourself can possibly help. It must be so painful.' He gave an involuntary shudder. 'Why do you do it?' He ran his hand over the skin of his head. 'I thought all this had stopped. Are you still writing down your thoughts? Where's that diary you used to keep?'

'I stopped doing that.'

'Why? It helped, didn't it?'

'Everything I wrote sounded so stupid, so weak, so needy.'

Michael shook his head again. She could see how hard he was trying and that made it all much worse.

'Who are you angry with this time?' he said, betraying his frustration.

'Myself. Only ever myself.'

He walked around the room, one hand on his hip, the other taking a slow route from his scalp, back down over the white tonsure of hair above the nape of his neck and round to his clavicle where he gently massaged the muscles at the base of his throat. 'Finish dressing,' he said, his voice now warm with compassion. 'Let's pray together.'

When Maureen came out of the bathroom Michael was already on his knees. He held a hand up, she took it, and he guided her down until she was kneeling beside him. He released her hand, folded his together in front of him and closed his eyes. 'Jesus, help my beloved Maureen to know that You shed Your blood in her place. Show her that every reason for cutting herself that she has held on to, was every reason that You bled and died. Help her to understand that she is justified, by the blood of a pure and perfect sacrifice. Show her that no cut she makes on herself will ever be deep enough or ever bleed enough. Show her that she would have to keep coming back, like the priests of the Old Testament, to offer a sacrifice that would never be sufficient to atone for her sin. Which is why, dear Lord Jesus, You came to us. To offer the perfect sacrifice. To stand in our place, and suffer our shame, and die for our sins. Let her clothe herself in righteousness, and never bleed again. Amen.'

He opened his eyes and turned to look at her, his own filling with tears. She knew they weren't tears of compassion for her – they were tears of pride for his own goodness, his own ability to understand her, his neurotic, difficult charge. Satisfied he got to his feet, helped her up and said: 'All right now?' She nodded. 'You feel better?' She nodded again. 'You'll be OK today, won't you?' He lifted her chin up with his forefinger and scanned her face. 'You weren't the one in the wrong,' he said. 'Do you remember when we talked through anger, and I explained that it's all right to turn your anger outwards, to blame someone else, to feel angry with someone else?'

'I remember.'

'I want you to think about that today. We'll pray again tonight,' and he kissed her on her cheek, his lips dry and chapped, and to her relief, he left.

Michael's conviction that she was sinned against and not the sinner was wrong, so wrong Maureen felt embarrassed for him. She had robbed herself of the opportunity of blaming BS Moreton because she had done something far worse, something shameful, and because of it she was trapped by a secret she could never share. If you really want to keep a secret, her mother had told her, tell no one.

She made her way downstairs to the kitchen. She toasted several slices of bread, spread butter and syrup on each slice while they were still warm, and piled them one on top of each other until rivulets of gold dripped and pooled on the plate beneath. Taking the stack with her, she went into the office she shared with Michael. After laying a newspaper on the desk to stop it getting sticky, she put the plate of toast down and drew out a file from the cabinet beside the desk – a file she had not opened for two years. She had written 'The Indigo Library' on the front of the folder using a calligraphy pen which one of her sons had given her many years ago, and as she looked at the careful lettering she recalled the pride she had felt when BS Moreton agreed that her idea was a good one and that she should follow it through.

It was an idea that had developed over several seasons as a result of questions the visitors asked her when she was on security in the library. Most of them wanted to know how many books there were and whether they were ever read, but others asked more interesting questions. What was the oldest book in the library? The most valuable? Had the books been catalogued? Could they view the catalogue online? Were the books all in English? She sat on security in the other rooms as well, but the visitors there didn't ask questions in the same way.

'Have you ever thought,' she said to BS a few days before that Christmas two years ago, 'of writing a booklet about the indigo library?'

Apparently delighted to have an opportunity to lay down his pen, lean back in his chair and chat, BS mulled her suggestion over and said, 'It's all in the guidebook, isn't it?'

'Not really,' Maureen replied, and she brought the guidebook over to his desk and stood behind him looking over his shoulder as he scanned the page she had opened for him. She loved the way he smelt – clean, soapy, no hint of that musty denture smell she associated with being close to her husband. She went to point at the paragraph about the library and her index finger brushed across the top of his hand. He didn't seem to notice, but she felt the burn of physical contact run up her arm and flush her cheeks.

'It is brief,' he said, 'I'll grant you that.'

'You know so much about the library,' she said. 'You could write a brilliant little booklet – it could be sold as a companion to the guidebook, like they do at Wilton House for the art collection. I'm sure it would be successful.'

BS had chuckled at her compliment then shook his head. 'If only I had time,' he said.

Christmas was approaching and Maureen saw stretching ahead the prospect of almost two weeks of unending boredom, trapped in her home skivvying for Michael's elderly parents with only the occasional church service as respite. Instead she explained to the family that her new boss could spare her for only two days over the break, and volunteered to come in on the days before New Year's Eve to deal with any messages that might have been left because BS said he wouldn't be coming in until the first week of January. But when she started to climb the spiral staircase up to his office she heard him moving around above her, and she took it to be a good sign that he also preferred to be here rather than at home over Christmas.

'I've put a great deal of thought into your idea, Mo,' he said, 'and I think you should be the person to carry it forward. Ask for as much help as you like. Look,' and he struggled with the keys at his hip. 'Take the key to the library cabinets – keep it. I won't need it over the next week. I've dug out the catalogue for you,' he went on, pushing a plastic ring binder across his desk towards her. 'Start with a plan – different headings to categorise interesting aspects of the library. Break those down further, then hunt through and see if you can find an example or two of each. I'll ask Laurence to bring his camera in – he can take pictures to go in the guide. You might want to do it chronologically or by themes – you know, maybe sport, architecture, botany. All sorts of ways you could cut the cake. It's up to you. I will ...' he paused as if he was recalling a word, '... mentor you. That's what I will do – mentor you.'

Maureen was so happy. She could talk of nothing else. She told anyone she saw at the church that she had been commissioned to write a book, albeit a short one, but her name would be on the front cover, BS Moreton had said that to her. She would be a published author. When midnight came on New Year's Eve she raised a glass of champagne ostensibly to the members of the family clustered around the table but in actual fact she was toasting her own success at the start of this new exciting year.

Despite BS's assertion that he had no time to work on the project, he spent a great deal of time down in the library with her. A number of the books were in the wrong place, on the wrong shelves, but BS had an uncanny memory and would abandon whatever work he was doing and hobble down with Maureen, holding the library steps for her and pointing with his stick to where he was sure he had seen a particular tome. At the end of each day he liked her to print up the text she had written for him to read, and she sat watching his expression as he checked it through, monitoring his reaction, hoping his frown was one of concentration, not disapproval. He corrected the pieces as if he was still a schoolmaster and she was his pupil, and this casting fuelled other fantasies in her mind – fantasies of him sweeping down corridors with his gown boiling around him, his cane whippy in his hand.

By the middle of February she had completed almost twenty thousand words of copy. Laurence Cooke, the guide who liked to think of himself as a resting actor but was also a rather accomplished amateur photographer, had taken the pictures, but still BS hadn't spoken to the CEO or the shop manager. She didn't understand his delay but he assured her he would speak to them when she was away on holiday, and he thought the book could be out in time for the August celebrations. She bought herself a smart new file from Smiths and wrote 'The Indigo Library' on it using the calligraphy pen, and printed out a set of pages to take away with her to Scotland. She never tired of reading through them and she hoped that Michael would take a look too.

When the book finally came out, she was no longer speaking to BS and besides, she already knew his name was going to be on the cover. Michael was furious on her behalf and speculated about putting the matter into the hands of a local solicitor. Maureen said she couldn't prove she had written it – it was all done on the computer in BS's office, and all in Duntisbourne Hall's time.

She never told him what had happened a week after BS had humiliated her in the library, when she had seen him leaving with Donna for – she assumed – one of his intimate lunches. Instead of taking a break after her tour, she had slipped through the door and up the stairs to BS's office. She hadn't been sure what she hoped to find – maybe a memo from BS to the CEO perjuring himself. The hot file was full to bursting again, and she flipped through the pages, every now and then glancing up at the window overlooking the courtyard to make sure he was not on his way back. She found nothing. And then she saw his rucksack leaning against the side of the chair behind his desk. She stared at it for a full minute and gave an involuntary glance over her shoulder. She could feel her heart beating rapidly at the base of her throat. She knew it was wrong to look through someone else's things and she struggled with her conscience.

She lifted the rucksack up and put it on the desk. She looked in the main compartment. Inside were the proofs of *The Guide to the Indigo Library*. For a moment her heart lifted – it was a thrill to see the double-page spreads laid out, the pictures in position, the captions she had written beneath. BS had made a number of small corrections on the proofs and when she came to the proof of the front cover, she saw that he had put a line through her name as author and written instead 'by BS Moreton, Archivist to The Right Honourable The Earl of Duntisbourne'.

Maureen slumped down in BS's chair. The rucksack flopped forward, the mouth open towards her. What was she to do with this information? But there was a part of her that was thrilled, delighted she had real evidence that he was a mendacious old goat, and this feeling of heady victory made her want to search further, find more. She tore open the side pocket of the rucksack and recoiled. There was an apple core, oxidised and flecked with mould, shoved into the pocket, beneath it a black banana skin and behind that a sandwich in a packet. She drew them out on to the desk one after the other and tilted her head to read the expiry date on the sandwich. It was a week old. She grimaced with disgust and posted each piece of detritus back into its original position.

Then she opened the small pocket on the other side of the rucksack. A wad of paper towels had been thrust into this pocket and she drew it out and began to fold back the layers. She expected to find another apple core, the stone of a plum perhaps, but the first thing she saw was a square of foil, a packet with the top torn off, and it looked familiar – it looked like the packets Michael used to keep in the drawer of the bedside table when they were first married. She could hardly bear to carry on, but she was drawn by the horror of her discovery. Picking up a pencil from the desk, she used it as she had seen police doing in television dramas, turning back the next fold, and sure enough, there it lay like a piece of sausage skin, damp and spent and behind it another opened packet. However many were in here?

Her stomach gave a great heave and saliva poured into her mouth. She had thought she was going to vomit all over the desk and ruin everything, but she hadn't. She panted and swallowed several times in quick succession until the retching died down, but she hadn't been able to look at the execrable parcel again. She remembered fixing her gaze at a point somewhere above it as she refolded it, using the pencil to poke it back down into the rucksack, and then she had tottered down the spiral staircase and gone straight away to wash her hands.

She finished her toast, its sweetness comforting, then took the file marked 'The Indigo Library' outside and pushed it down the edge of the recycling bin. There was no point in keeping it, and there was no point in trying to explain to Michael why she couldn't turn her anger outwards. Another mantra her mother used to repeat was 'Eavesdroppers seldom hear any good about themselves', and although it wasn't completely apt, it did have parallels. Two years ago she had made a pact with the devil. She had pried, hoping to find something useful to use against BS, and had fallen foul of her own Faustian pact. She could speculate as much as she liked in her own head, but she could never discuss it with another living soul. What was a man of that age doing with used condoms hidden in his rucksack?

# - 10 -

Max had forgotten he was doing the last tour until Laurence reminded him. Now he was hanging around the front door watching the mist rise in the courtyard through the chilly gloaming, willing it to remain empty. He had put his outdoor coat on because it was bitterly cold, a few wisps of dry snowflakes had curled down during the afternoon and the smell of the air had changed. The tips of the Black Mountains in the distance were pale against a black and seething sky.

Five minutes before he and Noel were due to shut and lock the front door, he saw a father holding his seven-year-old son by the hand sprinting towards them. Behind him an earth mother lumbered, her landing-craft sandals slapping the gravel, the child tied to her hip with a large Indian scarf, lolling and screaming.

'Shut the door, Noel, for God's sake. I'm on last tour.'

'Oh, I don't think I can do that, old chap,' Noel replied gleefully. 'They look ever so keen.'

'Bull shit,' muttered Max, turning away.

'Ah, better and better,' called Noel as he looked out of the door. 'The whole family seems to be joining them. That must be the aunt, a couple of teenage children (they look a bit rough) and – oh and that's the grandmother in the wheelchair.'

Max was at his side in a heartbeat. 'You're not serious,' he said, wrenching the door out of Noel's hand and looking out.

'Course not, old chap. Load of porkies. Serves you right for making me stay on for those mythical ten Koreans last week when I was on last tour.'

Max waited in the Hall like a doomed man and watched his colleagues collecting their bags and escaping for the evening. He saw Roger Hogg-Smythe and Weenie leaving together. They looked over towards him, Roger said something to Weenie, who laughed like a hyena and clung on to his arm. BS Moreton limped past him on his way up the stairs to the minstrels' gallery. The family pounded up the steps, their breath forming clouds of vapour as they panted. Noel locked up the front door once the family were in the great hall and bade Max a cheery farewell.

The tour was every bit as bad as Max had feared. He loathed small groups – he wasn't able to use his expansive style to amuse his audience. The father was interested in a number of things but the son kept asking questions about how long it took men to die once they'd been shot in the face by a musket, what the fifth earl looked like when his nose was blown off, and how big buboes grew before they burst when you got the Black Death. Max could smell the mother from several feet away, a mixture of patchouli oil, sweat and hair. What woman, he thought, came out on a freezing March day wearing sandals? He was halfway through explaining the tenth earl's passion for taxidermy when the child on her hip began to mewl again. To his horror she sat herself down on a seat in the watercolour room and flopped out a large-veined breast around which the child clamped its lips and proceeded to make the most repulsive sucking noises, squeezing and massaging the breast with its upper hand like a cat prinking a cushion. Max struggled on manfully with his description of the third earl's trip on the *Mayflower* including a number of references to the physical effects of scurvy to enthral the younger member of his audience. The baby dropped off to sleep and its head fell away from its mother's bosom, leaving the large glistening nipple clearly visible. Max hurried them on to the indigo library and saw Maureen, who was waiting in the library for the final tour to come through, get up and leave through the library bedroom.

Eventually the tour was over and he let the family out into the twilight through the small door at the end of music room. By now the snow was falling steadily and the courtyard was whitening. A few flakes of snow swirled in around the door as he shut it and locked it with a sigh of relief. Pugh had been following quietly behind him, closing shutters and turning off lights as Max left each room with his group, and the building was now dark and quiet as the grave. He made his way back along to the foot of the stairs up to the guides' room to collect his things, and pulling on his gloves, he wound his scarf high on his neck before stepping out into the freezing evening. The wind had got up and he tucked his face downwards and walked briskly to his car, flakes of snow stinging his cheeks and brambling on his eyelashes. Away from the shelter of the courtyard the snow was beginning to settle and his feet squeaked as they compressed it. He looked up. The flakes were coming thick and fast, grey against the clouds above.

He swung his Land Rover out of the staff car park and across the great courtyard. The snow was starting to drift along the left-hand margin of the drive and as he accelerated he felt the tyres slip before they took hold and he followed the route around the top of the lake towards Dolley Green Gate. The drive was virtually impassable and he wondered if his had been the last car parked in the staff car park because he doubted anyone else would be able to leave the Hall this evening. Ahead of him his lights picked out a figure stooping against the wind, and as he drew near, he recognised the gait and stature. It was Claude Hipkiss. He was wearing a viyella shirt and corduroy trousers. He had tucked his trousers into his socks and wrapped a towelling cravat around his neck, but these were the only concessions he had made to the weather. Max drew up alongside him and rolled down his window.

'Can I give you a lift, Claude?'

The old man stopped and leaned towards the window. Snow was building up in Claude's ear on his windward side and his comb-over was trailing in the wind like a banner. His nose was crimson and had a bead of moisture quivering on the end. 'Why?' he asked.

'The weather, of course. I could give you a lift into town.'

'Better on foot,' he said, stepping away from the car to continue his journey. Max cruised beside him.

'I've got an old coat in here you could borrow,' he shouted.

Claude waved his hand dismissively at him.

'Are you sure?' Max called out, but Claude waved again as if shooing him away. 'Well, if you're certain.'

'Yes, yes,' the old man shouted back over the wind. 'Leave me be.'

Reluctantly Max drove on, but pondered that perhaps Claude was right about it being better to walk. He couldn't believe the weight of snow that was falling. His windscreen wipers were having trouble keeping it clear.

Eventually he broke free of the park and was able to pick up a bit of speed in the lee of the valley running down towards the River Lugg, but it wouldn't be long before this road too was impassable. He checked over his shoulder to make sure his wellington boots and shovel were in the back. The trusty Land Rover hadn't let him down in fifteen years of living on the Welsh borders, but tonight might just be the night. He moved gingerly up the gears, relaxing into the bumping rhythm of the vehicle, and began to think about Sam. He wondered what she was doing right now – he hadn't seen her in the Hall all day. He hoped she wasn't out in this terrible weather – that silly little car of hers would be hopeless in these conditions. Already the road in front of him was a white ribbon, a single set of parallel lines had formed along the narrow lane away from the drifts where a few other vehicles had passed before him. She would probably be home by now. He wondered what her flat looked like. He should ask her – he wanted to imagine how she spent her evenings. Did she pour herself a drink the moment she had put down her things and hung up her coat? Did she have someone waiting for her in London and would she call each evening to say 'Hi, how did your day go? Mine was terrible, and now it's snowing'? He wondered if she ever thought about him when she wasn't at work. This is ridiculous, he said to himself. Why on earth would she think about me?

And suddenly, there she was. In the split-second that it took his headlights to illuminate a car tipped at a crazy angle on the other side of the road, he registered a flash of lime green paint, warning lights blinking and Sam's blonde hair whipping around in the gale as she stood beside the open door talking on a mobile. He began to slow, his mind racing. Had she stopped to answer the mobile? No, he realised with mounting excitement – the warning lights were on. His happiness was almost beyond endurance. She needed rescuing. He searched desperately for a place to turn, braked and felt the back of the Land Rover skitter and slip before he came to a halt. He battled with the gears, the old engine revved and coughed but it never let him down, and he was back on to the packed snow of the road and heading towards Sam.

'Can I help?' he said, rolling down his window. 'I just happened to spot you as I came along, and it looked like you could do with some help.'

'Oh, Max, it's you.'

Max squeezed the Land Rover past her car and pulled off the road as far as he dared before climbing down. He felt his feet sink into the snow and begin to melt into his socks. He should have put on his wellingtons. He turned his collar up against the wind. Sam was hopelessly under-dressed for the weather. She plunged around in the snow to reach him and he put a hand out to help her.

'If you could just get me back on the road,' she said, 'I can't be that far from the Hall.'

'Hopeless,' Max said. 'I hardly made it out of the park myself.'

'I was trying to raise the AA,' she said, waving her mobile at him. Max shook his head. Townies. 'I'm sure I'll get through to them in the end. Don't worry about me. I'll be fine.'

'That's ridiculous,' he said. 'You'll freeze to death. Anyway, I don't think you should be waiting here in the dark on your own. Someone odd might spot you.'

'Like you?'

'Good heavens, Sam, you do say the most extraordinary things. Of course not like me. You know me. No, I mean someone unpleasant. There are a lot of very unpleasant individuals in this world at the moment, and they all come out after dark. Look, my house is only ten minutes up the road from here. Come back with me. Sort this out from there, in the warm. The rescue services are going to be stretched to the limit tonight.'

Sam hesitated. 'Oh, I don't know, it seems an awful imposition.' She peeled a strand of soaking hair off her forehead and turned back to look at her car on which several inches of snow had built up in the time they had been talking. Shivering, she went on, 'You're probably right. If you don't mind.'

'Marvellous! What do you need to take out of your car?'

Ten minutes took half an hour. Sam didn't say much as they drove but sat staring out of the side window. Every now and then her body gave another shiver, and she tucked her hands under her thighs. Max reached back and pulled across an old Barbour coat which he pushed into her lap, and she rustled around with it to cover her front and hands.

'Cold?' he said.

'Frozen.'

Eventually Max turned into a quiet lane and crunched the gearbox into a lower ratio to climb an ascent through woods until they reached a hamlet of houses. He parked in front of a small row of modern timber-framed cottages and came round to help Sam down. She began to shiver again and he grabbed the coat from her seat and wrapped it around her shoulders, retrieved her handbag and briefcase and offered her his arm to help her up the path to the door. The snow was heavy on the trees above. The crunch of their footsteps and the gentle ticking of the cooling engine was muffled as if they were already indoors, then the high-pitched barking of a small dog sounded from inside the house. Sam turned and looked at Max.

'That's Monty,' he said with a slight shrug.

'I wouldn't have had you down as a dog person at all.'

'He's not my dog – he belongs to my daughter. I ended up with him by default.' Max opened the front door and stood to one side to let her pass into the warmth of the compact hall. A brindle Cairn careened up the passage, his claws clicking frantically on the tiles to get a better grip, his tail wagging every part of his little body. Max squatted down on his hunkers and scrabbled his hand across the dog, 'Hello, you old stumper,' he said before straightening up.

He shook the snow and moisture off his coat and hung it up on one of a row of cast iron hooks. 'Let me take yours,' he said. 'Come on through, you'll soon warm up.'

The sitting room, which took up most of the ground floor of the cottage, was at the end of the corridor and turned back on itself into the kitchen. Max flicked open the doors of the wood-burning stove and dropped in some more logs. 'Sit down,' he said gesturing towards the sofa. 'These will soon blaze up. I'll get some wine.' Monty sprang up on to the sofa beside Sam and responded to Max's glare and pointed finger by circling round a couple of times and settling into the corner against a cushion.

'I'm really sorry,' Sam said. 'What a night! Is spring always like this?'

'Not always,' Max called through from the kitchen, reaching into a tall double-doored fridge. 'Sauvignon?'

'I'd better not. I ought to call the AA again. I may have to drive.'

'One won't matter.'

'OK then, just a small glass.' Sam dialled the number and wandered over to the fire. She finished her phone call and came into the kitchen where Max was leaning back against the worktop, a glass of chilled wine in his hand.

'Hopeless,' she said. 'Unless I go and wait with the car, they say they can't come out. If I'm not in any danger, they say wait 'til the morning. They're unlikely to get here tonight.' Max tried to affect a look of frustrated despair on her behalf to cover his delight. She looked around the kitchen and added, 'Goodness, Max, you live well.'

'Don't sound so surprised,' he laughed. 'What did you expect? Middle-aged bachelor squalor?'

'I don't know really.' She took the proffered glass of wine. 'I don't know very much about you. In fact, I don't know anything about you. What do you do?'

Max disliked this question for a number of reasons. He had done well for himself in the eighties, but recognised that the decade had damaged the reputation of stockbrokers to such an extent that many of his breed were regarded with suspicion at best, disgust at worst. When his marriage failed he was pleased to give up his high-octane life and go back to where he'd grown up on the borders of Wales, but found that for a man the role of single parent brought with it other difficulties. He lacked a support network to help him, there were no other single dads in the area, and he was wary of socialising with young mums in case his motives were misconstrued. This didn't pose much of a problem when Charlotte was younger, but when she hit her teenage years with a vengeance he would have valued the sounding board of other parents going through the same experiences. However, by this time he had carved out a niche for himself as a loner and was content to deal with parenting as best he could on his own. Around this time the first e-broker developed and for the next four years he devoted his time to trading from home, spending all his days and most of his nights puffing away at his Rothmans upstairs in his study and making a great deal of money. This stopped him worrying too much about the things Charlotte was up to, but he didn't regard his career as admirable. In light of this, his answer to Sam's question was, 'About what?'

'Come on, Max, you know what I mean. No one could work at Duntisbourne Hall unless they have another income source. What's yours?'

'I retired young.'

'And well, by the look of it. What did you do?' she persisted.

'Very little indeed, if I could help it.'

'Max!'

'Oh all right then. I was a stockbroker and now I top up my income with a little day trading.' And he gave her a smile of resignation accompanied by a shrug of the shoulders.

'Interesting,' she said.

'Let's go back next door, that fire should be going now.' He put his glass on the table by the sofa and went over to the French windows to close the curtains. The outside light penetrated several feet into the garden which was heaped with soft mounds of snow. He saw in the reflection of the dark glass that Sam was watching him from behind, and he felt a flutter of excitement that she was appraising him. 'It's getting nasty out there,' he said as he drew the curtains shut and returned to the sofa. Sam sat down beside him.

'Not much point ringing for a cab then?'

Max stared into the fire and shook his head. There was only one solution to her dilemma, but he needed to handle things carefully. He turned towards her, resting his arm along the back of the sofa. 'I hope this isn't going to sound all wrong,' he said, 'but could I suggest that you stay the night?' He raised his hand and hurried on. 'No, don't get the wrong idea. I've got a perfectly safe double spare room with its own bathroom and I'd be honoured if you would consider it. Then I can run you back tomorrow and you can wait with your car for the AA. Or I may even be able to pull you out with the Land Rover. I could probably get the tow bar on in the daylight and take you back to the Hall. These spring dumps don't tend to last. And you can have another glass of wine. And I could fix us a bit of supper. And,' he smiled, 'I could tell you all about my sad and complicated early life and get to know you a bit better.'

He could see her struggling with the suggestion and guessed that the glass of wine on an empty stomach, together with the comfort of his warm home was tempting.

'Are you sure?'

'I insist.'

So Max got up again and went through to the kitchen to rummage around in the fridge until he found some cheese and packets of cold meat which he started to lay out on a serving plate. As he worked he leaned back a little to enable himself to see what Sam was doing. She had tucked her stockinged feet up on to the sofa and was relaxing. Max was happy.

Monty trotted into the kitchen and sat under the table watching the floor in the hope that a few scraps of food might drop in front of his nose. When Max started making toast, the smell brought Sam through to the kitchen again, and she opened a few drawers until she found the cutlery and started to lay the table. It felt so comfortable, the two of them moving around the kitchen, making a meal together, that Max had to resist the temptation to walk over and hug her as she chatted about her meeting that day in Hereford with the council and the architects, finalising the details of pushing the walls of the sealed chamber out to the west above the dining room to create an exhibition space beyond the room above the minstrels' gallery.

'But I have yet to see any of the pieces that might go into the exhibition,' she said. 'BS Moreton is a charming fellow, but working with him is like knitting jam.'

Max opened a second bottle of wine and they settled down to eat. She talked about her work at the British Museum, her divorce, her flat in London and her daughter. He told her about Charlotte and Monty and day trading. Over the years he had found that courtship was similar to an interview for a job except that it generally ran for longer than a few hours. When he had first spotted Sam he had been interested in her, and this evening confirmed that he wanted the job. However, he knew he would probably have to go through a process of tests and vivas until she decided he was the right candidate and gave him the post.

He thought this analogy had probably begun to form during his adolescence. He was academically lazy and his parents hadn't been confident he would pass his Common Entrance, but they found a progressive boarding school in Hampshire which offered hordes of hopeful boys and girls the chance to impress over three days of the summer holidays. Max, a keen sportsman, had injured his leg and attended this three-day marathon in a plaster cast, and he was certain this had gained him the sympathy vote and got him a place.

He wondered if regaling Sam with the story of his recent hospital adventure would have a similar effect, and he was on the point of opening the subject when she looked at her watch and said, 'Goodness! Is that the time? It's half past one.'

'Is it? Would you like a coffee?'

Sam smiled and reached out to rub the top of his hand. 'No, I think it's time I went to bed. We'll have to be out early tomorrow to get that car out of the ditch. It's been a lovely evening, I couldn't have hoped for a more gallant rescuer, but I'm shattered.' She patted his hand affectionately and he knew it signalled an end to the evening and that he had no option but to capitulate. Reluctantly he showed her up to the spare room.

Half past one was not late for Max. He seldom slept well. After he had found some towels and a spare dressing gown for Sam, bidden her goodnight and come back downstairs to shut down the stove, he put his coat on and walked out into the back garden with Monty to have a final cigarette. It had stopped snowing and he could hear a gentle rhythmic dripping in the woods at the back of the garden. It wasn't going to freeze tonight – as he had suspected, the snow would not last. He looked back towards the house and saw the light of the spare room extinguish. Sam would be turning in the bed, pulling the duvet over her shoulders ready for sleep. Had she slipped under the covers naked? Probably. Rather crossly he threw the lighted butt away and heard it hiss as it hit the snow.

## - 11 -

Earlier that same evening, BS Moreton reached the great hall a trifle early. Several members of staff bade him a cheery goodnight and the new guide, Max Black, was waiting at the front door while Noel checked the tickets of a family who had arrived in the nick of time. BS couldn't understand people paying all that money to come into the Hall when it was about to close. Tonight he felt particularly irritated – it would take Max half an hour to get them through and out. He would just have to risk slipping down to the muniments room while the tour was at the other end of the building.

He hesitated in the shadows of the gallery and watched from above until Max disappeared into the statue corridor, then he unlocked the door of the sealed chamber and began a painful ascent of the stone steps. He was feeling extremely puffed. Halfway up there was a small slit window which looked out across the park, and here he rested a hand on the sill to get his breath back. A dim glow came through the window, and bending to peer out he realised it had begun to snow. He sighed and started to climb once more.

The table was exactly as he had left it, the foolscap notepad covering the great leather tome, and BS sat at the desk for a few minutes, his hands knitted across his belly, his eyes closed. He thought perhaps it was nerves that were making his heart thump and that it would be a good idea to use a short meditation on the Hail Mary to relax. He took a deep breath and imagined it travelling up into his head, then exhaled and felt it running down into his feet. His shoulders began to soften and on the next inhalation he said quietly, 'Hail Mary, full of Grace,' and breathed out the words 'The Lord is with Thee', and so on, up and down, in and out, 'now and at the hour of our death ...' and his lips formed a wordless 'Amen'.

He woke with a snort. How long had he been asleep? He checked his watch. Not long, only fifteen minutes or so. He pulled himself forward, pushed his hands down on the desk and rose to his feet. He felt much better – invigorated, refreshed. Gathering up the heavy volume, he started back down the stairs. All was quiet below.

When he reached the door into the undercroft he spent a few minutes of exasperation struggling with the security key – there was a knack to turning it – and he had to stand the inventory up against the wall with his stick beside it to leave both hands free. Eventually he opened the door and stepped down into the half light where the air was even colder. He patted the powdery wall until his hand felt the bakelite switch which he flicked on. A small blue spark spat inside the switch, making BS jump and curse. He hobbled down the stone steps into the bowels of Duntisbourne Hall.

Swaying heavily on to his stick with each step, he started to make his way along the corridor, the inventory tucked underneath his right arm. Passages disappeared into the gloom to left and right of him, while a dank breeze lifted the sheets of cobweb and every now and then he stopped to wipe one from his cheek. He was heading into the darkest middle section of the corridor. The locked door to the wine cellars was on his right, and ahead of him in the distance he could see a yellow oblong of light, the glass panel of another locked door leading to the cellars of the private apartments at the other end of the building. The light from the base of the hopper windows set low in the wall was already obscured by a bank of snow building up outside. Feeling his way along for the second switch, he began to curse again.

'Oh blow me down to the ruddy ground,' he said as, supporting himself against the wall with his hand, he tried to inspect the sole of his shoe as well as he could with his limited mobility. Even in the darkness he knew what had happened and the smell confirmed it. He had trodden in dog shit. When the weather outside was cold, Dean couldn't be bothered to take the earl's dogs out for their exercise, so he let them run around in the undercroft beneath the Hall. BS had tried to reason with the earl about this, but had made little headway. With a heavy sigh he located a discarded piece of wood on the floor, and pinioning it down with his stick he began to scrape his foot across the edge reflecting that if a dog had done that up in the park the earl would have fined the owner heavily, but in his own household, what did it matter if someone stepped in it? He treated his employees like dog shit anyway.

Taking a corridor to his right, BS eventually reached the door to the muniments room and began to fumble with the keys at his hip. He paused momentarily, his attention caught by a barely perceptible disturbance in the silence. He thought he had heard the door at the end of the corridor  open and felt a brush of air across his face.

'Hello!' he boomed out. 'Dean? Is that you?' But his voice echoed away and died unanswered. He hobbled back towards the intersection of the passageways, his stick hooked over his arm, the book still pinned to his side, and strained his eyes into the darkness. The yellow oblong of light from the glass panel in the door at the end of the undercroft had been replaced by a grey oblong. That was what he had heard: someone must have gone down to the basements in the private apartments to turn the lights off on the other side. He hobbled back towards the door of the muniments room, but just before he turned the key in the lock he paused again, breathing through his mouth to listen. He was sure he had heard something, and there in the drumming darkness of the passageway running off behind him he thought he could make out an even darker shape. He blinked hard and stared and it was gone.

'Come on, you silly old fool,' he muttered to himself. 'It's just your eyesight. Jumping at shadows!' and he unlocked the door and let himself in.

Once inside he felt more settled. The room had been created for him by one of the estate carpenters underneath the domed ceiling of the cellars, and over the years BS had been collecting up all the old books and files and letters and papers from around the Hall and slowly and laboriously stockpiling them here in the muniments room before beginning the task of cataloguing. He had found stacks of letters in the most unlikely places: abandoned rooms up in the disused servants' quarters, trunks stored in the attics, once fabulous pieces of furniture stacked broken and twisted and waiting for restoration.

There was no window down here, but the carpenter had painted the brickwork white to make the room brighter, and although the moisture had already caused the paint to start peeling and crumbling in places, it did give the room the appearance of care. As soon as the cold weather began BS had smuggled a fan heater into the basement hidden in his rucksack, and the first thing he did on entering the room was to plug this in and turn its purring mouth towards his feet so that the air underneath the desk warmed and washed over his shoes and up his trouser legs. The room was stuffy and smelt of mildew and the chipboard shelving that had been installed last autumn down one side. The shelves were piled high with parcels of papers tied with string and labelled in his own spidery handwriting. Tucked between them were treasures from the earl's uncatalogued collections which BS had carried down here over the years: a photograph of the Grand Duchess Anastasia Nikolaevna in the original Fabergé frame, a Meissen figurine of a semi-naked young woman, an exquisite little bronze of Leda and the swan.

Dropping the book on to a table near the door, he inspected the room for the best possible hiding place for the inventory. He lifted a few boxes aside until he came to a tin trunk which probably dated back to the 1850s and bore a patina of age. The blue paint had been chipped and scratched over the years, and although it had a lock, the key had gone missing long ago. The inventory would fit very nicely into it and he could leave it at the back of the room and cover it with other boxes. It was a particular favourite of his, and he was confident he wouldn't forget where he had stowed the book. He pulled his chair over to the trunk so that he could sit as he emptied it, but as he leaned forward his attention was caught again by a sound, quiet but clear, just outside the room. He stared at the gap beneath the door and saw a shadow pass first one way, then the other. He tried to keep completely still and listen, but as he leaned forward just a fraction of an inch, to his horror he felt the chair beginning to move under his weight, and to stop it he took the strain on his bad knee. A stab of pain shot up through his leg and he pushed sideways with a groan to relieve it by straightening it and fell noisily on to a pile of boxes opposite him, twisting and rolling as he fell. As he flailed around like an upturned tortoise on his back, books and papers and seals clattered on to the floor around him. He lay for a few moments until the shower

of documents ceased, then laboriously rolled backwards and forwards until he could get an elbow down on to the floor and begin
to lever himself up into a sitting position. He listened, but everything was quiet once again. He wasn't surprised. He had probably made enough of a din to scare away even the most hardened
eavesdropper.

Getting slowly to his feet, he steadied himself on the back of
the chair before taking up his stick and opening the door into the
passage. He leaned his head around the door. 'Hello!' he called,
and was surprised that his voice sounded high and weak. He
cleared his throat noisily and swayed a few steps down the corridor
towards the intersection. 'Hello?' he called again, using the full
volume of his barrel chest to push out a strong, confident voice.
'Is that you, Dean?' He looked left and right into the dark portals
along the passage. The harder he stared into the darkness, the more
it seemed to clot as if something was forming in the shadows.

Behind him BS heard a creak followed by a loud bang and the
passage was plunged into darkness. He swung round and stood
panting and blind for a few seconds until his mind slowed. With a
great wave of relief he knew that the door had swung shut behind
him as it had done many times before. Taking a deep breath to
steady himself, he moved as quickly as he could back towards the
door which he could just see by the pencil line of light glowing
at its base. His large hand felt nervously up and down the wood
until he located the handle, pushed it down, and let himself once
more into the sanctuary of the muniments room.

He paused for a few moments leaning his back against the door.
He found he was panting. This wasn't surprising – he had just
hauled himself up from the ground – but he also felt jumpy and
his hands were shaking. Perhaps his coffee had been too strong

this morning after all. He needed to get that book stowed and head home. It was getting late, the snow could have worsened. Sitting down again, he plunged his hands into the trunk pulling out the contents in three great handfuls which he dropped on to the floor. He could get it all cleared up tomorrow. He unhooked his stick from his chair, pushed himself up and was about to make his way across the room to collect the inventory from off the table when he heard a thump directly outside his door as if someone had tripped and fallen against it. 'Who's there?' he called. There was no reply. He could feel that irritating tightness in his chest again as he made his way over to the door. He opened it, his heart pounding, and peered out into the gloom of the passage. 'For God's sake, who's there?' But the cannonade in his chest was getting louder and louder, he could feel the blood rushing through his ears, and as he stared into the darkness it turned thick and viscous and flowed into his eyes. He shook his head to clear it and saw the silhouette of a figure standing a little way up the passage in the darkness – someone who might have been fleeing, but had turned.

'Pugh?' he said weakly, 'Is that you?' And a horrible pain rose in his chest and sprayed across to his shoulder and arm and up into his face. He tried to catch his breath but it felt as if a carapace was forming around his rib cage, a breastplate of solid bone and try as he might he couldn't get another breath in. Blackness deeper than the dark of the cellars rushed into his peripheral vision and clamoured in his ears, and the pain in his chest was so strong he knew he was going to swoon. The figure in front of him began to come forward, he heard a voice but couldn't make out the words, everything was distorted, the noise boomed as if he was under-water, then the blackness at the edge of his vision rushed forward and overwhelmed him and he thought, Pray for us sinners, now and at the hour of our death, and he thanked God this awful pain was going to stop.

## - 12 -

It did not freeze overnight. Sam was woken just after seven by shafts of low sun sliced into lines by the louvred blind at the window. She reached out for the dressing gown Max had lent her and pulled it half on before she stepped out of bed, gathering the rest of the oversized garment around her as she made her way towards the window. The towelling was soft against her neck and there was a faint tang of citrus and musk beneath the smell of cigarettes. She changed the angle of the louvres and looked down on the garden below. The snow underneath the trees was pockmarked with drips of melting water. She could see Monty's paw marks circling and traversing the middle of the lawn, a spray of earth and mud radiating out across the white where he had kicked and scuffed at the ground.

Max was downstairs smoking. 'Coffee?' he said.

'Can I make myself a cup of tea?'

'Of course,' and he opened a cupboard and fetched down a box of tea bags. 'Are you a breakfast person? I've got some bread in the deep freeze.'

'You're obviously not,' she said, nodding at his cigarette.

'Sorry. Filthy habit. Would you like me to go outside?'

'Not in your own house,' she said.

Despite this Max walked over to the French windows and opened them. 'Thawing, much as I thought,' he said. 'Did you sleep well?'

'Great. You?'

'I never sleep well,' he said.

Sam sensed that both of them felt awkward. Last night their conversation had flowed easily and warmly, probably as a result of the wine but also because of the shared drama of their meeting. They were now playing out a scene which traditionally followed a night of intimacy, and she wasn't entirely sure why last night had ended on such a chaste note, but in the cold light of day she was glad it had.

'When you've finished,' Max said, 'I'll take you up to your car.'

'Aren't you working today?'

'No. I do every other day. I'll be in tomorrow.'

The roads were wet with slush and her car, although still tilted at an angle and filthy dirty from mud thrown up by passing vehicles, started on the third attempt and was back on the hard standing of the road with little more than a few rocking pushes from Max at the back. He came round to her window. 'I'll see you tomorrow then.'

'I can't thank you enough,' she said, and he patted the soft top of her car. She watched him in her rear-view mirror as he walked back to the Land Rover, his hands thrust deep into the pockets of his coat. Monty was bouncing around in the front trying to see what was going on. She saw Max worry the dog's head in his hands before pushing him over to the passenger's seat and setting off back to his house.

The flat was icy cold. Sam dropped the files and papers from her meeting with the planners the previous day on to the dining-room table and checked her watch. There was still time to have a soak in a hot bath before the working day began. Her unplanned night away had left her feeling unkempt and grubby. While the bath ran she stood at the window and looked out across the lake to the Black Mountains beyond, sepia and white against a weak blue sky. She felt truly homesick. When she accepted the post at Duntisbourne Hall, she had underestimated how stateless she would feel. She envied Max his comfortable home filled with his own things – she even envied him his dog. She resolved to get the exhibition to a point where her daily intervention was no longer needed, to enable her to commute from her home in London on a more sporadic basis.

The steam in the bathroom was so thick she could only just make out the ghost of the tub. She had forgotten this aspect of living without central heating – something she hadn't experienced since her days at boarding school a few decades before. She lowered herself into the bath, her skin goosebumping above the waterline as she submerged – a feeling so seductive it was almost worth getting frozen to the bone to experience it. The bath was huge and the taps poured like geysers, the hot water bubbling and spitting as if it was boiling. That was one thing to be said for old plumbing – people never use to worry about the green issue. Sam had to hook her elbows over the side of the enamelled cast-iron rolltop to stop herself from disappearing completely under the water. She watched her legs float up and bob just below the surface. She needed a pedicure – the varnish on her toenails was chipped.

She smiled at the thought, it reminded her of something which last year had been incredibly painful, but now struck her as comical. She had begun to suspect her boyfriend's infidelity when she realised he had been for a pedicure. Was her awareness of her own toenails a sign that her restless companion was stirring again? It had settled prior to her divorce, but when she met Paul, the thrill of a younger lover projected it on to a higher plain. Here was a man who had not witnessed the compromise of her sexuality through childbirth. He met her when she was no longer responsible for Claire's daily care or happiness, when she no longer felt frustrated with herself or with life, and when, after a series of serendipitous house sales, she was comfortably financed, but the relationship was accompanied by such nervous energy and suspicion that the price eventually became too high and she handed back to him the burden of his delicate psyche. Although highly sexed men undeniably liked a lot of sex, they usually liked it with a lot of different woman.

'When did you start to dislike Paul?' she had asked her daughter when she had finally been strong enough to end the affair.

Claire had looked surprised then rolled her eyes at her mother's stupidity. 'When he started to be horrid to you, of course.' Claire was right – it had been a stupid question.

Sam dressed quickly to retain the heat of her bath. She fastened a long necklace round her neck, wrapped and arranged a scarf above it and then slung her glasses chain over both. She had enjoyed excellent eyesight for the first forty years of her life before it started to deteriorate. When she could no longer hold the menu far enough away to render it legible, she found a pair of tiny reading glasses in a shop in Paris which were so chic they invariably provoked comment, but within the next few years she found it increasingly difficult to do her job without spectacles. Finally she could look back and understand her father's hysteria about his ageing eyesight. It was dawning on her late in life that elderly people were not a race apart, and she calculated that when her father was obsessing about the inadequacies of spectacles he must have been the age she herself now was. He had been dead for nearly thirty years, but she vividly remembered him soaping his spectacles with washing up liquid and rinsing them under scalding water before buffing them with a clean handkerchief, and, as she followed a similar routine herself, she wished she had appreciated the gift of being able to read 'hot' and 'cold' on the top of a tap without first finding her spectacles.

Bunty intercepted Sam on her way to BS's office. 'Not looking for BS, I hope,' she said.

'I was.'

'He had a bit of a do last night.'

'What sort of a do?'

'Poor chap collapsed in the undercroft, had to be rushed to hospital. Terrible business. The ambulance took an age to get through the snow.'

'Oh dear, I'm sorry to hear that. Is he at home again?'

'Heavens no! He's still in hospital. We've no idea when he's going to be fit enough to come back, but as luck would have it, we were talking only yesterday, and he was saying that because of his heavy workload he thought Noel could deputise for him and give you any help you may need. Noel doesn't usually come in today, but I've called him and he should be in shortly, and Maureen has handed BS's keys into the office.'

'Maureen?'

'Didn't I say? She found him, and a good job she did. She was on security for the last tour and noticed that the door down to the undercroft was open, went down to investigate, and there he was, the poor old fellow, lying in a heap outside the muniments room.'

'Coronary?'

'Too early to say, but Maureen thought he looked very unwell.'

'We are going to push through this wall here,' Sam explained, patting the plaster with her hand, 'and extend the exhibition room out into the void above the dining room, effectively increasing the room's size by two-thirds.'

'Excellent,' Noel said. 'Nice views out across the park to the west then?'

'No,' said Sam. 'We want to retain the integrity of the sealed chamber, and according to the planners, the lintels you can see above the west terrace were not being used as windows when the Hall got its Grade I listing, so they have to stay bricked up.'

'Potty planning policy working in our favour. That's a first.'

'Certainly is. Now, I want to retain these original drawers and plan chests and put the smaller items in the drawers for the visitors to pull out and have a look at. It'll add to the clandestine feel of the place, and also underline this theme I'm building on of the Victorians pushing normal human drives underground which, of course, spawned the rise in pornography.'

'Capital,' Noel said. 'Really clever. I had no idea how you were going to make an exhibition out of all this stuff. But isn't it a bit risky having the things in drawers? People could just help themselves.'

'Oh no – you'll pull the drawer out, but the pieces and the description will be under glass, maybe acrylic, rather like a boxed picture frame. There'll be no chance of anyone helping themselves. Also, the exhibits are protected from light and dust and all those other things we curators hate.'

'Like the general public.'

Sam smiled her assent. 'Then, once past this sort of Victorian scientist's-cum-gentleman's-club entrance, visitors will make their way down to the left and round the exhibition in a roughly clockwise direction. I intend to arrange the cabinet exhibits in chronological order, but as well as the continuous displays running around the walls, the space will be broken up by several large island cabinets of pieces. I can't really plan much further than that until I've gone through the inventory with you.'

'There's no inventory,' Noel said.

'No inventory?'

'No, never has been.'

'There must have been an inventory. The earl who created this room, and these cabinets, would surely have catalogued everything as it was stowed.'

'Maybe, but I've never seen one or heard of one. It's all in BS's head. He's an encyclopaedia of knowledge.'

'Unfortunately, that particular encyclopaedia has fallen off the shelf now.' Sam sighed heavily, put her hands on her hips and surveyed the piles of boxes. 'Blast! That really complicates things. This is going to be a monumental task.'

'I know quite a lot about it,' Noel said consolingly. 'And BS had obviously started making a list for you here.' He picked up a foolscap notepad divided into two columns. 'This must be a list of things he knows are up here, and these must be things he thinks are down in the muniments room.'

'It's not all up here?' Sam was worried.

'I don't know,' Noel said cautiously.

Sam peered down at the spidery writing. 'He didn't make much of a start, did he?'

'No.' Noel stared at the pad, then added, 'If BS was here, he'd probably be able to dig out some of the lists that visiting scholars made of the things they studied – I think the St Andrews lot made a pretty extensive list.'

'I hope we've got more here than the Beggar's Benison.'

'I'm sure we have – I'm just not sure how much more.'

Sam scanned the room. 'What to do, what to do ...' she wasn't asking Noel a question. 'OK, here's the plan. Until the building work starts, we're pushed for space. Apparently I can have the music room temporarily while the builders are up here, and removals are booked for the beginning of next week. There's no point in us unpacking and cataloguing the boxes just yet – they can just go over to the music room as they are. We need to get stuck into the stuff in the drawers, make a note of it, and repack it securely before next week.'

'I thought the drawers were staying.'

'The room needs to be completely gutted first. The underfloor heating's got to go in, wiring for the lighting, all of that, and the drawers need taking out, restoring ...'

'Thought we were only allowed to 'conserve' these days,' Noel said with a cheeky wag of his head.

'These aren't special enough – they're much later than the Hall. I'll make sure they don't look brand spanking new.'

'Perhaps they should, for this exhibition.'

'Indeed,' Sam said. She took her laptop out of her case and set it up on the table. 'Let's start with this,' and she held up the Fabergé plate which BS had left lying next to his notepad. 'Do you know what this is?'

'Pudenda display tray of Peter the Great,' said Noel.

'Which works how?'

Noel held the dish at crotch level. 'BS thinks the Emperor held it in this position and placed his pudenda on it before entering the room, possibly with the royal member covered with a piece of silk until the moment of reveal.'

'BS has quite an imagination.'

'He's very knowledgeable.'

'So you say. What about this?'

'Pudenda display tray of Catherine the Great.'

Sam studied the glass platter and conceded to herself that the applied decoration at the centre of the plate could possibly be interpreted as labial. 'Are you sure?' she said.

'I'm fairly confident. Have a look at this one,' and Noel opened a deep drawer and pulled out another plate, simple in design and made of a comparatively cheap material. 'BS always said that this particular tray belonged to Captain Cook and accompanied him on all his voyages. It is believed to have played an unfortunate part in his demise in 1779, when the natives of Hawaii were grossly offended by the display he offered and promptly killed him.'

Sam laughed. 'That can't be true.'

'BS swears it is.'

She leaned back in her chair. 'It's all very subjective isn't it? These could just be large serving plates. It's not like the pewter test platter up in St Andrews. They've got the Beggar's Benison club minutes from 1737 – 'Twenty-four met ... all frigged."

Noel began to chuckle. 'Really?'

'Yes, really. But that's provenance. There's no provenance here.'

'I'm sure there are papers about the Thomas Lawrence painting over there of the ninth earl.'

'Fair enough. But show me some other pieces. Prove to me that this isn't some colossal eighteenth-century dirty joke. Because if it is, fine, that's how we create the exhibition. But we can't present artefacts on hearsay.'

Noel opened several drawers in succession, finally picking up a piece of lace work pinned on a velvet cushion.

'What does our archivist say that is?' Sam said.

'A perineal polisher apparently. The spiel goes that due to the frail nature of the fabrics of which these were made, very few examples have survived.'

'You don't say.'

'The ninth earl was only able to secure one authentic example – a particularly fine one in Belgian lace thought to have belonged originally to Rabelais and dating back to the sixteenth century. The ninth earl paid the colossal sum of £400 for this particular artefact.'

'Bollocks.'

'Shiny bollocks?'

'Very shiny bollocks. But bollocks all the same. It's a piece of Belgian lace, Noel, and a badly conserved one at that. Those pins holding it in the cushion are rusty.'

Noel shrugged in a 'fair enough' way and returned it to the drawer. 'Aha! You won't be able to argue with this one,' he said, placing before her a carved framework of scrimshaw, small enough to sit on the palm of a hand. There was an cranked handle made of ivory on one side and the central column was filled with sheets of soft suede on a spindle. It looked like a miniature Rollodex. 'Clitoral palpator. Turn the handle here and look – the little suede paddles beat away. You can't argue with that. What else could it have been used for?'

'It is rather charming,' Sam said, leaning forward for a closer inspection, 'but without any provenance ...'

Noel returned to the drawers. 'Penile stiffener with pearls round the top there.' He held the object aloft for Sam to see. 'Lift and girth, all in one.'

Sam shrugged. 'Maybe.'

Noel struck the heel of his hand against his forehead. 'Of course!' he said. 'Come over here – come on,' and he led Sam to the back of the room, pushed aside a screen of faded baize and whipped a dust sheet from the top of a cabinet with the flourish of a matador.

The sheet had concealed an ornate box standing on stout conical legs. It was about waist-high, and Sam recognised the intricate marquetry pattern of brass inlaid with turtle shell. It was definitely Boulle work. In the centre, on a raised and ornate piece of gilded woodwork, a deep dark hole disappeared into the depths of the box. Rising above it was a sweep of Boulle work decorated with a small mirror.

'And this is?'

'The brass-bound buggery box.'

'The what?'

'The brass-bound buggery box, circa 1725.'

'Noel! This could be anything. It could be a writing slope.'

'With that hole? There are remnants of silk and damask around the edge which probably flopped down into the box which BS thinks was filled with sawdust, maybe sand, or even goose down. And these handles,' he grabbed them and pivoted the box towards his crotch, 'give you the grip and the mirror in front of your face,' and he grimaced into it.

'Great imagination. But it could easily be a sewing box, the hole somewhere to push offcuts, or even a campaign shaving table. It could be a dozen possible things.'

'No it couldn't.' Noel let the box rock back into an upright position. 'It was commissioned at the beginning of the 1700s by Peter the Great as a gift to the Danish sailor, Vitus Bering, the chap who found a way through the Bering Straights proving that Siberia and America were not joined by land. Bering took it with him on all his voyages. But later it was acquired by the Scottish pirate, Angus MacDirk, who uttered the immortal word:

*Take these boys away, they split -*
*Bring me my Brass-Bound Buggery Box!'*

Sam experienced a combination of frustration and a feeling that she was watching a warm-up act for an end of the pier show. 'Those are lines from a version of "The Ballad of Eskimo Nell", Noel,' she said.

'Based on this.'

'Not a shred of evidence. Pure speculation.' She took off her glasses and let them swing down on the end of their chain. Running a hand up her face and through her hair, she frowned with irritation – not at Noel, but at the situation. 'The problem for me is that I can't curate an exhibition around speculation.'

'It's only for the general public,' Noel said. 'How accurate do you have to be?'

Sam flung her hands up towards him. 'You only have to put the wrong medal on a uniform in a television costume drama to bring an avalanche of complaints down on your head. Never underestimate the general public. If I make a single error – a date, the spelling of a name, anything – in an exhibition board, at some point someone will see it and write to the British Museum. Apart from the cost implications of having to redo information boards, the reputation of the museum is paramount. If I create a stunning, compulsive exhibition based on nothing but canards and scandal, Duntisbourne will be a laughing stock, and I probably won't get to curate another exhibition ever again.' Noel looked back at her with a dazed expression. 'I'm sorry,' she said. 'It's not your fault.'

'What do you want to do?' he asked. 'Carry on, or wait until BS gets well again?'

'I suppose we'll have to carry on.'

'Then perhaps this will cheer you up,' and Noel dived into a box and drew out a peniform vase, a gloriously harmonious shape of male external genitalia. Sam smiled. 'This,' Noel said, 'is a bronze copy of a Greek terracotta vase which is in the Metropolitan Museum of Art in New York, and this,' he snapped open a letter which had been stowed with the bronze, 'is a letter to BS from the museum's curator confirming its accuracy.'

'OK,' conceded Sam. 'Now we've got something to put in the exhibition.'

# - 13 -

Patricia's voice was the first thing BS heard in hospital, and he opened his eyes to see his wife's concerned and comfortable old face looking down on his from above. He was in the coronary care unit, his naked chest wired up to a number of monitors. The ward was clean and bright and smelt of male sweat, but he was comfortable and content. He found the drama surrounding his collapse stimulating as opposed to frightening, and was intrigued to recollect that as he swooned he had had a strong conviction that he was dying but felt an incredible calmness sweep over him, a reassuring knowledge that death was the most natural thing in the world, and here he was facing it with no fear whatsoever. And his hearing had been the last thing he lost. He remembered a voice radioing out an urgent request for help. He had slipped into a deep and dreamless sleep from which he stirred when he heard the metallic clatter of the wheels of a gurney trolley coming nearer and the comforting voice of Pugh saying it wasn't as bad as it looked before he slipped away completely. But after Patricia left the hospital at three o'clock in the morning and the drapes were drawn around to enclose his bed so that he could sleep, he began to remember other things. He remembered a woman's voice talking to him, but he couldn't remember what she had said. And he remembered someone struggling with his waistband and the clatter of his bunch of keys. He raised his head, opened a lizard eye and peered over at his bedside table. He was too tired to stir any further and check that he still had his keys with him. He hoped Pugh had locked up the muniments room after he had been taken into hospital. The thought of the inventory sitting on the table made his heart begin to beat hard and fast again, and he sank back on to his pillows. He needed to rest. Little wonder this had happened. He pushed himself too hard.

The following day he was surprised to be moved on to an ordinary public ward for observations. Patricia arrived with some books and a bottle of squash.

'I don't know why they've put me here, my love,' he said to his wife. 'I'm really rather ill.'

'Apparently not, BS,' she said. 'You just had nasty turn.'

'Nasty turn?'

'The doctor says you had a panic attack.'

'Panic attack? Of course I didn't. If I'd had a panic attack, why did they have me in the coronary care unit? Answer me that?'

'Because you're over sixty and overweight, I should imagine. They said you can come home this afternoon.'

'Surely not.'

At least they had the decency to wheel him out of the hospital in a wheelchair, one of the nurses pushing him and Patricia following along behind carrying his clothes of the night before in a plastic bin bag. He had refused to get dressed. He said he was too exhausted and was feeling breathless again, but the twelve-year-old doctor didn't seem to be taking him seriously and told him to try some relaxation techniques.

When they got home, Patricia insisted he spend the rest of the day in bed where he lay trying to read and feeling thoroughly bored and agitated. His wife didn't reappear until the afternoon when she came up with a cup of tea for him. He asked her to get in touch with Donna and tell her to bring his work diary over.

'You're meant to be resting, BS,' Patricia said. 'And that doesn't mean entertaining a horde of adoring women from the Hall.'

'It's not a horde. It's only Donna.'

'Your Donna kebab, you mean.'

'That's not very kind, dear.'

'Really?'

'Why are you being so disagreeable?'

Patricia whipped the pillows away from behind him, thumping and puffing them up before shoving them back in position. He meekly submitted to her manhandling, trying to work out why she was upset. She caught his eye and stopped fussing with the bedding, then sat down heavily on the foot of the bed. 'I'm sorry, BS.'

'It's so unlike you,' he ventured, reaching forward to touch her shoulder.

She looked up at him, and her eyes were moist. She burrowed a quivering hand into the pocket of her cardigan and pulled out a cotton handkerchief. He caught the faint smell of lavender as she shook it out and blew her nose. 'I thought we weren't going to make forty years after all,' she said in a small voice.

'Forty years?'

'Our anniversary.'

'That's weeks away.'

'I got such a fright last night.'

'So did I!' She looked sharply across at him and he regretted bringing the subject back on to himself. 'But equally alarming for you, my love,' he added.

She looked out of the window and continued, 'I saw the snow was worsening. I rang your office and the answerphone was on and I thought you were on your way home, but the time ticked on, and still you didn't come. And I looked out into the drive and the snow was getting so bad I began to think you must have had some sort of accident, or worse. And then the phone rang. No one rings after ten o'clock at night unless it's bad news. And it's that supercilious Maureen on the phone, and she keeps on prevaricating and spinning things out and I can't get her to cough up the story. I know she's enjoying every minute of my agony, but she's wrapping it up with all that cod sympathy and condescending claptrap about Jesus, and I want to scream "What's happened?" But I don't. I wait. I refused to thank her for her pompous condolences, but she blathered on for so long I honestly thought she was building up to telling me you were dead, and she was there with you. She didn't say where you were, where she was, or why she was with you at that time of night. Honestly BS, my imagination was running completely wild.'

'Patricia!' BS exclaimed. 'I can't stand the woman, and she can't stand me.'

'But she did find you, and if she hadn't, you could have died.'

'I know, dear. I know.'

Patricia looked down at her hands and massaged her knuckles. 'She found you, and now I have to be grateful to her. I fully expect her to be on the phone again this morning, crooning in that haughty way of hers, pretending to be full of concern for you, and, even more nauseatingly, for me.'

'Well, let's forget about her now. It was only human nature for her to help me – anyone would have. If she hadn't been ...' and he paused, remembering the figure in the dark, the figure who might have been fleeing but who didn't, and something made him not want to tell his wife about it. 'If she hadn't come along, Pugh would have found me. Or even Dean. She did what any normal human being would have done. Heavens above, you'd have to be fairly inhumane to walk away and leave someone lying in the sort of state I was in.'

'I can't bear to think of you lying there, on that cold stone floor.'

'I know. It was awful.'

'And I don't want that wretched woman on the phone every day asking how you are.'

BS sighed. 'It's probably best to feel sorry for her, really. She's hoping this will put her at the centre of attention, but she's making a fool of herself by milking as much drama out of it as she can.' He leaned forward in the bed and patted Patricia's knee. 'We know the truth. We can see through her.'

He sank back into his pillows and reached out for his teacup which rattled in the saucer as he moved it towards him. Sipping the tea, he watched his wife to monitor her mood. Over the last few years she had developed a very slight tremor which caused her head to move like that of a toy dog in the back of a car, and this made her body language difficult to read.

'I would, however, like to make contact with Mrs Westbrook, just to make sure that she has everything she needs to carry on with the exhibition.'

Patricia stared at her husband and the movement of her head increased until he realised she was now shaking her head at him, her expression one of extreme irritation. She got to her feet and re-moved the teacup from his hand in a movement akin to a snatch. BS knew he had read the body language incorrectly. 'You're the limit, BS. The giddy limit. I am not contacting the Hall, and neither are you. That job puts too much strain on you and too much strain on me. You reneged on your promise, BS. You promised me nearly twenty years ago that you would retire.'

'I did. From teaching.'

'You did not. You were pushed.'

'I was not pushed. I took early retirement.'

'What about Candida Cochrane?'

BS rolled his eyes and sighed. 'That was years ago. How many times have I got to say it? The girl was lying.'

'That's not what her mother thought.'

BS took a sharp breath in and placed his hand on his chest to strike an anguished pose. 'Oh dear,' he said. 'Another little twinge, I think.'

The following morning Patricia agreed to him getting up and dressed only because he promised to take it easy once downstairs.

'I can't find my keys, dear,' he said.

'They'll turn up.'

'I think I may have dropped them when I fell in the undercroft. Could I just give the Hall a quick ring to make sure they're safe?'

'I'll do it, BS. You rest.'

'It's bothering me a lot. If they fell into the wrong hands, someone would have security keys for anywhere in the Hall.'

Patricia dried her hands on a tea towel and took off her apron. 'I'll ring them now for you,' she said. 'Quite safe,' she called through from the hall a few minutes later. 'Bunty said they've been handed in and she'll hold on to them for you.'

'Thank you dear,' he called back, modulating his tone to prevent himself sounding as irritated as he was.

For the rest of the morning he bided his time, knowing that Patricia would eventually have to leave him alone for a few hours at least if only to carry out the weekly shop which she always did on a Wednesday afternoon with their daughter-in-law Jane. He sat in the small conservatory reading his newspaper and watched her moving around the kitchen trying to keep his waves of impatience at bay. She showed no signs whatsoever of getting ready to go out. When she came through again with his cup of decaffeinated coffee he could stand it no longer.

'Shall we make a list, my love?' he said casually.

'What for dear?'

'Well, I thought we could make a shopping list for you for this afternoon. There are a few things I wouldn't mind you picking up for me.'

'No, dear, you mustn't worry yourself about that, it's all organised. I phoned my list through to Jane and she has ordered everything we need online. Very clever. They will deliver any time today between one and three o'clock.' Patricia smiled over at him and he sensed a flicker of victory in her face. 'So you see, I don't need to leave you alone for a minute.'

'Well, thank you, my love, that's very thoughtful of you,' he said, bringing his paper up between them with a snap to disguise his expression of pique. After about five minutes of listening to the gentle click of her knitting needles he crumpled the paper noisily into his lap and said, 'For goodness' sakes Patricia, let me ring the Hall.'

Patricia removed her reading glasses and looked him straight in the eye. 'BS! I have told you once and I will tell you again, every day if necessary, you are not ringing the Hall. It may be a difficult concept for you to grasp, but you are not indispensable at the Hall. You are, however, indispensable to me. You are going to rest and you are going to get better.'

'How can I get better if you put me under this sort of strain?' he shot back crossly.

Patricia replaced her reading glasses and recommenced her knitting. 'You're being peevish BS, and it doesn't suit you.'

'Nastiness of the very worst order!' he muttered, scrabbling for the remote and turning on the cricket.

Noel reluctantly called it a day at five because he and his wife were off to see a performance of *The Caucasian Chalk Circle* at the Guildhall in Oswestry. 'A favourite of the amateur theatre companies,' Noel said gloomily to Sam. 'Can't stand the play myself.'

Sam worked on for another couple of hours before leaving the sealed chamber and making her way carefully down the spiral staircase, her laptop case slung across her back to leave both hands free for the descent. She locked the door and looked down into the great hall beneath. Pugh had left a dim light on for her on the desk below to illuminate her way down the staircase, but when she started along the statue corridor towards the music room she wished she had taken a torch with her in the morning. The marble statues loomed out of the darkness to left and right of her, punctuated by deep shadows and she felt a tingling in the hair follicles at the sides of her head. She paused and turned, fearful of what she might see, but all she could make out were the profiles of stone gods and goddesses staring with their white and sightless eyes. She hurried on towards the door into the music room and out through the exit on the other side into the great courtyard.

The mist from the Red Lake had once more stolen silently up the valley and into the courtyard. The night air hung motionless and tangy with a mineral odour, water from a gutter somewhere in the courtyard was tapping out a metallic *bock-a-da-bock*. With the aid of a weak light above the exit, Sam locked the door and made her way over the gravel towards the stairs up to her flat. The sound of her footsteps bounced around the old stones and she looked across to her right at the cheerful yellow light flooding from the windows of the private apartments on the opposite side of the courtyard. She imagined Dean and the rest of the staff below stairs having a meal together, and envied them.

Once inside her flat, she put a match to the fire and went into the kitchen to fetch a glass of wine. She could hear the kindling cracking and spitting next door and caught the scent of resin as a wraith of smoke puffed into the room. Pugh had been right when he assured her that the fire would draw properly once the chimney warmed and she had come to like the smell of woodsmoke in the flat. She was soothed by the sight of a full fridge – it looked almost as good as Max's.

Max. She was thinking about Max again and she realised she was smiling. She wondered if she should reciprocate his hospitality and kindness by offering to cook a meal for him tonight, but then decided he might read the offer the wrong way. He wasn't her type at all.

She carried her wine back into the sitting room, closed the curtains on the night and wondered why Max wasn't her type. He made her laugh and he was undeniably a nice looking man, intelligent, clearly interested in her. In fact the candour of his pleasure to see her was very appealing, so much more attractive than a man who retains a cool aloofness when in reality you know he is boiling with desire. Perhaps it was nothing to do with type, perhaps it was more to do with an overwhelming feeling of ennui that enveloped her at the thought of investing all that emotional energy into yet another relationship that would most probably end badly. Friendship seldom ended in that way.

The moment Sam heard the knock on her door she was sure it was Max. She sprang to her feet, hurried over to the door and flung it open without a moment's hesitation.

A woman swathed in layers of clothing, her head covered with a scarf that swaddled her hair, stood in the dark a few steps down and away from the door. She must have knocked and then retreated before the door opened. Sam couldn't see who it was.

'Do you have company?' the woman asked.

'No. Who is that?'

The woman came back up the steps towards her and as she travelled into the light flowing through the open door Sam recognised the pale face as one of the guides.

'Maureen Hindle?'

The eyes, heavily lined in kohl, loomed out of the darkness and Sam had to stop herself from retreating back a step. 'Won't you come in?' she said.

'No. No, I won't. I wanted to give you this,' and from beneath the layers of clothing she drew out a large leather-bound book which she held towards Sam with both hands.

Automatically Sam put her own hands out to receive it. 'What on earth is this?' she said.

Maureen did not immediately let go of the book, so the two of them stood facing one another and holding the great tome between them. Eventually she released her grip and Sam caught the full weight and gathered it up on to the crook of her elbow. She looked down at the book and back up at Maureen, waiting for an answer.

'I think it's a list of the Dywenydd Collection, but I didn't like to read it.'

'Where did it come from?'

'The muniments room. I found it the night Mr Moreton was taken ill.'

Sam paused. Something was wrong here. 'Why didn't you hand

it in to the office?' she asked. Maureen took two steps backwards and put her foot on a lower step.

'I thought you should have it. Things have a habit of getting mislaid here. It's safer with you.' She moved a few steps further down. 'I have to go now,' she said.

'No, wait. Please come back,' but Sam was calling down the dark stairwell at a retreating figure. She heard a car door slam and an engine cough into life and accelerate away, and silence flowed back up the stairs towards her with the mist from the Red Lake.

# - 14 -

The events in the undercroft the night the snow came catapulted Maureen back into those dramatic surges of buoyancy and despair that she had hoped and prayed she had vanquished. Once more, thoughts of BS Moreton filled her mind, unbidden and without warning. It seemed that every waking minute was an opportunity to revisit evidence from the past and the romantic obsession – her limerence – which she had fought so hard to keep at bay, blossomed once again under this new stimulus. She wondered if perhaps she was going mad, but comforted herself with the thought that if she was struggling with a psychosis she should feel like a normal person in a crazy world, and this was not how she felt. She knew her behaviour had no logical explanation, but it gripped her with such ferocity she could not set it aside.

It was initially triggered by a series of sensory events that drew her back to the evening two years ago when she had had her accident. There was something about the light in the Hall that evening, the smell of snow in the air, the emptiness of the great hall, that stripped back time. That night two years ago Bunty had left early and asked her to stay behind until Pugh had finished locking up. She agreed to do so, but in fact it was incredibly inconvenient because she had promised Michael she would be home on time to take over the elderly parents while he went to preach. She remembered feeling stressed, rushed, out of control. Whatever the reasons, when she saw that Pugh had missed one of the shutters in the lower dining room, she was furious. His duties weren't exactly onerous, he was a salaried member of staff on a good wage with benefits, and he had that lovely house at Dolley Green Gate all for free. It was beyond unfair. The least he could do was remember to close the shutters at the end of the day before he slunk off for his tea.

She battled with the leaden wood and eventually managed to unfold each stubborn side and as she struggled to raise the heavy locking bar, feelings of ferocious helplessness overwhelmed her, so much so that when she slammed the iron bar down across the shutters, she knew the middle finger of her right hand was still on the bracket. As the noise of metal clanking into position shocked along the state rooms, an exquisite pain flung her away from the window and on to the floor. For a moment it was so intense that it disconnected her utterly from everything – her stress, her hatred, her fury, and this disconnection was even stronger when she looked down at her hand and didn't recognise it. The tip of her finger was missing and as she watched, blood as thick and black as pitch pushed out from the wound and the pain, already unbearable, washed in sickening agony up her arm and she filled the room with a full-throated animal roar.

It was BS Moreton who found her. Back then she only knew him by sight and this great man, this oracle of the Hall, fell to his knees beside her and gathered her up into his embrace. He rocked her and soothed her, he helped her up and along to the office, he praised her for her bravery and stayed with her all the way to the hospital, leaving only after her husband Michael had arrived. He visited her daily at home, short visits to bring her a book she might like to read, or just to sit with her and share a piece of gossip about the Hall. When her own guilt forced her to admonish him for the time he was spending, he explained to her that as a Catholic this pastoral care was a duty required of him which he was happy to give, but she knew it was more than that. No one, not even Michael, and certainly none of her family, cared for her the way BS did. That had been the start of her feelings, and even though subsequent events had warped them, BS Moreton remained extraordinarily important to her.

Why she had followed him the night of the snow she hardly knew. Her suspicion was piqued by his behaviour towards the end of the working day when she spied him looking down from the minstrels' gallery, watching Max Black set off with a family on the last tour. She began to make her way slowly along the statue corridor to the indigo library to take up her position until Max came through, but she lingered in the shadows to see what BS would do once Max and his group rounded the corner to the south of the great hall to start their tour in the brown drawing room. Max had the reputation for moving his groups along swiftly so she couldn't delay for long, but within a few minutes of him moving out of sight, she spotted BS making his way down from the minstrels' gallery. Before descending each step, he planted his cane on the one below to support himself because he did not have a free hand to use on the banisters; he was using his other arm to hold a large leather book tightly to his side. She made her way slowly along the statue corridor, looking back all the time, and when BS reached the foot of the stairs and turned right towards the morning room, she knew he was heading down into the undercroft.

She came to the conclusion that the archivist was up to something, and she had an irresistible need to find out what it was. When Max entered the library, she didn't hand the radio over. She made a sign to him implying that it had gone dead, and mouthed that she would put it on charge for him in the office, then she slipped back through the library bedroom so that she wouldn't meet Pugh, who she could hear closing the shutters on the west side of the Hall.

When she entered the undercroft the light was on, but as she crept along the far wall, her shadow slipped away from the light and was swallowed up in the darkness. She could hear the click of BS's stick on the stones – he was only yards ahead of her, down the corridor to the right. She heard him stop and pressed herself against the shifting shadows of the wall. His footsteps were coming her way. 'Hello!' he called out before he came into view. Maureen pressed herself flatter against the stone as his head peered into the passage, his shock of white hair bright in the gloom. 'Dean? Is that you?' he called, stepping out into the corridor with his back towards her. He had hooked his stick over his arm and was still holding the book against his side. Maureen turned her face away, fearful that her pale skin would reveal her presence, and remained in this position until his footsteps receded.

When she heard the door into the muniments room close, she allowed herself a deep breath of relief and stood away from the wall to brush the dust off her clothes. She made her way cautiously round the corner and towards the room, her eyes becoming adapted to the dark. She wished she was brave enough to take off her shoes, but she feared treading on something sharp. Instead she placed one foot in front of the other with great care and did not transfer her weight until she was sure there was no piece of loose gravel or grit to scrape out a warning of her approach. By the time she reached the door, she could hear BS moving around inside. It sounded as if he was dragging something across the floor, and as she positioned her feet for maximum stability in order to sink down to her haunches and peer through the keyhole, she heard him cry out and curse, and she fled back up the corridor and returned to her position in the shadows, panting in shallow breaths like a frightened animal. Once again she heard his approach, once again he called out for the butler. She heard a door slam, felt herself jump, and when she had the courage to roll her head slowly to look, he was gone.

Despite the thundering of her heart and the icy prick of sweat along her hairline and under her arms and breasts, she could not stop now. She had sensed trepidation from his voice, his movement, and she had to find out what he was doing. The journey down the dark corridor seemed easier this time, the snow had stopped falling outside and the moon must have risen because a sliver of weak light was reflected up from the hopper windows in the main corridor behind her, but as she took up her position once again to look through the keyhole she became disorientated – the door was nearer than she imagined and she struck her forehead against the wood with some force. The next moment she was fleeing, the light was flooding out into the corridor and BS was moving towards her, but something about his breathing, the shuffle of his feet, made her wait at the intersection. As she turned, she saw him looking at her with such longing, such need, that she felt herself drawing near to him, and as she did so he reached a hand out towards her and sank to the ground like the envelope of a hot-air balloon emptying.

She flung herself on to the cold stone beside him and drew his head across and up on to her lap. His lips were trembling, his eyelids fluttered open and shut, and she placed her hand on his forehead which felt cold and clammy to the touch. His fingers worried the fabric of his shirt with a feebleness that squeezed her heart, and she reached down and folded them into her palm. His lids steadied, his eyes looked up at her, and she felt a tremor in his fingers as if he was striving to return the intimacy of her clasp. Two whole winters had passed since she had been in such close proximity with him, and the similarity of the situation brought everything flooding back again. He was there for her when she had her accident, and now she was here for him. She released his hand to stroke the hair across his forehead, and in the muted light of the undercroft she looked at the bent and stunted middle finger of her hand as it moved across his skin. The intense anxiety she felt about the seriousness of his condition was leavened by the exquisite pleasure of knowing that she had been right all along – he did have feelings for her. His eyes closed again, his trembling and fluttering abated, his breathing became steadier and she felt his neck relax against her thigh. She knew her succour was flowing into him, and as she watched him slip into a seemingly untroubled sleep, she was enslaved once again. He was putting his trust in her, his life in her hands – he needed her, he could not reject her.

Maureen had no idea how long she sat on the cold stones nursing the head of BS Moreton, but her yearning for the moment to last forever was tempered with anxiety. She had to get help, or she could lose him altogether. Struggling through the folds of her fleece she drew the radio out from her pocket and turned it on. She looked down again at BS; 'Anyone who can hear me,' she said. 'BS Moreton has fallen in the undercroft. I repeat, BS has fallen in the undercroft.'

Pugh was the first to arrive. He made a pillow from his overcoat and lifted BS's head off Maureen's lap and on to the coat before helping her to her feet. Her back and legs were stiff from sitting on the cold flags, and the front of her thighs felt a chill where they had been in contact with the warmth from BS's body. Pugh demanded she hand over her fleece, and he covered BS with this then felt his wrist for a pulse, shook his head, and pressed his fingers into the side of BS's trachea. BS stirred. A ghostly blue light began to move along the ceiling, and she realised the ambulance had arrived, the headlight's beam bouncing up from the snow of the courtyard through the gloom, and minutes later she heard the sound of metal wheels on stone.

Relieved of his responsibility, Pugh stood to one side next to her as the paramedics worked. 'It's not as bad as it looks,' he said. 'His pulse was quite strong,' and she felt herself shrug off the consoling hand he placed on her shoulder. He moved away from her, and she knew she had made him feel awkward.

When BS was comfortably on the trolley Pugh asked one of the ambulance men if he could take the security keys off the patient's belt. 'Here,' he said, handing them to Maureen. 'I'm going in the ambulance with him. See these are returned to the office.' Picking his coat up, he shook it out and pulled it back on again. Before he set off behind the convoy he added, 'And lock up the muniments room will you?'

Maureen stood in the empty corridor. The only sound she could hear was a distant tapping of water on to lead. The snow was beginning to thaw already. She collected her fleece from the floor and went into the muniments room, propping the door open with a chair. The room was in disarray. An open trunk stood in the corner surrounded by papers and books which had been carelessly flung on to the floor. On the table by the door was the book she had seen BS carrying. She turned it round to face her. In all the time she researched the indigo library, she had never seen this book. She wondered if it was from BS's own private collection, but when she opened it, she saw an engraved stamp of the earl's coat of arms on the frontispiece. A cursory skim through a couple of the pages acquainted her with its contents and she thumped it shut and sat down heavily on the chair beside the table.

If only she could understand her feelings, but they dipped and turned with such frequency it exhausted her. She looked down at the book and knew BS had hidden it for one of two possible reasons. The first was to stop Sam Westbrook succeeding, just as he had stolen her own idea for the publication about the library, but she also wondered if it explained that horrible find she had made in his rucksack. Could it be that the descriptions scrawled on these pages had stimulated his carnal desires to such an extent that he had been unable to control himself and had found it necessary to seek instant relief high up above the indigo library in the sanctuary of his office? She pushed the image away. How, she asked herself, could her feelings of caring affection towards a man turn back within minutes to suspicion, perhaps even disgust?

## - 15 -

Dr Patterson was a lovely young girl, but BS didn't have an enormous amount of faith in her. For a start, she didn't look old enough to have completed her training – more like one of the work experience girls who arrived at the Hall at the end of each summer for a couple of weeks, and they were only fourteen. She listened to his chest, took his blood pressure and weighed him. 'You are overweight,' she said, 'but generally you are in quite good health.'

'How much longer do you think I need to be off work?'

'You're fine to go back now, if you wish.'

'Shouldn't I have some more tests?' BS asked.

'No. Everything seems OK, but there are a few self-help things you can do. Do you drink a lot of coffee?'

'Yes,' BS said cautiously, seeing the demise of his belters before she continued.

'Cut that right down. A lot of caffeine can exacerbate the condition in many patients. And watch out for very strong tea too. That can add to a caffeine overload.' BS groaned inwardly. 'Do you drink a lot of cola?'

'Never,' he replied with pride.

'Good. That's one thing you won't have to give up then.' She smiled at him, but he didn't feel cheered. 'And I do think you would benefit from some cognitive behavioural therapy. It's an extremely helpful treatment for panic attacks.'

'I didn't have a panic attack.'

'I think you did.' She looked at her computer screen. 'Yes, I've got your notes through from the hospital. You had all the classic symptoms: breathlessness, light-headedness, a feeling of impending doom.'

'I was having a coronary.'

'Not according to your tests.'

'Supposing you've missed something?'

'Lots of patients who suffer from panic attacks make repeated trips to see us or go straight to casualty trying to get treatment for what they believe is a life-threatening medical problem. I promise you that we have ruled out any possible physiological cause of your symptoms.' She wheeled her chair away from the desk and turned to look at him. 'Interestingly, it's often panic that is overlooked as a potential cause – not the other way around. But if you think a few more days off work would help, take them. Most men of your age have retired by now. Just be sure in your own mind that you're not avoiding a situation because you're afraid you could have another attack in public, away from home.'

'Attack? Heart attack?'

'No. Panic attack.'

Nonetheless, BS adopted a grave expression as he came out once more into the waiting room. Patricia rose to her feet when she saw him and looked worried.

'I'll tell you outside,' he said quietly, pulling her arm through his and patting her hand consolingly. Patricia gazed up at him, her head making that infinitesimal movement back and forth which squeezed compassion from BS's heart. Once in the car he dropped his charade of doom and said: 'She thinks I'm on the mend, and that it's a good idea if I get back in the saddle straight away.'

'Go back to work?' Patricia looked dismayed. 'Is that really such a good idea? You still seem very frail to me.'

'Frail? Of course I'm not frail,' he said, dropping the hand that he had reached across and taken once they were seated. 'I've had a nasty scare, of course – a shot across the bows one might say. I'll just do a couple of days a week to begin with.' The look Patricia gave him drained his compassion away. She put the car into reverse and revved the engine to a high pitch before jerking backwards into the pall of smoke generated at the back of the car.

Be that as it may, here he was a few days later driving up towards the Hall, his car window rolled down and the crisp spring air blowing full on his face, free at last. He felt quite emotional when Pugh's friendly face popped out from the gatekeeper's box.

'Mr Moreton! How wonderful to see you again. How are you feeling? I must say, you're looking remarkably well.'

'I am feeling fit as a flea, Mr Pugh. Fit as a flea. What's been going on since I've been away?'

Pugh thought for a few moments then said, 'Nothing particular, I don't think. Everything's been running quite smoothly. That nice assistant of yours, Mrs Westbrook, has turned out to be a very resourceful woman. Things are singing along nicely upstairs with the new exhibition apparently. We've had men tramping up and down the stairs with boxes – the music room is packed to the gunnels. It's been temporarily roped off from the general public. And I've a note here that the skip is arriving sometime this morning – they're putting it in the senior staff car park, so you'd better get round there and make sure you don't lose your space.'

'Skip?'

'They're ripping stuff out upstairs. A whole wall's coming down this evening once the Hall is closed.'

'A wall? A whole wall? Whatever for?'

'Not sure exactly. Just what I've heard.'

BS accelerated away and spun round through the courtyard and out to the senior staff car park beyond. He was met by a scene of devastation, piles of rotten floorboards smouldered away in one corner on a builders' bonfire, jumbled heaps of laths and plaster lay in another. Even the old baize screen was there, leaning drunkenly against the pile of spoil. He parked up, struggled out of his car, and set off towards the entrance of the Hall. He was waylaid by Sharon the cleaner, who dropped her cloth and toilet cleaner back into the bucket outside the Ladies, and tearing off her rubber gloves as she wobbled over towards him, planted a huge smacking kiss on the side of his face.

'Blimey, Mr Moreton. You've had us all that worried! Should you really be back at work? You look awful. You've lost so much weight, it makes you look ten years older.' BS managed a watery smile and assured her that he was feeling fitter than he had for months. 'Take it easy,' she shouted after him. 'We don't want you falling flat on your face again all over the place.'

He tried to get in through the music room door, but it was locked and he didn't have his keys. He swung along and up the main steps where Max Black was standing on the door. Max shook BS warmly by the hand and patted him on the shoulder; Laurence came flapping across the Hall waving his hands up and down with the excitement of seeing him; Major Frodsham, woken by the commotion, raised a languid hand from behind the bookstall and said, 'Great to see you back again, old fellow. Had a good break?' BS looked up towards the minstrels' gallery. The left-hand flight of stairs was cordoned off, each step shrouded with dust sheets.

'Good grief,' BS said to Laurence. 'What on earth do the visitors make of all this?'

'They've been wonderful. That curator has done some brilliant information boards about the development of the new exhibition, she's even produced some little flyers about it. It makes them feel involved in some sort of way I suppose. We've had hardly any complaints at all – mostly people want to know when it's going to open. Sam Westbrook certainly knows how to generate interest.'

BS harrumphed and started to make his way up the statue corridor towards the office. He needed to find Rosemary and get his keys back. Up ahead he saw Donna, the voluptuous northern guide, who abandoned her group with a yelp of delight before rushing along the corridor towards him, her magnificent cleavage boiling up above her blouse as she ran.

'BS! You're back! I have been so worried about you. We just weren't getting any bulletins whatsoever. It was as if you had completely disappeared from all our lives, and the Hall just isn't the Hall without you.' She pressed her large bosom against him and held on to him for a good minute before releasing him. Some of her group had caught her up by now, but instead of looking irritated by her abandonment, they smiled affectionately at the scene. 'How lovely,' one of them muttered. The only person who didn't show a childish gladness to see him back was Maureen who smiled coldly at him without using her eyes and nodded an acknowledgement.

'Your usual coffee, BS?' Rosemary said when he came into her office.

'No, thank you. I need to take care of my heart now,' he replied.

'Your heart. Of course. We were all wondering what the diagnosis was. Patricia was insistent that no one from here bothered you during your convalescence and was obviously too upset to talk about what exactly it was that had struck you down.'

'Look, Rosemary, I would love to stop and chat, but I really popped by to pick up my keys.'

'Your keys? Oh, I gave them to Sam. Seemed to make sense.' BS felt a swift plummet deep in his bowels and he knew in a sickening instant that Sam Westbrook had the inventory. Rosemary chattered on: 'She was very keen not to let the grass grow under her feet while you were away. As were the trustees for that matter, the amount she charges per day.' BS hadn't been listening, but this last piece of information pulled him away from the rising crescendo of worry about the inventory and on to a wave of resentment. Naively he had assumed Sam Westbrook was on the same sort of pay as himself, after all she was doing a job he could easily have done.

'Where is she?'

'Upstairs in your office I should think. She's rather taken that over, her and Noel, until the workmen have finished knocking seven bells of hell out of the sealed chamber.'

'Good grief!'

He cut towards the west side of the passage into the watercolour room and entered the indigo library just as Walter Willis, a retired music scholar who had taken responsibility for the mighty Wurlitzer, was blasting the organ pipes through at the end of the room which was devoid of visitors. BS particularly disliked Bach's Toccata and Fugue in D minor, and Walter was not a skilful enough organist to pull it off. Even so, as the opening bars swelled and shook the room with their rising crescendo, BS felt he was in a film about himself, striding down to meet his doom as the mighty Wurlitzer organ played him towards his destiny. Walter wasn't aware of BS's approach until he came level with him, at which point the small man jumped and the organ coughed out a strangled squeak.

'I do apologise,' Walter said. 'I thought I was alone.'

'Carry on,' BS said irritably as he opened the door and began to make his way up the spiral stairs. He could hear Walter recommence the twiddly bits of the piece, but he sounded as if he was playing with the backs of his hands. As BS ascended the stairs, the notes receded and the sound of voices from the room above became clearer. He took some comfort from the fact that by the time he reached the top he still had plenty of puff. Perhaps his time away had done him some good.

Sam was seated at his desk and leaning over her was Noel. As he feared, they were studying the inventory, but he had already decided on a tactic. 'Good morning,' he said cheerfully. 'I am so glad you have that. What a find! I had been down in the muniments room on that dreadful night searching and searching for the wretched thing when I was taken ill. The quest for it has been a long-held ambition, my belief that it existed a certainty, so much so that I have wondered often during my convalescence whether in fact it was the excitement of its incredible discovery that brought on my horrible attack. I cannot tell you how worried I have been that it was still lying locked away down there while I was ill, and you two having to struggle away without this incredible asset.'

Both listeners had looked up when he entered, but apart from that, neither of them moved throughout his speech. Silence flowed back into the room as he stared from face to face. It was as if they were dumbfounded. He wondered if he should continue in the same vein, but before he could Sam said, 'Hello. Are you better?'

'Much. Thank you.' He looked around and saw that his desktop had been cleared and on every side of the room the shelves were topped up with neatly stacked stationery. The bookshelves were devoid of the volumes he had carefully purloined from the library over the years, and with a feeling of intense irritation he guessed they had been returned to their rightful places once more.

The computer was on again, and a labyrinthine pattern of colours coiled and whirled on the screen. 'Well, you've certainly made some changes up here,' he said.

Sam got to her feet. 'You must have your desk back,' she said, but before coming round, she gathered up the inventory.

'Thank you,' and he manoeuvred around and past her, catching his stick on the table leg as he tried to squeeze himself into his old leather chair at an odd angle. Sam retreated to the other side of the desk where a new chair stood, and Noel sat himself down on the swivel chair next to the computer. The room did seem exceedingly crowded.

'I'd offer to make coffee,' Noel said, 'but we've run out. Been too busy to replenish it.'

'Have you now?' BS said. He was determined to maintain his breezy demeanour. 'Right. Fill me in. Tell me how it's all been going. What have I missed?'

# - 16 -

Maureen Hindle loathed the drive up to Scotland, and this time she resented it more than ever. It was as if each gaudy motorway stop marked another tranche of miles further away from BS Moreton. Michael liked to leave after the rush hour, which meant most of the journey was made in darkness, and although Maureen preferred to watch the countryside in the daylight as it slipped by and metamorphosed from the quaint fields and modest valleys of the south to the hulking shoulders of the mountains as they pressed on up through the Lake District to Carlisle and on towards the borders of Scotland, that Thursday evening she was content to gaze at the lights sliding past them out in the darkness and replay her waking dreams over and over again. The images she conjured up were like short trailers for movies on the internet, and she had to keep rerunning them because she didn't want to forget a single detail, and as she reran them, she was rewarded by recalling other components of the event that she had hitherto seen as irrelevant.

She was beginning to explain to herself why her feelings seemed to switch back and forth between cherishing BS and ardently hoping that he would be discovered. At times her devotion had seemed so unlikely to be returned that she tried to convince herself that instead of being the great man she initially thought he was, he was a man of straw, flawed like everyone else, and her fear of rejection spurred her on to watch for deficiencies in his character and behaviour which might, she hoped, eventually extinguish her feelings towards him. When the final rejection came, she was riven with such fury that she replaced her quest to see and interpret loving signs with a search to prove him false and disingenuous, fraudulent even, not only towards herself, but to the world in general. However, recent events had made her review the opinion she had held so tightly to herself for the past two seasons. She had invested so much thought around the events of Monday night, she could not believe it was only two days ago. She filled her mind with thoughts such as, This time last night, This time the day before yesterday, and as a result, time slowed. She recalled feeling his trembling fingers return her consoling grip, and realising that his feelings hadn't altered, she formulated a plausible explanation for his rejection two years earlier: he had not been able to trust himself with her.

And in a flash another thought struck her with such force that Michael turned to her, the headlights of the car behind reflected in the rear-view mirror and falling across his eye like a glowing mask. 'Did you say something, dear?' he asked.

'No.'

'I thought you said something,' and he turned back to the road in front. She felt a wave of intense irritation that her train of thought had been broken. 'Would you like a little radio?' he asked.

'No, thank you.'

'Were you sleeping?'

'Sort of.'

'Why not put your seat back, have a proper snooze?'

'I'm all right like this.'

'Daydreaming?'

'Just thinking.'

They slipped back into what Michael referred to as companionable silence. This usually meant he didn't want to have a conversation. Maureen never found it companionable. She had learned, however, not to try to kick-start a conversation with a series of questions as this generally resulted in Michael getting irritated and even quieter. Tonight she was quite happy to leave him mulling over whatever it was he liked to think about.

The past few days had been frustrating. The morning after BS's collapse in the undercroft, she had intended to offer him the same kindness he had shown her after her own accident and she was eager to get out of the house and over to the hospital. She didn't feel like confiding her plan in Michael, and as the morning ticked by she began to feel that he would never leave for work. He read his morning paper from cover to cover and then decided he wanted another cup of coffee. It spilled into the saucer when she put it down in front of him, and he looked up from his paper with an expression of mild contrition at a perceived scolding. The moment she saw his car turn out of the drive and into the rush-hour traffic she rang the hospital, but they wouldn't give her any information because she was not a relative and it appeared that being a work colleague wasn't seen as important. She wondered if she should contact Patricia, but she now had the odd feeling that she was a rival for BS's affection, and she didn't think she could trust herself not to leak her emotions in the tone of her voice. She thought about ringing Pugh, but she had never telephoned him before in all the time she had worked at Duntisbourne and would have to ask Rosemary in the office for his number, so she spent an irksome day at home trying to fill her time catching up with housework and the garden when she had expected to spend it sitting at the bedside of BS Moreton.

She was on the rota for Wednesday and hoped to find Pugh on the gate in the morning when she turned up for work, but it was being manned by a scrofulous youth she had never seen before.

He had the affront to stop her and ask for a ticket; without a word she jabbed her finger at the parking sticker in her windscreen and drove on through.

The gossip in the Hall was that BS was home again. 'Donna got a right bollocking from Patricia,' she heard Weenie telling Roger Hogg-Smythe during her tea break. 'She went into the hospital on her way to work to bring BS his diary, and Patricia fell on her like a circus tent. Said he wasn't to have anything to do with work or the Hall, and please could she pass that message on and leave the poor man time to get well again.'

'What's wrong with him?' Roger asked.

'Heart attack, I think.'

Maureen rolled her head away and looked out of the side window of the car at the lights moving slowly by in the distance and wondered if they were near Glasgow yet. Michael must have thought she was sleeping because he leant forward and turned the radio on, leaving the volume low. To her astonishment the sombre clarinet solo that preluded *E lucevan le stelle*, the aria from *Tosca*, filled the car with a sweet sadness. She felt sure it was a sign. This was the piece of music she had introduced to BS, the song he had included in his radio broadcast as one of his desert island discs. She didn't understand Italian, but she was able to make out certain words: *languide carezze* – languorous caresses, and *braccia* – arms. Her heart soared with the passion in the tenor's voice and she saw the stars shining over the snow and BS Moreton reaching out to her in the undercroft before he sank to the ground. She conjured up new images, taboo and exciting, remembering the weight of BS's head as she raised it on to her lap. It seemed exquisitely intimate to have cradled his head, to have stroked the hair from his forehead, and she returned to the thought that had jolted her moments before – a thought so crucial yet at the same time so terrible she had to approach it carefully. The thought of a man pleasuring himself had always disgusted her, but she realised she had found the solution to the mystery of the rucksack. BS Moreton had pleasured himself as he thought about her, and he had made the act as dignified as he could in the circumstances. She could think of no other explanation.

At the same time as these thoughts brought relief and satisfaction to her tumbling mind, she felt guilt sliding in again, hand in hand with her sin of carnal interest. It seemed to her that every time she pushed these notions aside, they strengthened. If she indulged them, just for a short while, would they pass more quickly? She thought it worth trying, and as they passed over the borders of Scotland and on up through Perthshire, she let her imagination step cautiously from the idea to the image of a room high up above the great hall at Duntisbourne, a room warm and dimly lit, a man lying back, the expression on his face one of self-transcendence, the kind of rapture that had shuddered from the throat of the tenor and which still rang in her mind, and a moment of release that she now shared with equal exultation.

# - 17 -

The day was bright and chilly, cumulus clouds were scudding over from the Black Mountains. When the wind veered around to the north, it tore down the Lugg valley and walloped itself against the Hall's stout doors, moaning as it squeezed through the gaps around the architrave. Max leant back on the marble radiator cover which was mercifully hot. He was on the door today.

'On behalf of the thirteenth Earl of Duntisbourne, ladies and gentlemen,' Bunty began, 'I would like to welcome you all to Duntisbourne Hall, one of the finest examples of Tudor architecture in the country. '

An enormous gust of wind hit the front door at the precise moment Claude Hipkiss, arriving a little late for work, turned the handle from the outside. The wind caught the door and whacked it open with tremendous force, yanking the old man off his feet. He maintained a tenacious grip on the handle, and Bunty paused in her introduction as Claude sailed across the threshold in a horizontal position, crashed to the ground and slid a short distance on his front, papers fluttering around him in his wake. The visitors gasped in horror. He lay motionless, his bony limbs spread out at awkward angles like a squashed insect.

'Heavens above, Claude,' Bunty said. 'What are you doing?'

Roused by her hearty tones, Claude raised his face from the floor, shook his head a couple of times like a dog drying its coat, mumbled something, then began to get to his feet as Max came forward to gather up the old boy's belongings and replace them in the Tesco bag from which they had issued.

'Fine, fine,' Claude grumbled. 'Nothing at all. Just a little trip.' Snatching the bag off Max, he stumped away down the statue corridor. Bunty clapped her hands sharply to regain the attention of her audience and continued: 'And now, ladies and gentlemen, I am going to hand you over to your guide, Edwina, and I just know you will enjoy your tour.'

As the group of visitors shuffled off down the corridor behind Weenie, Bunty hailed Max across the hall. 'Good morning, Max. How do you find yourself this morning?'

'Just threw back the bedclothes, Bunty, and there I was.' Major Frodsham, who had been nodding off behind the guide book desk in a patch of early spring sunshine which flooded through the windows and on to his back, came to with a snort and began chuckling.

'Well, something's tickled Frodders,' Noel said, moving round the corner of a pillar inside the door to shelter from the draught. 'Hard to believe it now, but the Major was a brave man in his day. Saw action over in Borneo in the sixties.'

'What's your history?' said Max. 'How did you end up here?'

'Oh, blew in one day, like the rest of the guides. No, truth is my wife's from this part of the world. We met out in Hong Kong, but when I retired we came back; then I realised that playing golf every day was getting as tedious as going into an office every day, so I came to work here. They get a motley bunch applying for jobs, and they never turn anyone away. You, for example.'

'Of course.'

'Claude there,' and Noel pointed in the direction the old man had gone, 'was a big noise in London – worked as a lawyer up in Lincoln's Inn. Now he gets the bus in from Leominster because his wife needs the car. Laurence was out in Manhattan in the sixties –

did a stint at Lee Strasberg's Actors Studio, he was a contemporary of Robert De Niro.'

'Really?' Max said.

'He made a reasonable living – I sometimes see him popping up in old reruns of *The Saint*. Bunty looked after horses for the rich and famous. Her niece dated Lord Montague for a time, years ago.'

'And Weenie?' Max could see her silhouette in the morning room – tiny body, huge lollipop head topped with a mane of brittle hair dyed a desperate blonde. She was giving her all to her group.

Noel raised his eyes heavenward. 'Weenie! Hard to believe a thing that woman tells you, but she swears she was a top model in London and shared a flat with The Shrimp. Eats like a shrimp. In fact, I've never actually seen her eat. You keep an eye open, Max. See if you can catch her putting food into her mouth. I've never seen it. Oldest anorexic I've met. Fancies herself as a maneater though. You'd better watch it. When she squeezes herself into those leather party pants, no man is safe.'

Max shuddered.

'Wait until the summer party. Guarantee she'll be wearing them then.'

'What summer party?' Max hated parties.

'Nothing to worry about yet. It's not until August. It's to celebration the 1575 Summer Progress, when the queen first pulled the second earl into bed with her. He wasn't a earl then, of course – he was only thirteen, she was nearly forty. Ah, here comes our venerable archivist.'

Max and Noel watched BS's progress across the courtyard. His head was down and he seemed deep in thought, but a peal of laughter from a group of schoolgirls sitting on the steps to his left drew his gaze and as Max and Noel watched, he veered over towards them and ascended the steps on which they sat. He greeted them to left and right, pausing to talk, and the girls tittered and tugged their plaid skirts over their knees.

'Look at the old goat,' Noel said. 'Can't resist the schoolgirls. You can tell when his blood's up. Wears his tie flopped out over his jumper, like an escutcheon. You are witnessing the full display of the Great BS Moreton.'

'You've been upstairs too long in that exhibition Noel,' Max said.

'Perhaps.'

'Good morning Noel – and, Max isn't it?' BS said as he eventually came in through the front door.

'Yes. We met when I was being shown around,' Max said.

'Of course.' BS swung his rucksack up on to the marble of the radiator box and leant back against it with his hands spread out. The archivist was looking well despite his recent illness.

'I like your tie,' Max said. Noel rolled a jaundiced eye towards him.

'Why, thank you,' BS said. 'It's from my old alma mater, as a matter of fact. Always seems such a shame to cover it up,' and to emphasise the point he flicked it towards Max between his first and second fingers. 'However, my business today is with Noel.'

'BS?' Noel said.

'I just want to know how things are getting along upstairs. I've been snowed under with work, I'm afraid – you know what it's like. Take a week off, and you need a month to catch up. I haven't had a moment to join you. Got everything you need, you and Sam?'

'I think so.'

'What stage are things at the moment?'

'We've got about as far as we can without access to the sealed chamber. Sam's up in London today, seeing contractors about the display cabinets. She couldn't find the right people down here. She'll be back this evening.'

'Been through all those boxes yet?'

'No. We won't start that until the builders have finished upstairs.'

'Looking good?'

'Yes. Go up and see.'

'I don't like to get in the way of the workmen.'

'You wouldn't recognise the place. The wall's down – it's a great space – and the underfloor heating's being laid. They're plastering at the moment, putting lighting in next week. Sam's kept them right on schedule and she's got a good idea of what's going into the exhibition.'

'Without checking the boxes?'

'From the inventory.'

'Ah, yes. What a good thing it was I found that.' BS gazed down at the floor. 'Anything missing?' he said.

'I don't think so.'

'Excellent. Keep up the good work,' and scooping his rucksack up on to his shoulder, BS swayed off down the statue corridor. Halfway down he came to a halt, then plodded back towards them. 'Completely slipped my mind,' he said. 'The whole time we were chatting, I knew I had something to tell you – just couldn't remember what it was. Patricia's coming in this afternoon – we've got family in a few weeks' time, and she wanted to get some staff tickets in case they want another look around the place. Show her down to the office, will you, then call me on the radio and let me know she's here.'

'We certainly will.'

'So explain to me, Noel,' Max said after BS had gone. 'Why

doesn't the old boy go up and see for himself how the exhibition is going?'

'The great archivist moves in mysterious ways,' Noel said. 'Basically, I think his nose has been put out of joint, but between you and me, Sam's doing a much better job than he could ever do. She's whip smart, that woman, if you'll excuse the pun.' Max felt a swell of proprietorial pride for which he admonished himself. 'BS is out of touch with the modern world. He's a charming fellow, but if I've heard his mantra about the quill pen once, I've heard it a hundred times.'

'Quill pen?'

'Haven't you heard him? "Technology ended with the quill pen"?' Max shook his head. 'You surprise me, Max. He trots it out whenever you mention the internet, or emails, or Skype. There are much older men and women at the Hall who have come to grips with new technology in their twilight years, me included. BS has spent his professional life admired for his intellect. In order to learn a new skill, he would have to admit his ignorance – he would have to put himself in a position where he didn't know what he was doing, he wasn't best at something, he wasn't superior. It's much easier to affect an arrogant aloofness, as if it's beneath him to get involved in something that's a passing fad. If someone else used that same aloofness to cover their ignorance of, say, literature or the history of art, BS would berate them for their inflexible attitude and admonish them for robbing themselves of an educational opportunity.'

'Would he?'

'Course he would. He's fallen into an age-old trap.'

'Which is what?'

'Staying safe. There are many excellent things about getting older and one of them is that we have control over our lives and can pretty much avoid putting ourselves in a situation where we might take a monumental pratfall. I took them all the time in my youth. The only time I've taken one recently was when I learned to ski.'

'You did?'

'Of course. It was terrible, but I did it, and I'm bloody glad I did. The French give us a free ski pass in a few years' time.'

'Do they?'

'Free if you're over a certain age. Absolute bargain. The French are clued up, you see. They've done the maths. Janet and I ski to eat, so we spent lots of money eating and drinking and put a very light load on the pistes and chair lifts.'

'I hate skiing,' Max said with feeling. 'My ex-wife took me down a black run on my first day out. She was a good skier, of course. I had one morning of lessons, and she took me out and promised me there was a green run from the top, but when we got there it was closed and the black run was the only way down. I made one agonising plough turn at the top, and went the rest of the way down like a Catherine wheel thinking – I'm sure these skis are meant to come off – as they scythed past my head. It was humiliating. I took my skis back the next day.'

'But that's exactly the point I'm making. You were too wet to face up to a monumental pratfall.'

'Really, Noel, you do say the most extraordinary things.'

'You should have persevered. Janet and I had to spend two seasons being scoffed at by adolescents, but we soldiered on. You couldn't face it. And in his own way, neither can BS. He would much rather belittle an interest in new technology than go through the humiliation of trying and failing, then trying again and again until he succeeded. Hence his side-lining of the exhibition. Sam arrives, she knows her job, she's really good at it. He could see humiliation looming and down he goes, spluttering and writhing on the floor in the undercroft.'

'Come on, Noel. He didn't put that on.'

'Didn't he?'

'He had a coronary.'

'Did he? Then he's made a remarkable recovery.'

'You're talking bollocks.'

'Well, if that man had a coronary, my cock's a kipper. Anyway, enough of this, I'm taking a tea break while Weenie's out on tour. Can't bear getting stuck up there with her. Happy to manage the door on your own?'

'Of course.'

The morning rush of booked groups had abated. Max checked the tickets of a handful of visitors as they came in, but the stream was slow enough for him to wander away from the door and look out across the courtyard from the window where he could rest the front of his legs against the pedestal radiator. It was too hot to lean on for more than a few seconds, but he adopted a gentle rhythm of rocking forwards on to the heat and away from it to maintain a constant temperature. The sky was washed with dramatic greys and blues against which the lime green of the early trees zinged with an acid contrast. As usual, his thoughts moved on to Sam Westbrook.

His early adventure in the snow had not accelerated their relationship as he had hoped. He had thought she might phone him the following evening using the pretext of thanking him for helping her. He even lifted his telephone receiver a few times during the evening to make sure it was not out of order. He wondered if he could ring her to see if she had made it back to the Hall without further mishap, but he didn't want to come across as desperate. He discussed his dilemma with Monty whose lack of interest in the subject gave him the impression that a cool approach was the one most likely to succeed. The following morning he was soothed to see Sam's car, still dirty from its adventures, standing in the staff car park, and when he heard about BS Moreton's collapse, he consoled himself with the thought that this was the reason Sam's attention had been hijacked. She probably had every intention of ringing him, but was too busy picking up the pieces after this apparent catastrophe.

The next few days at work had been similarly frustrating, particularly as his friend Noel had been propelled into the enviable position of Sam's assistant. Max sighed heavily. It was another piece of incredible bad luck that it was Noel, and not himself, who had been picked to help Sam with the erotic collection. He accepted that Noel was more qualified, but even so. He had never been a lucky man. He saw luck as a line running through life, the people on the right of the line enjoying more luck than anyone else while those on the left were crushed by the bad breaks. He, however, was so far over to the left of the line he was out in the stratosphere, the cold icy edges of the dark side of the luck universe.

He often wondered if this was the reason he had become such a successful day trader after he retired. His belief in his own poor luck was so strong that he had never gambled, never played roulette or blackjack. He had never placed a bet on a horse, definitely not a dog, and had never bought a lottery ticket. He accepted that despite his experience from years as a stockbroker, day trading was gambling, but his belief in his own bad luck meant he applied stringent physical stops on his trades and had managed to make a comfortable living, even with the huge handicap of having the most atrocious luck imaginable. In fact he was convinced that had he enjoyed even normal luck over the years, he might well have become reckless and his day trading would have bankrupted him.

At that moment he saw Sam Westbrook enter the courtyard through the arch to his right, making her way, he assumed, across to her flat on the opposite side. He couldn't believe his luck. There he was thinking about her, and as if conjured up by the force of his thoughts, she had appeared. He accepted that nowadays he spent most of his idle hours thinking about Sam, but surely it was a good sign – a sign that this was the right moment to follow Noel's advice, risk a pratfall, take his courage in both hands and ask her out for a drink.

He left the window and walked briskly over to the front door. As he opened it and stepped out into the wind, the door was whisked away from his hand, banging back against the marble radiator cover. Sam must have heard the report from the door and turned, halfway across the courtyard. He raised his hand and beckoned. Come over, he mouthed. Come over. And she waved back, and she smiled, and she kept on walking in a straight line towards her flat. And he waved again. Come here. Here! And she laughed and waved again, and then looked away towards her flat.

Max glanced around. There were no visitors, no one needed to have their tickets checked, and he was down the first three steps away from the Hall to intercept her when he heard a voice behind him. 'Max! Where on earth are you going?' He spun round. Bunty was standing on the top step in the double teapot position, a hand on each hip, full square.

'I had to give Sam Westbrook a message,' he said. 'She's just down there.'

'You can't leave the door unmanned,' Bunty said.

'She's there. Just there. I won't be minute.'

'Back to your post. It'll have to wait.' With leaden feet, Max re-traced his steps. 'What were you thinking?' Bunty said. 'Good job the earl didn't see you. Or Rosemary. Still, you're new. They may have cut you some slack.'

Just my luck, he thought. My usual stinking bad luck.

# - 18 -

The phone rang and BS picked up the receiver. 'BS Moreton speaking,' he said. 'Archivist to The Right Honourable The Earl of Duntisbourne.'

'It's Sam here.' His heart sank. Why was she ringing him at the weekend? 'I got an anonymous letter this morning,' she continued. That was not the problem he was expecting.

Still holding the phone to his ear, he peered down the dark passage towards the kitchen. He could see Patricia in the room beyond, silhouetted against the spring sun coming into the conservatory. His wife was watering the plants. He moved the phone nearer to his mouth and said, 'I'll ring you back in a minute. On my mobile.'

He hung up before Sam could answer, unhooked his stick from the edge of the hall table and, swaying heavily on to it with each step, started to make his way down the passage. Passing through the kitchen, he leaned a hand on the architrave of the door into the conservatory and said, 'Just getting something from the car, dear.' Patricia straightened up and pushed a strand of white hair away from her eyes.

'Was that the phone?' she asked.

'Not even a real person – a recording trying to sell me something.' He shrugged.

'Irritating, aren't they?' she said.

BS smiled at his wife before leaving the room and shut the door behind him only after he saw her bend to resume her task. He made his way out through the utility room and into the garage where the car was parked. The cold made him shiver. Before he climbed into the front seat, he patted the right-hand pocket of his trousers to make sure he had his mobile phone with him. He did. He took a moment to position himself for the drop into the driving seat and carefully closed the car door to prevent it from clunking shut. After fumbling to put on his spectacles, he began to poke the rubber keys on the mobile phone. He couldn't find that confounded bit which had a list of phone numbers on it.

'Oh blow!' he muttered as the phone began to launch something inexplicable. He tried again and a message came up: 'You can make your own notes.' 'Oh blow me down to the ruddy ground,' he said, pressed another key and was told he had saved a message. He sighed heavily and shifted his weight to take the pressure off his back. He had another go. 'There you are,' he said. 'At last,' as he chanced upon the list of contacts and found  Sam's number right at the top under the title he had given her of Assistant Archivist.

'Ah, BS. Finally.' Sam said. 'Why all this cloak-and-dagger stuff?'

BS looked across to the door back into the utility room, then checked the garage door behind him in the rear-view mirror.

'Well,' he began slowly, 'the thing you have to understand, I'm afraid, is ...' He paused. What could he say to make sure this went no further? Sam's tenacity was one of the reasons she was good at her job and he knew she would need careful handling. He believed that the gravitas and charm he had cultivated so carefully for sixty-odd years was hard to resist, but not over the phone. And certainly not on a mobile phone in the front seat of a car in a freezing cold garage. 'I think under the circumstances,' he said, 'it would be better if I came over and talked to you about this.'

'But it's Saturday.' Although the appearance of Sam Westbrook at the Hall had caused him a great deal of trouble, he couldn't help imagining her relaxing on a Saturday morning. Was she still in her nightwear, her skin clear of make-up, her hair loose across her shoulders? Was she having breakfast in bed reading the weekend newspapers?

'If I set off now, I could be with you in about fifteen minutes,' he said. There was a long silence on the other end of the phone. BS felt compelled to explain further. 'You see, when all this unpleasant business developed ...'

'What unpleasant business?'

'I can explain that when I see you. But it caused Patricia a great deal of discomfort and unhappiness.'

'Patricia?'

'My wife.'

'I know who Patricia is,' Sam said, 'but why should she be upset by a letter to me?'

'Well, the thing is that the boys are planning a big family get-together for our fortieth wedding anniversary ...'

'What are you talking about?'

'... and she's got a lot to do getting the house ready for the grand-children, et cetera et cetera, and I am extremely reluctant to cause her any more stress or upset.' Sam was silent, but he soldiered on. 'We both thought this painful episode was over ...'

'What painful episode?'

'I'll explain all that,' he said. 'I just want her to enjoy next weekend and not be reminded of all that nastiness coming on top of my horrid health scare.'

He heard Sam sigh. 'Honestly BS, I don't want to sound rude –' but you're going to, he thought – 'but I haven't the faintest idea what you're talking about.' BS looked anxiously over towards the door into the utility room. How long had he been? Would Patricia be looking for him?

'Are you still there?' he said.

'Yes, yes. I'm still here.'

'It really would be more satisfactory if I could come over.'

He heard her sigh. 'Well, if you really must. But give it a good hour. I'm not completely up and doing just yet.' The line went dead.

He was over the first hurdle. He leaned back against the headrest, puffed out his cheeks and closed his eyes. He snapped them open the moment he heard the latch of the door into the utility room. He let the mobile phone slither down from his lap and into the footwell.

Patricia tapped on his window. 'BS! What are you doing?'

He rolled the window down. 'Still looking, dear.'

'Looking for what?' Patricia frowned and twitched her head to the side as if she was trying to catch a noise, and BS realised she was waiting for him to speak and got the impression that she had been waiting for him to speak for some moments. Then a thought struck him.

'It's a secret, dear.'

'Secret?' she said. 'It's nothing to do with your health, is it?'

'No, no. I wouldn't keep that a secret from you. No, it's a nice secret. I really can't tell you any more about it but suffice it to say all will be revealed very soon when the boys and the grandchildren are here.'

Patricia smiled through the window at him. 'I see,' she said.

'But because I couldn't find something ...'

'What? Oh, sorry. Secret.'

'... I'm going to have to go out this morning for a bit.'

Patricia pulled her head back from the window and stood up.

He knew he had her on the horns of a dilemma. He was bad at presents and surprises – she wouldn't risk thwarting a genuine attempt on his part to treat her. He allowed himself a moment of self-congratulation until he saw disappointment in her face. He also knew she expected their weekends to be sacrosanct, particularly now that he had promised to take things easy and spend less time at the Hall. He quashed a flutter of regret. It couldn't be helped – needs must and all that.

Once he was on the open road he began to feel more hopeful that he would resolve at least this problem once and for all, but as the drive continued he began to fret. He knew the route to the Hall like the back of his hand, but his distraction caused him to take a wrong turn somewhere outside Oswestry and he spent an anxious twenty minutes travelling through an ugly built-up area. By the time he broke free of the suburbs again, the weather had changed. The sky ahead looked heavy and featureless and the countryside had been devastated by the recent snow which had left pockmarked grey lumps on the verges. He checked the time on the clock on the dashboard, and to his horror saw that it was nearly two o'clock in the afternoon. Then he remembered he hadn't managed to work out how to reset it last October when the clocks changed. Even so, he was running much later than he intended.

Eventually he arrived at the Hall. He weaved through the weekend trippers who were scattered around the courtyard and drove on towards the part where Sam had her flat. In his early years he and Patricia had been offered this very flat over the stables, but he had persuaded the land agent to let them have one of the cottages on the north of the estate down by the river walk, which he felt was more fitting to the job he had been appointed to do. He didn't want to be associated with the staff on the private side who lived in. He wasn't going to seen as a servant to the earl. Patricia had hated the cottage. It was damp and only saw the sun for a few hours in the morning during the summer. She would have preferred the flat in the Hall.

He pulled himself out of the car, manoeuvred his stick from between the seats and made his way into the arch and slowly up the stairs. He heard the door above open and Sam leant over the banister to greet him. She was looking crisp but casual – he wasn't used to seeing her away from work. He couldn't help wondering what she had looked like when she was young. 'Come on in,' she said. He followed her into the flat and caught her scent – fresh shampoo and mint. He found it hard not to gaze at the tight fabric of her jeans as she walked ahead of him, but then he stumbled over the small step into the sitting room a split-second before she said 'Mind the step' over her shoulder to him. 'Can I make you a coffee?'

'Yes, please,' he said, feeling a little puffed.

'Straight or decaf?'

'Let me see.' He paused for a moment to give an impression of indecision before he said, 'Go on then, make mine a belter.'

Sam left the room to make the coffee and he sank down into the corner of the old sofa to get his breath back. He stretched his leg out to the side of the coffee table – it was more comfortable if he could keep it straight. The fire in the grate had been lit recently and the kindling was still cracking. An ember sparked out and landed on the rug, red hot. BS leant forward and extinguished it by mashing it into fine charcoal with the ferrule of his stick. The smell of burnt wool crept into the room and he scanned the rug to make sure there were no further smouldering pieces. The fire cracked again and he tried to manoeuvre the spark guard across to protect the rug, but he couldn't do it with his stick. He sank back into the sofa and looked around.

Sam had made an effort to personalise the flat. There were some new cushions on the sofa, a faux fur rug draped over the back of the armchair, a vase of lilies on the top of the bookshelf, and some photographs of Sam with an attractive young girl – her daughter, he assumed. Then he noticed the letter on the table in front of him. He recognised the type, the short staccato sentences. He could feel his heart beat beneath his rib cage. 'Is this it?' he called through to her, surprised at the tightness of his throat.

'Yes,' came a voice, 'that's it. Have a read. I won't be a sec.'

With difficulty he pulled himself forward on the sofa and reached out for the letter. Goodness, it was hot in this room.

*Mrs Westbrook*
*We understand your boss's health is not good and will get worse.*
*The archive department will face many taxing challenges soon.*
*This may be a splendid opportunity for you to leave.*
*A wellwisher*

He felt so relieved he almost laughed out loud. It wasn't bad at all. It was clearly aimed at him, not Sam. It would be a bitter blow to the Hall if she abandoned her work on the exhibition. He would be left to pick up the pieces, and if he was completely honest with himself, he wouldn't be able to make as good a job of it as Sam planned to do. On a personal level he would be sad to lose her: she was witty and efficient and, he didn't mind admitting to himself, extremely attractive for a woman in the autumn years of her life. Not that he would have acted on that attraction. He was a man of letters, an intellectual, but that didn't mean he wasn't able to appreciate admirable qualities at a baser level.

Sam came in with two mugs of coffee and sat on the armchair facing him. 'Horrid, isn't it?' she said. 'What do you make of it?'

He laid the letter back on the table and stroked it flat with his hands, balancing in his mind the best way to explain. Sam picked up the empty envelope which she had also left on the table and said, 'You can see that it was franked at the Hall yesterday, and it's been typed on the Chief Executive's notepaper. But it can't possibly be from his office.'

'No, no,' said BS, 'of course not. Of course not.'

'I tried to ring his office this morning.' BS's gut gave an uncomfortable lurch. 'But it's Saturday – no one's there.'

'He doesn't need to know,' said BS. 'I can assure you it's nothing to do with him.' He sounded more abrupt than he meant to.

Sam looked straight at him. She was frowning. 'Nothing to do with him? Someone has written to me on his paper, and you think he doesn't need to know?'

'How are you anyway?' BS asked.

'I'm fine. You're the one we should be worried about. But why do you think the CEO doesn't need to know?'

BS was beginning to feel annoyed. He must control his temper, keep things calm. On the way over he had convinced himself that with a lot of sympathy and understanding he could persuade Sam that this was some kind of silly prank, and the best possible course of action was to ignore it completely.

'Because,' he said, 'it's probably some kind of silly prank, and the best possible course of action is to ignore it completely.'

'Prank?' said Sam. 'This isn't a prank. It's a poisoned pen letter.'

'Now look here, dear,' BS said. 'You are a very capable, intelligent woman and you know that on a number of issues I will defer to your opinion. But on this occasion I feel very, very strongly that we shouldn't overreact.'

'Shouldn't we?' Sam fixed her gaze on the old archivist and went on, 'but you're the one who leaped into his car and raced over here to discuss it.' BS felt stung, then offended. How dare she be so short with him.

'That's absolutely no way to speak to your boss,' he retorted. He could feel his breath coming more quickly as he stared back at her implacable gaze. He saw a tremor crease the lines of her forehead, and then she laughed softly, shook her head and looked away.

He reached out for the mug of coffee and said; 'Mustn't let this get cold.' The hot liquid went down like prussic acid, and he pressed his fingers into his solar plexus. A flame flared then subsided in the grate and the logs shifted and settled making the fire spit again. 'Don't you think we should put the guard across that?' he said. 'I've already had to snuff out a spark on the rug.'

Sam looked across at the fire. She got up and dropped a couple more logs into the grate before putting the fireguard in front of it and returning to her seat. She waited for him to continue. 'I suppose,' he said, 'that I may possibly have overreacted but that's only because –' he reached forward and put the mug carefully down on the slate coaster in front of him – 'this is not the first time it has happened.'

'Really? Are you serious?' He had her back on his side again now.

'Completely, I'm afraid.' BS paused to gather his thoughts before continuing. 'I have to tell you that over the last year or so I –' he stressed the last word heavily then continued – 'and, I am sorry to say my wife, have been victims of similarly scurrilous and unpleasant missives which have been – how shall I put it – even more disturbed and vicious in nature.'

'Good heavens! How extraordinary. So who's writing them? Do you know?'

'In matters such as these it is almost impossible to establish salient issues as absolute facts.'

'I know, but you must have some idea.' BS had a very good idea. 'Can I see them?' she said.

BS raised his right hand to calm her. He closed his eyes and furrowed his brow as if he was weighing up the pros and cons of her request, when in reality the very last thing he wanted was to have anyone else read those blasted letters.

When he opened his eyes Sam was sipping her coffee and watching him. 'Well?' she said. 'Can I see them?' She put her cup on the table and picked the letter up again. 'Look, BS,' she said, 'I don't like this,' and she flicked the page with the back of her fingers, 'and I haven't been at the Hall long enough to guess who could have written it. If you have other letters, we could compare them and narrow down the field. In the meantime, I've a good mind to pin this on the staff room notice board. Then the letter writer can listen to your colleagues roundly condemning them.'

'No, no,' BS said, 'don't do that. You really shouldn't do that.'

'Why ever not?'

'Because ...' If Sam did make hers public it would force his hand and when he thought of the letters he felt shamed, abused. 'Because,' he said, 'I think you would regret it terribly. After all, you don't want people to think that you're the sort of person who would get a letter like that.'

'What?' And he knew he had explained it badly. 'With the greatest respect,' she said, 'I am not prepared to take this lying down. What possible reason can you have for keeping this thing under wraps?'

'Prudence?' he tried.

Sam flung her hands up in the air and brought them heavily back down on to her knees.

'All right, all right. I'll tell you what we will do,' BS said in order to placate her. 'If you can assure me that for the moment this will go no further than these four walls, then I can't see the harm in you reading them. If I can find them.'

'If? You must know where they are.'

'I do. I think I do.' He could feel her frustration. 'The thing is, I didn't like keeping them at home. Patricia found the whole thing very upsetting. She's bound to, isn't she? Someone writing scurrilous letters filled with accusations and lies. Some were sent directly to Patricia at our home address, some were sent to me here, at the Hall. Simon Keane got one too.'

'The CEO?'

'Yes, but about me. I have a copy of that one too, I think. Look, I'm sorry, filing isn't my strong point, and I haven't looked through them for months. Why would I? I just kept hold of them in case I needed them for evidence, that sort of thing, but the more I thought about it, the less I wanted to make them public.'

'I can't understand why.'

'You will when you see them.' BS stared across the room. His eyes alighted once more on the framed photographs. 'Is that your daughter? The one who's in America?'

'Yes. That's Claire.'

'Pretty girl.'

'The letters.'

'Yes, yes.' He pondered a little longer, then said, 'Why don't we meet down in the muniments room sometime on Monday morning? I should have rounded them all up by then.'

'And that's easy to find?'

'Yes, it's down in the undercroft ...' and BS paused. Surely she knew where the muniments room was.

'Are you all right?' Sam asked.

'Yes. Yes, I'm fine. It's just that I thought you knew where that was.'

'Why should I?'

BS could feel negativity rising in him again, soaring to another crescendo of anxiety. 'Because you've been down there?' he said slowly.

'No.'

'Then how ...?' He paused again, trying to gauge if his next question would throw them down another bumpy path of speculation, but he had to know. 'How did you find the inventory?'

'I didn't. Maureen Hindle gave it to me.'

## - 19 -

The days were lengthening but on Monday morning that cunning east wind followed BS along the empty corridors and down into the undercroft, robbing him of any sense of hope that summer was around the corner. He was chilled to his core – his internal thermostat had given up the ghost. He had woken before the dawn chorus and lain in bed suffering as his body was swept alternately with shivers as if someone was dripping iced water down the back of his neck, and intense waves of heat which slicked his flesh with a flop sweat. Now that he was up and dressed and limping along the icy corridors in the undercroft, he would have welcomed the return of that heat, but all he could feel was gelid tremors running through his bones. He was seized with a terror that there was, in fact, something mortally wrong with him. Could it be, he wondered, withdrawal symptoms from the caffeine he had been forced to give up? Or had they missed some vital clue about his collapse which would only be revealed when they did an autopsy?

His morbid train of thought jolted to a stop when he reached the door of the muniments room, unlocked it and pushed it open. He turned on the light, and it spilled out into the corridor and on to the flags of stone where he had lain, clutching his chest, trying to make sense of the bubbling, booming voices washing around him. He was able to recall now with total clarity the woman's voice he had heard calling for help: Maureen Hindle. It was she who had taken his keys, who had slipped into the muniments room and removed the inventory. What else had that virago done while he lay helpless and dying on these cold flags?

Collecting the letters hadn't been an easy task. He had squirrelled them away in various locations. A few turned a few up at home in the attic, the ones that had been sent to Patricia were locked away in their desk. He spent a fruitless afternoon searching the house for the one to Simon Keane (he only had a copy), but eventually tracked it down in the office at the Hall on Sunday afternoon, having concocted another story for Patricia to explain his trip. She would be expecting a spectacular anniversary present at this rate.

He lumped his rucksack up on to the table and checked his watch to see how long he had before Sam arrived. He hadn't read some of the letters in over a year and wanted to have a look at them first. He remembered the gist of them, but as he took them from the rucksack one by one and reread them, he was shaken anew by the contents. He had remembered certain sentences in one of them:

> *Bull Shit Moreton and his harem of adoring women ...*
> *Too arrogant and proud to guess we see right through you. Great*
> *intellect? You can't be trusted, shouldn't be trusted ...*
> *Man of God? Servant of Satan ...*

and in another:

> *Corrupter of flesh. How old was the pupil in Manchester? A lot*
> *younger than Donna who has fallen now ...*

and more recently in one addressed to Patricia:

> *Do you know he is at it again? Probably not – wives are the last to*
> *know. Tired of Donna and on to Sam. He doesn't care who knows.*
> *It stokes his pride that we all know, the great Lothario. Have you*

*found his Viagra? He must need it with you. Or does he just think about the others ...*

He stared at the laid vellum envelopes he had learned to dread, identical to one another except that some had stamps, others had been franked and one delivered by hand. He looked at the pages themselves, these neatly typed pieces of bile which he was about to share with someone else. He knew his own mind was capable of inflicting far greater brutality and judgement than other people's perception ever was, but the reason he felt so uncomfortable was because deep down he recognised that the letters held more than a grain of truth. He knew he had made mistakes – who hadn't? But he did his job to the best of his abilities and he never forgot the privilege he enjoyed as archivist. He had never been unfaithful to his wife – at least not in the last twenty years, he was a good Catholic, but he had on more than one occasion been guilty of the odd impure thought. However, he didn't feel it was wrong to have an attractive female assistant, given the choice. He liked to put his new assistants at their ease, so he felt the occasional lunch at The Blue Acorn to discuss work was justified. But these vicious letters took his innocent practices as some sort of proof that he was calculating and mendacious, lascivious and manipulative.

He was startled out of his reveries by Sam's arrival. 'Good morning, BS,' she said. 'No, no, don't get up,' and he sank back down on to his chair. 'Is that them?'

'I'm afraid so.' Momentarily he had the urge to gather them up out of her sight, but as she swung her coat over the back of the chair, she pulled them over towards her. He watched her reading and as she read she shook her head, looked up at BS in astonishment, moved on to the next one and gawped; and the next which pushed her back into her chair.

Eventually she said, 'Oh BS, these are just horrible. Horrible for you, horrible for Patricia. Heavens, they make mine seem pretty tame.'

'I believe,' BS said, 'that the degree of disturbance in this person's mind is reaching a serious level. I believe she is a very damaged individual who, perhaps when life becomes intolerably stressful, begins to do this.'

'So you do know who wrote them?' Sam said.

'I have a good idea.'

'Do I know this person?'

'Yes, you do.' He felt his heart beating fast.

'Are going to tell me?' Sam said.

The struggle in his mind made him shut his eyes, then he opened them and looked up towards the ceiling before his gaze fell once again on Sam. Her expression was one of such tender sympathy that he felt his eyes moisten and he was gripped with an urgent need to share his suspicions.

'Maureen Hindle,' he said, and a great wave of relief swept through his body like a shot of strong alcohol.

'The guide who gave me the inventory?'

'Yes.'

'Good heavens,' Sam said. 'How extraordinary. Why would she do this?'

BS took a deep breath to compose himself before he embarked on his saga. 'The earl has never seen fit to let me have a permanent assistant,' he began, 'so I used to recruit helpers over the winter on a more casual basis.' He paused again. He wanted to make sure that he laid out the sequence of events accurately so that Sam could get a true sense of escalation and understand how he had ended up in this bind. 'You may or may not have heard that Maureen Hindle had a horrible accident a few years ago.'

'No. I didn't know that. What sort of accident?'

'She trapped her finger in one of the locking bars in the state rooms.'

'Ouch.'

'I found her, helped her, and for whatever reason, asked her to help me out that winter. I think I felt sorry for her, but I quickly realised I had made an error.'

'Why?

He leaned back in his chair and knitted his fingers across his stomach. 'She wasn't discreet enough.'

'Discreet?'

'Not like that,' he said quickly. 'I have access to all sorts of things concerning His Lordship's personal life, and she couldn't be trusted.'

'Oh, I see,' said Sam. 'But I suppose we're all inclined to gossip.'

'That wasn't the complete reason.' The palliative rush of confession was waning and the room was beginning to feel stuffy, close. 'There was something – how can I put it? – Something arch about her.'

'Arch?' Sam paused. 'Well, in the short time I've been here, I haven't noticed anything playful like that about her. She strikes me as a rather unfulfilled woman – distant, bitter even.'

'Ah, there's the rub. She has very low self-esteem. She once described herself to me as 'lumpy'. I think she has lived a life of regret. She feels life has dealt with her badly.'

'It sounds as if the two of you were close.'

'Not at all,' BS said. 'I only know this because over the winter she confided in me' (he thought of Maureen heavy on his shoulder, her face turned away), 'probably too much' (he thought of Maureen crying). 'I would certainly not have taken advantage of such a confidence, but I got the impression ...' BS paused again to organise his thoughts, '... I felt that she was – how shall I put it? Trailing the bait.'

'Trailing the bait? You mean she had designs on you?' BS thought Sam was about to laugh.

'Probably not as strong as that,' he said, feeling an unwelcome warmth moving up from his neck. 'Anyway, the following winter I asked someone else to help me, ostensibly because I needed some documents translated, and Mrs Falkender – '

'Our northern guide?'

'Precisely. Mrs Falkender took over until you arrived. And, at the risk of paying a clumsy compliment, both of you epitomise everything Maureen Hindle is not.'

Sam sighed. 'But this ...' She indicated the letters spread on the table in front of her. 'Surely this is a pretty extreme response?'

'Not for someone like her,' BS said. 'She was already deliberately spreading pricks of rumour that I had unceremoniously got rid of Donna because you were arriving even though she stopped working for me last year. I carefully raised this with Donna and she was vehement that she had told me of her intention to go back to guiding at the end of last season, long before we even knew an exhibition was being planned.'

Sam picked up her handbag, drew her own letter from it and placed it on the table with the others. 'If you're right,' she said, 'what do you plan to do next? There's very little hard evidence here.'

'I have a meeting with the CEO at four today. I will lay the salient pieces of information before him and recommend that Maureen

Hindle be dropped from the rota with immediate effect.'

'Get her sacked, you mean?'

'That's not the way we do things here at Duntisbourne.'

'Explain.'

'The guides aren't on contracts. They are dismissed at the end of each season, and then invited to apply again the following year.'

'Why?'

BS sensed disapproval and was annoyed. 'It's the way it's always been done. It keeps things flexible.'

'Well, if it's meant to make getting rid of people easier, it doesn't. All the guides have the same statutory employment rights as any other employee.'

'Rubbish.'

Sam laughed at him and shook her head. 'I'm telling you, you can't just sack her.'

BS leant back into his chair and puffed out his cheeks before he closed his eyes and rested his hands the top of his stomach. When did women get so pugnacious? There was a time when his team of female staff positively quaked as he bore down the corridors of the Cathedral School. Back in the sixties they knew their place. There were a couple of argumentative ones, women's rights and all that, but he learnt early on how to goad them into making fools of themselves by losing their temper. He opened his eyes and met Sam's gaze. 'I won't be sacking her,' he said. 'She will be dropped from the rota, that is all.'

'It amounts to the same thing. She could make a lot of trouble for you.'

'Hasn't she already?' he said, waving an impatient hand over the letters.

'If it's her.'

'Of course it's her. Look at the language.' He stirred the letters around and pulled one out from the bottom of the pile. 'Look: 'Beyond unfair!' It's written right here. The number of times I've heard her say that.'

'I understand, I really do, how difficult this is. But your suspicions are all circumstantial. You could be imagining connections that aren't here.'

'No, no, because outside that lies my quite profound awareness of things such as motive, nature of personality, factual knowledge of malice in at least some areas.'

'In which case, you need to be one hundred per cent certain that these are from Maureen Hindle because if she feels she has been unfairly dismissed, it sounds to me as if she is just the type of person to make things extremely difficult for both you and the Hall.'

BS knew Sam's heart was in the right place, but he had been here for years and knew how things were done. Guides were getting dropped from the rota all the time for the weakest of reasons and he had never heard of a single instance when one of them came back with an accusation of unfair dismissal. It just wasn't done.

'I thank you for your excellent advice,' he said, gathering up the letters to return them to his rucksack, 'but you must let me handle things my way.' He was aware that Sam was watching him with an air of resignation, but something roused her and she stood up and shot a hand forward over the table towards his bag. He clutched it to him squeezing the mouth closed.

'Don't worry,' she said, 'I just want mine back,' and her hand pushed into the opening. BS swung it away from her, putting his broad back between them and hugging the rucksack to him. He felt a flash of anger – or was it panic?

'I'll find it,' he said over his shoulder, drawing it out and handing it back to her. She took it with a smile, but her eyes betrayed an undertone of suspicion.

# - 20 -

Max had found it hard to sleep all weekend and Sunday night was no different. At two in the morning he gave up trying to sleep and went downstairs to scan his bookshelves for a book he knew he had read a number of years ago about the Valley of the Kings, which he thought he should revisit in case he was asked about the Bomford Collection at the Hall. Having found it, he went back to bed and read until five when he eventually slipped off into a restless sleep. His radio alarm clicked on Radio 4 at seven but he continued to snooze and his dreams merged with the news bulletins of the day. He finally woke with a start from a deep sleep, dragged himself up through the syrup and staggering down to the kitchen to make himself a cup of coffee. He listened to the news and fancied that he had had a premonition not only about an air crash in the Urals, but also about a wave of 'flu that was going to sweep across Europe that winter. Then he realised it was Mullins who had told him he had the vaccination in his fridge, and that he hadn't seen Mullins since he left Christchurch School in 1974 and Mullins' ears had been as large as those of Anubis when he showed Max the enormous golden syringe he was going to use to vaccinate his bottom, and that in fact none of it was a premonition – it had all been a dream.

'Bull shit,' he muttered as he lit his first cigarette of the day.

The weather was bright and cold, and as he left his cottage Max felt the stirring of spring. Some years ago a kindly neighbour had tucked some daffodil bulbs into the bank beside his drive, and the breeze was knocking their heads against one another in a jaunty dance. The day got brighter still when he arrived at the Hall and saw Sam's magnificent motor parking behind his. He wandered over to her car and held the door open for her.

'Good morning,' she said, looking up at him. 'You're well wrapped up.'

'That front door is the coldest place on earth, I swear to God. How's that exhibition of yours shaping up?'

'Slowly,' Sam said. She went around to the boot of the car but before opening it, she hesitated and turned to him. 'I haven't said thank you for rescuing me the other night.'

'Indeed you haven't, but as it was such a pleasure, I'm not sure you really need to.'

'If you're not rushing back home straight after work, perhaps you'd like to come up to the flat for a quick drink. I've just been into town,' she opened the boot, 'and I'm all stocked up,' and she lifted up a couple of carrier bags which clanked.

Max stood stock still in front of her. 'Could life get any sweeter?' he said expansively. She smiled. Max liked it when Sam smiled. 'What time would you like to see me?' he said.

'I'm not sure. What's the earliest one can legitimately have a drink?'

'I like six o'clock, and it's six o'clock somewhere in the world even now.'

'Come after work. I'll be back there from five onwards.'

Sam peeled off towards her flat and Max felt an extra shiver of comfort when he entered the Hall through the coke hole, heard the throaty roar of the huge steam boilers and smelt the sharp tang of fuel oil. The heating was on. Today was shaping up extremely well. He bounded up the stairs to the guides' room two at a time and burst in through the door, issuing a cheery welcome to his colleagues. It was met by a mumble of hellos. Major Frodsham was sitting in the comfortable chair studying his fingernails and Weenie was stirring a cup of tea by the kettle. Noel looked up from the back of the room, raised an eyebrow at Max and nodded over towards Maureen Hindle, who was standing at the side of Bunty's desk, staring down at the diary. The atmosphere was fissile.

'There's nothing I can do about it,' Bunty said. 'You are not down to work today.'

'I always work on a Monday. We drove back through the night so that I could be here for work this morning.'

'You're not down.'

'Why not?'

'Maureen, I don't know.' Bunty sounded exasperated. 'Take it up with the office. We've got our full quota for today.'

Maureen pulled the diary away from Bunty and spun it round to face her. 'What's she down there for?' she said, stabbing at the page with a finger.

'Who?'

'Sam Westbrook.'

Max felt a jolt of irritation. He didn't care for Maureen's tone of voice, and no one was going to criticise Sam in his presence.

'Take it up with the office,' Bunty repeated.

'She's not a guide. She's not even a guide. Why is that woman down on the rota if she's not a guide? Beyond unfair! It's completely beyond unfair.'

Bunty sighed and turned in her chair to face Maureen. 'You will have to take it up with the office. All I know is that we work to a limited budget. It's possible that BS Moreton felt that now we have Sam Westbrook here, we can't justify an extra person on a Monday.'

'BS Moreton?'

'Apparently.'

'Oh, I should have guessed. Trust him to stick his oar in. He's got his favourites, you know, and obviously I'm no longer one of them. How dare he get busy with the rota! It's none of his business. And what's he doing putting her forward as a guide? He knows she's not a guide. Why has he had her put down? What's she going to do?'

'Maureen! Calm yourself. My hands are tied. BS is management, I'm not and what he says goes. Perhaps they think she can cover security if we're stuck because she's here in the building anyway.'

'She's on a salary. A great big fat salary. And you're telling me that on top of that she's going to be paid by the hour for sitting on security? Do you think she's going to do that? Sit in the indigo library with a radio? It's preposterous. She doesn't need the money, I do. This is beyond unfair. I'm not going home, you know – they can't get rid of me just like that.'

'That's up to you. But don't think you can fill out a time sheet and expect to get paid for today.'

'What about the rest of the week?' and Maureen began to flick feverishly through the diary. 'I'm not in at all! I'm not in for the whole of April or May. Is Sam Westbrook still going to be here in May? I thought she'd be finished by then. What's going on here?'

'Talk to the office,' Bunty said. 'I beg you, talk to the office. I can't do anything to help you.'

'I've brought my lunch and everything.'

'I'm sorry. Oh, come on now, Maureen. Don't cry.'

Maureen waved away Roger Hogg-Smythe, who had come forward to comfort her. She pulled a creased handkerchief out from the sleeve of her cardigan and pressed it into the corners of her eyes. 'I don't know what to do,' she said in a little voice and another sob rose up and shook her. Bunty got to her feet and led her by her shoulders over to the wide windowsill and sat her down. She patted her hand and said, not unkindly, 'You can pull yourself together, Maureen. That's what you can do.' Bunty dropped her voice, but Max heard her add, 'Don't make an exhibition of yourself. Keep the tears for later. I'm sure it'll all be sorted out.' This advice made Maureen lose control of her mouth, which twisted and stretched into a gape of misery. Max glanced at Noel who, with the merest flicker of expression, encouraged him to join him in a quick exit from the guides' room.

The two men came to rest by the closed front door. 'That, my friend,' Noel said, 'was shaping up to become a simply extraordinary exhibition of emotion. A ridiculous carry-on for a woman of her age.'

'Seemed a bit extreme.'

'Showing off, that's all it is. Completely unnecessary.'

'How are you and Sam getting on with the exhibition?' Max asked. He was bored with Maureen Hindle's problems. He much preferred talking about Sam.

'Slowly.'

'That's just what Sam said.'

Noel peered beadily at him. 'Attractive woman, isn't she?'

'Yes.'

'I have a feeling, old chap, that our otherwise perfect friendship has been compromised somewhat by envy.'

'I don't know what you mean.'

'Wouldn't you like to be working in my stead on the exhibition with Sam?'

'I have something better to look forward to. She has invited me to join her this evening for an after-work drink at her flat.'

'Oh, really?' Noel flashed his eyes and added, 'You're a sly old dog, Max.'

'I take exception to every single word of that, Noel – sly, dog and old.' Noel raised a quizzical eyebrow. 'And I wish I could brag that those lewd and lascivious thoughts that you harbour in some blackened corner of your overactive imagination are correct.'

'A slow-burning fuse then?'

'I'm not sure it's even lit.'

The day had started bright and cold and by lunchtime the fragile clouds began to melt and patches of brilliant azure appeared. Max walked out on to the steps and looked up at the afternoon sky which was high and blue, thin clouds up in the stratosphere whipped into feathered horsetails. The wind had shifted round to the west and a warm, gentle breeze blew across the estate where the branches of the bare trees bulged with the potency of approaching spring. The buds of the horse chestnut trees were glistening, poised to flop out their first leaves like limp green gloves. By the afternoon the crowds had thinned, and as the day approached four o'clock the Hall was all but deserted.

There was no last tour. Max left the Hall promptly at five, but before making his way over to Sam's flat he slipped out into the courtyard for a cigarette. His favourite spot was near the wishing well, where he could tuck himself behind the plinth of a statue of a Greek gladiator energetically defending himself from an invisible foe using his invisible shield. Tonight, as Max gazed up at him and drew deeply on his cigarette, he noticed a strategically placed trunk of a tree disappearing behind the warrior. He circled around the figure trying to work out where this strengthening bough ended, and came to the conclusion that it was lodged firmly between the man's buttocks. His study was disrupted by a late visitor returning from the gardens to his car, who frowned at him as he passed. Max chuckled to himself, tossed his cigarette down the well, popped a strong mint into his mouth, and set off for Sam's flat.

'This is kind of you,' Max called through to the kitchen. He stood at the window looking out over the park as evening descended.

'Not at all,' Sam said, coming back into the sitting room with a glass of wine and a beer. 'A thank you which is long overdue. Things have been a bit hectic.' She handed him the bottle of beer. 'Are you sure you don't want a glass?' He shook his head and she sat down at the end of the sofa and tucked her legs underneath her. He decided to be bold and took his place at the other end.

'So, when are we going to get a look at this exhibition of yours?' he said.

Sam winced. 'Not as soon as I would have liked. The organisation here is extraordinary.'

'Or the lack of it.'

'Precisely. There are artefacts scattered all over the Hall.' Sam stretched her legs out along the sofa towards him. She had kicked off her shoes, and Max stole a glance at her bare feet, momentarily observing they had the same slender elegance as her hands. Anxious he might have been observed, he glanced back at her, but she was gazing into her wine. 'I thought BS was meant to be this oracle who could track down anything,' she continued, 'but a lot of the time even he's baffled. You heard about the inventory, I suppose?'

'Noel told me.'

'It's all very peculiar. I simply don't understand why it's only just turned up.' She looked over towards him, and he shrugged. As if he should know, or care, when he was sitting in Sam's flat and her bare feet were inches away from his thigh. He was battling with an overwhelming desire to lift one of them tenderly on to his lap and begin to massage it. 'Of course,' she said, 'it's made things easier in some ways but a great deal more difficult in others. It's thrown up a great list of things I didn't know were in the collection. Even BS seems to have forgotten they were ever here, but they're certainly on that inventory.'

'They're missing?'

'Well, mislaid at least.'

'By the way,' Max said, sitting forward on the sofa to distract himself from his fixation with her feet, 'I meant to tell you. You caused a bit of a stir up in the guides' room this morning.'

'Did I?'

'Yes. Astonishingly, you've been put down on the guiding rota.'

'Me?' Sam pulled a face. She obviously found the notion as comical as did he.

'I know. Extraordinary.'

'But why?'

'Apparently BS Moreton has put you down on a Monday instead of Maureen Hindle who waddled in today after a weekend away to find she had been dropped for the next couple of months. There was a terrific scene – keening, wailing, the tearing of pocket handkerchiefs. Noel and I made a pretty swift exit, I can tell you.' Max chuckled and took a sip of beer before looking over towards Sam. 'Whatever's the matter?' he said when he saw the seriousness of her expression.

'Oh dear,' Sam said. 'I didn't think he'd really do it.'

'What?'

Sam didn't reply straight away and Max sat listening to the clink of the charcoal in the grate and watching her face. He wished he could light a cigarette. Eventually she stirred, sighed and put her wine glass down on the side table next to her. She drew her legs up towards herself and hugged her arms around them, resting her chin on her raised knees. It made her look adorable. 'How discreet can you be?'

'Me? I'm the soul of discretion.' This made Sam laugh. 'What? I am.'

'OK. I'll believe you, because to be perfectly honest, I wouldn't mind running some of this through with a third party.'

'I'm your man.'

Sam stood, picked up her glass of wine and made her way over to the fireplace. She put the glass on the mantelpiece and bent forward to throw two more logs on to the fire. Max caught his breath. She had stretched one leg forward to take her weight and her shirt had risen up at the back. He could make out the line of her underwear defining the curve of her buttock and he found the sight unbearably erotic. She straightened up, pulled her top back down over her trousers with a dainty tug and turned back to face Max. 'Someone at the Hall is writing anonymous letters.'

'No. Good grief!' Her revelation was sufficiently spectacular to bring him back on track. 'This place just gets better and better.'

'Max, for God's sake.'

'It does. I love this place. It's the oddest place on earth to work, I swear it is. Anonymous letters? Who's writing them?' Sam began to laugh again. 'I know what you're going to say,' he said, 'you're going to say you don't know. They're anonymous.'

'Something like that, I suppose. But unfortunately, BS thinks he does know. He thinks it's Maureen.'

'Whoa! Maureen Hindle? She's really having a bad week.'

'He told me he was going to get rid of her. I do wish he hadn't involved me in getting her booted out. I was dead against it.'

'Why?'

'Nothing but circumstantial evidence.'

'I assume you've had some letters.'

'Well, one.'

'Can I see it?'

'OK,' Max got up and followed Sam over to the dining-room table where her laptop stood. She sat down in front of the computer and began to leaf through a pile of papers then drew out the envelope and handed it to Max. 'Others have been sent to the CEO and to BS, but all of them are an attack on BS, criticising his working methods, and his personal life. The writer thinks he's the Casanova of Duntisbourne Hall except that his tastes now are for rather maturer meat.'

Max looked up from the letter. 'Marvellous.'

'Seriously though, Max, we can have a good laugh about it, but it's a shabby situation on a number of levels. Writing poison pen letters is a cowardly and subversive way to get your own back on someone; but squeezing someone out of their job without a shred of actual evidence is also a despicable way to behave.'

Max was having trouble ridding his mind of the image of BS Moreton sprawled on a chaise longue and surrounded by a group of skimpily-clad female guides in their sixties. 'Can you really be a Lothario when you're that old?'

'I think you can,' Sam said.

'There's always the good news.' He folded the letter up again and put it into the envelope, glancing down at the postmark before tossing it on to the table. It floated a short distance across the polished surface and bumped the cordless mouse beside the computer which purred and the black screen irradiated into life. The screen was filled with archaic figures in black and white piled one upon the other in a tangle of buttocks, genitals, nuns' wimples and birch canes. 'Jesus!' Max yelped. The whole evening was becoming an onslaught of lascivious thoughts and images.

Sam didn't seem flustered. She looked at the screen and then at Max's expression and smiled. 'Just research,' she said.

'Of course,' he agreed, regaining his self-composure.

'Another mystery, I'm afraid,' she said. 'These are engravings from a later version of a novella by the Marquis de Sade, *Les Infortunes de la Vertu*.'

'*The Misfortunes of Justine*?'

'Yes.' Sam raised an eyebrow.

'They're familiar. Can't think why. Perhaps they formed the bread and butter of our burgeoning sexuality at school.'

'According to the inventory the ninth earl bought a number of these engravings and they're valuable.'

'Are they? They're pretty comical.'

'Yes. I suppose they are to the modern eye, but there's an interesting history behind them.'

'Do tell,' and Max drew a chair alongside Sam's and stared at the writhing bodies on the screen. Sam shut the lid and turned to face him.

'Well,' she said, 'when the extended version of the original novella was printed in Holland in around 1797, engravings of these types of illustrations were printed off the original plates and sold individually. Napoleon thought the book was – ' here Sam flicked through her notes and read – "the most abominable book ever engendered by the most depraved imagination", although in fairness to Sade, his original novella was fairly tame compared to his later writing. It was these subsequent and graphic revisions that pushed the book into rank obscenity, but that didn't stop Napoleon arresting and imprisoning Sade for thirteen years for being the anonymous author. The Cour Royal de Paris ordered the destruction of the books in 1815. Anyway, I wanted to use images like these as huge backdrops behind the cabinets in the exhibition.'

'But you can't find them.'

'Not yet.'

'Get them off the internet.'

'Can't do that.'

'I don't mean download them for free. I mean contact the copyright owners.'

'Copyright isn't the issue – these prints are over two hundred years old. The problem is that I don't know which ones were in the collection. I have the part numbers and a visual description, but I can't be sure which belonged to Duntisbourne.'

'Does it matter?'

Sam sighed. 'Yes, it does. It matters to me and, as I keep trying to explain to Noel, unless they're genuine someone, some day, will spot the error, and I don't want my name on an exhibition unless I'm a hundred per cent certain all the elements are authentic.'

'OK,' said Max, feeling chastened.

'I don't mean to sound pompous.'

'But it's important to you.'

'Exactly. Another beer?'

He should have said no.


Max let himself into his house with a heavy heart. Monty sensed his mood and tailored his welcome to suit it, trotting along the corridor behind his master as he went to the kitchen to make himself a cup of coffee. Max lit a cigarette, filled the cafetierre and stared at the grounds as they rose and fell in the blackening water. Monty put his paws on to his shin and stretched up towards him.

'Ballsed it up, Monty,' Max said. 'But I was defenceless against her charming little feet.' He poured his coffee and went through to his office. He didn't expect to get much sleep again tonight – he might as well fiddle around on the computer.

He'd taken a gamble and it hadn't worked. He had moved in for a kiss towards the end of the evening and been rebuffed. In fact the kiss had signalled the end of the evening, and without his attempt, he would probably still be at Sam's flat, chatting merrily in front of the fire, watching her bend to put another log into the grate, making her laugh with tales of eccentric work colleagues. And the reason she had rebuffed him was awful – a deal-breaker. She didn't want to kiss a smoker. That's what she had said. He had scrabbled for his mints, but she said no, it wouldn't help, it was coming from his lungs.

'My lungs?' he had said, recoiling in horror as she must have done from his gamey breath. It was humiliating.

He lit another cigarette before he noticed that his earlier one was still smouldering in the ashtray. He had smoked for England ever since he was a teenager – there couldn't be a more passionate smoker in the world. He was a two-pack-a-day man, sometimes three packs at times of high stress such as when he was squabbling with his ex-wife. He would have smoked his finger if necessary. The anti-smoking lobby appalled him – they summed up disapproving Middle England, the nanny state, everything he hated, and his beloved Sam was one of them.

'What to do, Monty?' he said. The dog stirred from underneath the desk and thrust his head up between Max's knees. He rubbed his fur and looked into the dog's eyes. 'Your breath smells. Does that put me off you?' Monty tipped his head from side to side, listening. 'Well, a bit, I must admit.' Monty dropped down on to the floor and Max stretched back in his chair. Could he give up smoking? It had defined him for so many years, he couldn't think of life without cigarettes. Even his recent health scare hadn't been enough of an incentive – he felt it was part of being in the twilight of his days and ill health was inevitable. Perhaps it wasn't. Could he really start taking care of himself this late in the day? If he could see a future with Sam, he certainly wanted many more years to enjoy it.

But hang on a minute – Sam hadn't said in so many words that if he was a non-smoker he'd be in with a chance. Perhaps she wasn't that keen anyway, and she thought the smoking thing was a good way out. But surely that was wrong. He couldn't have misread the signs so completely. She obviously enjoyed his company – after all, she had made the move and invited him up to her flat. She wouldn't have done that if he wasn't in with a chance. God, he thought, so many things get easier with age, but not this. He felt every bit as insecure as he had at sixteen.

He opened up the packet of cigarettes. It was a full pack bar four. He would make a decision in the morning.

## - 21 -

'Good morning,' Sam said. The hammering stopped and the carpenter looked down at her, brandished his hammer and smiled around a mouthful of nails. 'Carry on. I'm just checking progress.' The ceiling was plastered, the cables for the lights were hanging out of the holes above and the floor was back down again although covered with polythene to protect it. She lifted up one edge to check that the cabling had been brought under the floor for the power points beneath each display cabinet. Satisfied, she bade the electrician and carpenter good day and made her way back to her flat. The sun was shining, but the wind was from the east so she lit the fire early because she intended working throughout the morning where she wouldn't get constant interruptions. The conclusion of her evening with Max had left her mildly troubled and she knew that once she immersed herself in her task these concerns would be pushed to one side. Often, when she revisited worries after a certain amount of time, she had a clearer perspective.

Over the past few weeks, with Noel's help, she had been systematically opening each box in the music room, listing the items and repacking them in preparation for their return upstairs, and today she faced the monumental task of comparing her list with the inventory which Maureen had given to her. She had been forced to rethink her plan of using enlarged images from the prints in the collection as a backdrop to the cabinets because she was running out of time to have the panels manufactured and however many times she impressed on BS the urgency of the situation, he invariably had some reason for failing to unearth them. His initial delay was plausible – he did seem to be overstretched by his workload to the point that he had been taken ill – but Sam was beginning to wonder if something more sinister lay behind it. His handling of the anonymous letters had revealed a side to his personality that worried her. She couldn't understand his response, his secrecy and shame, unless there was some truth in their content, and his solution to the problem frankly appalled her. She wondered now if his inefficiency with the collection was in fact obfuscation and she was getting an uneasy feeling that a great deal more was missing than a few prints.

Sam continued to work through until lunchtime, fixed herself a sandwich and worked on until the light began to fail in her room and she stood up to turn on a few of the lamps. Her task today had been made doubly difficult because the inventory was more like the minutes of meetings and had been compiled chronologically, with descriptions of the items followed by handwritten notes and anecdotes which, if another item was not procured for a number of month, ran to pages. She had started by making headings, but it soon became clear that this was too cumbersome a way to list them, and instead she created a spreadsheet which enabled her to jump from box to box as she came across another item amidst the slanting handwriting of many different people.

Sam stretched and yawned, then went over to the window and looked out into the darkness. She wondered how Max was. She knew she had wounded him, but she hadn't meant to. She had been aware throughout the evening that he was following her with his eyes, and she was not displeased by his attention, but she still didn't have that knot of excitement in her stomach that she had when she was deeply attracted to a man. It was as if she needed that crazy feeling to override any characteristics that didn't fit the blueprint which branded itself on to her mind the moment she was captivated by someone. For months, sometimes for as long as a year, she could minimise a man's faults and glorify his qualities, but eventually the crazy feeling waned, and she was left with the bald truth that this was no dream man but someone who hung their jacket up on the hook in their car, who liked to watch world wrestling or who held his knife like a pencil, and one of these minor irritations would bring the whole edifice of delusion tumbling down. She didn't know how to operate romantically without that feeling. Her rejection of Max wasn't really about his breath. Heavens above, she had had excellent sex with someone for nearly six months who had tonsil trouble and the most awful halitosis and as long as she was nuts about him, she learnt to mouth-breathe. She just wasn't nuts about Max, and wasn't able to disregard any minor flaws.

She drew the curtains shut with a sudden violence, irritated with herself, and realised she was ravenously hungry. Seeing that it was well past seven, she went into the kitchen, poured herself a glass of wine and pulled out a packet of streaky bacon, a tray of eggs and some fresh pasta. A plate of carbonara was exactly what she felt like.

She stirred the onions and bacon around in the pan and watched them popping and jumping in the oil. The pasta bubbled and sent clouds of steam up into the kitchen. She gazed at them as they rose, her hand stirring the food but her mind was tripping away down a line of connections which were easier to unpick than her feelings about Max, easier to dwell on. Too much stuff was missing from the collection for it to have been mislaid – she had sensed that days ago, and her painstaking exercise today revealed the true extent of the problem. She had been unable to track down any of the fifteen engravings from *Justine*, and had not managed to unearth a single one of the twenty-five volumes of books that were discussed in the inventory. There was no John Wilmot, Earl of Rochester; no Charles Sedley or George Etherege; a first edition of *An Essay on Woman*, the obscene parody of the writings of Alexander Pope, along with collections of bawdy country songs and flagellation eclogues such as *The Flogging Block* were nowhere to be found. The most frustrating loss was a small portrait of the ninth earl in his youth painted in the style of William Hogarth's portrait of Sir Francis Dashwood as a Franciscan monk. From the description in the inventory, it would have been the perfect illustration of the growth of religious nonconformity and the rise of toleration which, in Sam's opinion, represented the turning point in western cultural attitudes to sexual behaviour.

She had just finished eating when her mobile rang.

'It's Max.' To her surprise her stomach gave a little flip. 'Am I forgiven?'

'Whatever for?'

'The lunge.'

Sam laughed, relieved. If anyone was at fault, it was her. 'Of course you are. Don't give it another thought.'

'Still chums then?'

'Definitely.'

'What are you doing?'

'Having supper.'

'Blast. I thought we could grab a bite to eat together this evening.'

'Too late.'

'Are you OK? You sound distracted.'

'Do I? Sorry.' Sam paused. 'Actually Max, you know what? I am distracted.'

'Thinking about me, no doubt.'

She lied, a bit. 'Thinking about BS Moreton, as a matter of fact.'

'Bull shit! A rival. He is married, you know.'

'That wasn't the direction my thoughts were rambling.'

'What a relief. So what were you mulling over about our venerable archivist?'

Sam picked up her wine glass and drew her legs up on the sofa. She found Max easy to talk to. 'The thing is, I've spent all day on that blasted inventory, and it appears a number of things have gone missing, and I can't understand why BS isn't more worried about it.'

'I expect he's extremely worried about it.'

'No, he isn't. He just keeps saying things have a habit of turning up and haven't I got enough for an exhibition already.'

'That's not what I meant. He's worried because he's probably had the stuff away.'

'Max! Of course he hasn't.'

'Of course he has. It goes on wholesale in places like Duntisbourne. Earl's a shit, doesn't care about his staff, rude to everyone, pays them very little, then puts them in charge of piles of treasures that have never been properly catalogued. Stuff must go missing all the time, and if BS has been in sole charge of the sealed chamber for the past however many years, who'd blame the old boy for flogging off a few pieces.'

'That's rubbish, Max. Why else would he want me to have the inventory?'

'Did he?'

'What?'

'Want you to have the inventory?' Sam was silent. 'Are you still there?' Max said.

'Yes. I'm still here.'

'If you want my advice, I'd leave it be. You've got a cracking exhibition already, so what does it matter if a few things have gone astray? It's no skin off your nose. I wouldn't get involved if I were you.'

'I am involved.'

'Your brief isn't to unfrock the old goat. No one likes a snitch.'

Sam felt a flash of irritation and a strong desire to bring the conversation to a swift conclusion. 'You know what, Max? I'm tired,' she said. 'I might see you tomorrow if you're in.'

She walked into the kitchen to refill her glass and seethed. She didn't have many allies stuck out here on the borders of Wales, but she thought she had found one in Max. Perhaps he was getting back at her for wounding him. His attitude incensed her. Of course she was involved. She had been employed by the trustees, under the direction of the earl, to curate a collection which wasn't complete, and Max was suggesting that if she continued to push for the truth she was nothing more than a whistle-blower, something she had always regarded as contemptible.

She paced up and down the sitting room in front of the fire taking angry sips of her wine and then she swung round and caught sight of herself in the mirror. She looked furious and, she had to admit, ludicrous. She stared at the reflection of her own eyes and a half smile lifted her mouth. She shook her head. Her fury was for quite a different reason. She was smarting because Max had criticised her, and Max's good opinion of her was rather more important than she had realised. She was behaving like a teenager. She had to stand by her own principles whether Max approved or not and despite his criticism he had thrown up a pertinent point, one that needed further investigation.

The following morning she got Maureen Hindle's phone number from the office.

'Maureen? This is Sam.' There was a long silence. 'Is that Maureen Hindle?'

'It is.'

The two words simmered with such venom that Sam wondered if Maureen had mistaken her for someone else, someone she loathed. 'Sam Westbrook, from Duntisbourne,' she said.

'I know who you are. You're the reason I've been dumped from the rota. You come up here with your nippy little car, and your sharp suits and your manicured nails, and they all flutter around you and bow and scrape to you and you sit up there in your comfy little flat looking down on the rest of us and you think, I know, I haven't actually got quite enough, so I'll just have her job as well. What have I ever done to you?'

'Goodness me,' said Sam. When attacked her immediate tactic was to apologise. 'I'm extremely sorry you feel that way, but without discussing ...' and here she paused '... all the details of that list of grievances, as far as the rota is concerned, you've got that wrong.'

'Then why am I at home without a job and you're still there earning goodness knows how much money and getting extra for filling in for guides?'

'Maureen, listen. I have no idea why that has been done. It was nothing whatsoever to do with me and I couldn't possibly guide here, and I wouldn't want to. You and your colleagues do an excellent job, I couldn't fill your shoes. That's not what I do. I've already got a job. I can't pretend to understand the way Duntis-bourne runs that rota system, but I can assure you, this is none of my doing.'

'BS Moreton's then.'

'I can't really speculate. You would have to ask him yourself.'

'Bunty said it was him.'

Sam had no intention of telling Maureen about her conversation with BS. Instead she said, 'I only found out two nights ago that it had happened, and I can assure you, I will speak to Rosemary in the office and explain, if you think that would help.'

'Two night ago? It's taken you a long time to do anything about it.'

'I've been busy,' Sam said, determined not to let Maureen's belligerence rile her. 'Would it help if I spoke to the office?'

'If you have a shred of decency in you.'

'Then I shall.' She paused in the hope that Maureen would give some indication that she was winning her round. 'That's not actually why I rang you,' she continued, and quickly added, 'but I'm extremely glad we have thrashed that out and hope that there won't be any more ill feeling between us. When the exhibition's done, I'll be away and gone from Duntisbourne. I promise you I have no ambition to upset the status quo.'

'I see.' Still no thank you, but Sam sensed that Maureen was calming down.

'I actually rang to ask you about the night BS had his accident.'

'Yes?'

'You brought the inventory to me.'

'That's right.'

'Do you know where BS found it?'

'Found it? He didn't find it. He was hiding it.'

# - 22 -

Max turned over and gathered his pillows up under his chest. Within seconds he felt that glorious sensation of his thoughts being plucked away and knew he was about to drop off to sleep. An owl screeched from the woods at the foot of the lane and Monty, who always slept under Max's bed, stirred and moved out from underneath, folding himself up in the far corner of the room by the chest of drawers. Max dreamed he was lying in a field of kale under a moonlit sky. The dew had fallen, the countryside looked wide and exquisite, but the smell of kale increased until it was almost unbearable. In his dream he saw headlights sweep across the kale and he stood and saw Sam's beautiful car whispering over towards him. He leant in through the car window to speak to her but the smell of kale mixed with a terrible aroma of shit and instead of Sam, he was face to face with Maureen Hindle, who was caked with excrement. Max woke with a snort and sat bolt upright.

'You stinker!' he hissed across the room at Monty. 'Jesus! I think my teeth are disintegrating. And you haven't even got the decency to lie in your own cloud of phosgene.' In the darkness Max saw the glint of a eye before it closed and the dog licked his lips and fell into an untroubled sleep.

Max sighed and turned on to his back and his thoughts, inevitably, turned to Sam. He didn't seem to be making any headway with her at all – in fact, he seemed to blunder along from one mistake to another and the swift end to their chat left him in no doubt that he had made a big blunder this evening. He felt like getting out of bed and going downstairs for a cigarette, but earlier in the day he had made a decision to stop smoking and had tossed the remaining cigarettes into the bin, where they now lay under the kitchen detritus of the evening. He puffed ironically; he had quit smoking to improve his chance of success and within a few hours he had blown them again. Perhaps he was too old to get back into the dating game.

'Bull shit!' he said, rolling over on to his side. He mustn't be too hard on himself, he thought, she had confided in him about the letters, so perhaps all was not lost. In fact ... and he sat up in bed with such vigour that Monty stood up on the other side of room and stared at him before coming over to the side of the bed and bounding up on to it. Max didn't bother to shoo him off – he had thought of something, the postmark on the letter that Sam had shown him. He liked numbers, he remembered numbers, and he remembered the date on the franked postmark. He turned his side light on, reached for his iPhone and opened his calendar. He counted the days back and laughed softly to himself. He had found a great reason to contact Sam Westbrook again. Maureen Hindle could not have posted that letter to her, she had left for Scotland before the date on the postmark.

Max was not a man to feel down for long. On the way into work he dropped off at the chemists and bought a packet of nicotine gum. The ritual of popping the top off the cardboard box, pulling out the sheet of lozenges and cracking up a niblet to put in his mouth had some parallels to the pleasure of opening a new packet of cigarettes, and as he crunched through the minty coating he concentrated on the sensation in his mouth, confident that he would get a nicotine rush within a few moments. He chewed away as he drove and soon realised it was not going to replace the pleasure of a cigarette. He pushed out another, then another, chewing and packing several of them between his lower lip and teeth for extra impact, but they began to make him feel a bit queasy. How, he wondered, could he have smoked so many cigarettes for so long and yet find the nicotine in a piece of gum nauseating? He rolled down his window and flung the box into the hedgerow.

Max strode across the great courtyard, looked over to the windows of Sam's flat and smiled. He had found a way of moving back into a favourable position and there was plenty going on that morning to amuse him until the right opportunity arose. The day began with a bang when Sharon the cleaner was set with the task of dusting the two suits of medieval armour which stood at the foot of the staircase, one on each side. Deciding she could get a better angle from which to flick away the dust and cobwebs, she had climbed half way up the stairs and was leaning over the banister. Unfortunately her duster caught on the sharp point of one of the helmets, and with a swift jerk she managed to start the suit of armour rocking. Her duster remained attached, and she continued to tug despite the cries of alarm from Max, Noel and Bunty who rushed across the great hall to try and divert disaster.

They failed. Like a house of cards the pieces of armour began to tumble and separate, falling on to the stone with a clatter of metal and swords, scattering visitors in different directions like a shoal of fish. Breast plates and shin plates skittered across the floor, the helmet struck the ground on one edge and rose up again like a cricket ball, spinning and turning before crashing back down into the pile of armour. Max, Noel and Bunty were joined by other members of the guiding team and they stood around the pile of tangled metal in silence.

The door into the private apartments opened with a crash and the earl, his breakfast napkin still tucked into his collar, stormed into the great hall. Sharon, crouched down on the stairs, covered her head with her arms as the earl pushed through the crowd. His ashen complexion slowly turned puce as fury overwhelmed him and, shooting a look of pure venom towards Bunty, he turned on his heels and left.

'Come along, everyone,' said Bunty briskly. 'Let's get this cleared up. Each of you take a piece.'

'Where to?' Laurence asked.

'I don't care. Pop it all in the office. Just get it moved!' They scuttled up and down the passage with dented pieces of armour. Major Frodsham carried the helmet and the moment he got to the statue corridor he tried to put it on. 'Major Frodsham!' Bunty yelled from the hall.

'Good God,' Frodders muttered. 'That woman has got eyes in the back of her ruddy head.'

On his way back from the office, Max heard a familiar jingle of beads behind him and without turning round he said, 'I know who that is.'

'I owe you an apology,' Sam said. She fell into line beside him and he slowed his pace. 'I was sharpish last night.'

'Were you?'

'And you may have been right.'

'I usually am.' He looked across at her and held her gaze to show her he was teasing. She smiled and he grinned back at her. 'Right about what?' he added.

'Pop in this afternoon on your way home, would you?' she said. 'I'm going this way,' and she left his side and ran lightly away from him and up the stairs towards the sealed chamber, her beads and scarves and spectacles jingling like horses' tack.

At the end of the working day, Max bounded up the stone stairs towards Sam's flat with an equal lightness of step. When she opened the door he saw that she had changed into comfortable clothes, which made her look softer than her working self.

'Max! How are you?'

'Embarrassed, ashamed, hoping for an early death ...' he replied.

'Stop it. I was snappish, you have nothing to apologise for, and besides, as I said this morning, you may well be right. Come on in.' He followed her through to the kitchen. 'Beer?' she asked.

'I must be drinking you dry.'

'I do seem to be getting through rather more alcohol than usual,' Sam said. 'Let's go through.'

The fire was burning merrily in the grate and Max dropped down into his usual end of the sofa. He liked Sam's flat. 'So, what's this apology all about?' he said.

'I thought a lot about our conversation last night and decided to ring Maureen direct.'

'Brave.'

'She's a very strange woman. My whole conversation with her was extremely tense, it made me very uncomfortable. The moment she realised it was me speaking, she began to spew up such a foul diatribe of bile about me, how I'd swanned in here and taken her job. Horrid stuff. And her manner ...' Sam shuddered.

'Classic passive aggressive, isn't she?'

'Oh, she'd dropped the passive, I can tell you. I was beginning to come round to BS's way of thinking. She told me he was trying to hide the inventory.'

'Did she now? That certainly seems compelling evidence,' Max said.

'Is it though? We know she hates BS. What about the letters?'

The thrill and excitement of Sam's apology had knocked his earlier plan completely off course and Max sprang to his feet and spun round to face her. 'I meant to tell you,' he said. 'The letter. Show me that letter you got,' and with a puzzled frown Sam went over to the table and pulled it out of the pile again. She handed it to Max, who flicked his nail against the postmark. 'There!' he said, 'Look at the date. Maureen Hindle was in Scotland. She couldn't possibly have got this letter into the post tray at Duntisbourne Hall. She was four hundred miles away.'

'Oh God,' Sam moaned. 'This is getting far too complicated.'

'You said yourself all the evidence against her was circumstantial,' Max said as he handed the letter back. 'She's exonerated on this one though.'

'Possibly. But she could have found a way round it – got a someone else to put it into the out tray for franking after she left for Scotland.'

'Is that really likely?'

Sam's mobile buzzed into life and she glanced down to see who was calling. 'Sorry, Max,' she said, 'I've got to take this. It's my daughter.' She scooped the phone up and went into the kitchen, partially shutting the door behind her for privacy.

To kill time Max pushed a log down into the fire with the poker and dropped another one into the grate. He brushed his hands together and turned around to warm his back. He could hear Sam making a few sympathetic noises in the room next door. He couldn't hear what she was saying, but he recognised the tone of voice and felt a kinship with her. She was comforting her daughter, there had been a crisis, but if her daughter was anything like Charlotte, the crisis would be minor. He hoped it was. He spotted some photographs on top of the low bookshelf and went over to investigate. They were of Sam, her hair much shorter and parted to one side, younger and, Max was interested to note, not nearly as attractive as she was now. With her was a girl, her daughter, Claire, he assumed. Pretty, but she looked high maintenance to Max.

Sam came through from the kitchen and although she was still holding the mobile to her ear, she caught Max's eye and mouthed the word 'sorry' to him. He shook his head and smiled to show that he understood.

'What darling? No, of course I was listening.' She paused, then added, 'as a matter of fact, there is someone here,' and she turned on her heels and disappeared into the kitchen. A few more minutes passed before she returned. 'Oh dear,' she said. 'That didn't go down very well.'

'Not me, I hope.'

'It's not really you, Max. It was my fault. Trouble is – and I know this will sound so unsympathetic – I could write the script for these phone calls. It's always the same problem: Jake.'

'Boyfriend?'

'Husband. And there's nothing I can do except listen and make the right noises. I feel so helpless – she's thousands of miles away, I'm stuck here. All she seems to want to do is go over all the times he's behaved like a jerk, but heaven help me if I agree with her and say he is a jerk.'

'Is he a jerk?'

'I don't know. I like the boy, but Claire pretty well supports him financially. She sensed she didn't have my full attention, but it's nothing. It'll pass. I'll call her back later when she's calmed down a bit. Anyway, where were we?'

'Much simpler stuff. The earl's archivist has just had someone sacked for doing something she didn't do.'

Sam laughed. 'It's up to BS how he pursues that one.' she said. 'I'll be gone from here the moment the exhibition is done.'

'Gone?' She had dropped it in so casually, and a heavy feeling of sadness washed over Max. 'You can't go.' She had joined him by the fire once more and he reached out and took her by the hand, pulling her towards him with the slightest of pressure. 'I couldn't bear it if you went.'

Sam looked down and said quietly, 'Max, don't.' She drew him over towards the sofa. They sat and she patted his hand before releasing it. 'We're the very best of friends, but we both have complicated private lives. I've got Claire, you've got Charlotte. And we live at opposite ends of the country.' She sighed. 'Besides, friends isn't a bad way to be: friends don't have crises and arguments, friends don't split up, friends don't tear each other to pieces. You meet a friend after ten years and you're glad to see them even if they haven't been in touch for all that time – meet an old lover after ten years and you approach them with a sense of dread.'

'I'm very grown up. I could risk it.'

'Stop it, Max, please.'

'Bull shit,' he said quietly, staring down at the recently released hand.

She pushed away from him into her corner of the sofa and carried on breezily, 'My pressing problem now is what to do about the Dywenydd Collection. Whether things are missing or mislaid, or even stolen and sold, my brief is to curate the collection – the complete collection – and I can't find it all. I'll have to talk to the earl – or snitch, as you so pertinently put it last night.'

Max winced at the word. 'Warn BS first,' he said. Sam wrinkled up her nose and shook her head. 'He's a nice old boy,' Max added.

'Is he? I'm beginning to wonder. I've seen a rather different side to him over all this.'

Max persevered. 'Give the fellow a chance.'

'A chance to do what? I'm not pointing a finger at anyone. You're the one who came up with the notion that he's had stuff away. That's not my problem. I haven't been brought in here like a private detective to find a thief. I'm simply here to do a job.'

'Tell him first.'

Sam looked away towards the fire, deep in thought. Eventually she said, 'I'll tell you what I'll do. I'll give him a copy of the missing things and tell him that I'm going to have to talk to the earl. Would that lift me above the rank of whistle-blower in your eyes?'

So my opinion of you is important, Max thought with satisfaction, taking it as an indication that the 'let's be friends' speech was not a complete rebuttal. His spirits lifted. 'I think that would be the kindest thing to do. Who knows, I may be wrong – I hope I'm wrong. It may make the old boy pull his finger out and track everything down, then we'll all be happy. Anyway, I'm bored now. I'm fed up with beating around the bush, so I'm just going to come straight out with it.' Max was amused by Sam's troubled look. 'When am I going to get a private view of that bloody exhibition of yours?'

Sam seemed relieved. 'You in tomorrow?'

'I'm not working, but I'll come in for that. Private viewing, mind. I don't want Noel up there acting as chaperone.'

They talked on until it was late and Max left, as he knew he would have to. He stopped at the fish and chip shop on the way home and ate in the car while the food was still hot. Monty was waiting for him on the other side of the front door when he let himself in. The dog bounced off merrily into the house to collect his toy and flung it at Max's feet. 'What have you been up to?' Max said as he tussled with him. 'Not blithering the plimby I hope.' Monty growled and ran off down the hall shaking the plimby in his small jaws.

He poured himself a whisky and as he sipped it, put together a plateful of cheese and cold meats with two thick slices of bread and butter on the side. Despite the hour and his late snack on the way home, he was feeling extremely hungry. Carrying his plate through to the sitting room, he settled down on the sofa. Monty leapt up beside him and watched each mouthful of food make the journey from plate to Max's mouth. When Max finished the plateful, Monty lost interest in him and began to remove an eye from his toy. 'Life is so simple for you, isn't it?' Max said as he worried the fur on the dog's neck. 'Do you ever lie awake at night and wonder what it's all for?' Monty stopped chewing the toy and looked up at him. 'No. And you shouldn't, old chap. You really shouldn't.'

# - 23 -

Sam was trying to decide if the smotherbox in the style of William Kent looked better open or closed. If she displayed it closed the leather interior, painted in an elaborate Italian baroque design of acanthus leaves and phallic buds, remained hidden; if open, the gilded mask and shell motifs could not be seen.

It was quiet in the exhibition, the only sound an occasional ticking which came from the floorboards moving a little as they heated and expanded – she had asked the electricians to leave the underfloor heating running. Every now and then the rising wind outside moaned in the chimney stacks overhead. A breeze came down towards her – the door at the foot of the stairs must have been opened – and then she heard footsteps coming up the spiral staircase. Leaving the smotherbox open she closed the cabinet and locked it before going through to meet Max. His hair had been tousled by the wind and he was eating a chocolate bar.

'How on earth,' he said, 'are you going to get visitors up those steps? They're lethal.'

'Luckily that's not my worry. You hungry?'

'Can't stop eating.'

'I think they're going to have timed entries so people aren't coming up at the same time as others are leaving, but no one seems to have given any thought to disabled access.' She could see Max wasn't listening. He was staring around, the chocolate bar held like a microphone in his hand.

'This is incredible!' he said. 'The real deal. It's as if I've walked on to the set of a Jack the Ripper film. I love it. I want this room.'

'But do you want the tour?'

'Yes please,' he said. He finished his chocolate bar and stuffed the paper wrapper into his pocket.

'OK. Well, the visitors come in first to this gentleman's club bit,' Sam said. 'It's not finished, there are some sofas to come up, but these wonderful mahogany cabinets were already here, so I wanted to start the story with the man who locked the whole collection away from prying eyes, but being Victorian, of course he did it in style. Visitors can open the drawers.' She pulled one out and beckoned Max over.

'Goodness, what pretty things. What are they?'

'Those are Burmese bells,' Sam said, her fingernail tapping on the glass which protected the treasures beneath, 'or ben wa balls. This set is made from hammered silver – they're Chinese, those are Perugian marble, and those ones there are tooled leather stuffed with sawdust.'

'What are they used for?' Max asked.

'Read the card!' Max looked across at her, his eyes bright with amusement.

'Christ! My mum had one of those,' and he pointed down at a pair of instruments with ornate porcelain handles at one end and small wheels with evenly placed radiating sharp needles at the other. 'She said she used them for sewing.'

'I'm sure she did. They're tailor's tracing wheels, called Wartenberg wheels by the medical profession but these are here because the inventory describes their use as sex toys. It's one of the few things from the realm of SM which I thought was appropriate for the show. There are the Japanese butterfly clamps too, but the workmanship on them is so exquisite I couldn't resist, especially as they came as a set with these beautiful little weights: the black ones with the flowers on are cloisonné beads, those are lampwork beads made of opal glass and these are faux pearls. I think they're lovely.'

'I like the dice.'

'Great, aren't they? They still make a version now – I think there's even an app – but these are incredible, mother of pearl, the lettering picked out in gold. I had a bit of trouble deciding which words to have face up: kiss and lips seemed the best choice.'

'I can still see blow on the edge of that one,' Max said, tilting his head to get the right angle. He looked at her again with a roguish grin.

'Come on,' she said, shutting the drawer, 'you can prowl through the rest of the drawers some other time. Right, back to the tour. I want to get people thinking about why these clubs began to spring up when they did, like the Medenham Monks ...'

'I've had such a sheltered upbringing.'

'It was popularly known as the Hellfire Club. Come on through.' She led him down a narrow and dark passage to the next room, which was laid out like an eighteenth-century tavern, stopping in front of a portrait of a youth with a weak chin. He was wearing a loose turban of silk, and his clear skin and hairless chest visible through the unbuttoned shirt made him look effeminate. Max stood beside her, leaning in towards the painting and in the airless room she caught the vanilla smell of chocolate on him, 'This fellow is Philip, Earl of Wharton, and he's credited with starting the Hellfire Club. There's little evidence of debauchery – it was much more to do with mocking religion and getting drunk.'

'It's rather a good painting. Was this in the original collection?'

'No, this is on loan from the Royal Collection. It's by Rosalba Cerriera, a woman who made a name for herself with miniatures.

She was a Venetian painter. I agree, it is rather a nice portrait. It's about the only help we've had from the earl – he pulled some strings for us. The next little room we come to takes the story further,' and they continued along a tunnel lit only by electric candles which guttered as if the flames were real. It opened up into a cave apparently carved from rock. 'This is meant to look like the inner temple underneath West Wycombe, where Francis Dashwood continued Wharton's legacy. Although the ninth earl missed this era by several decades, a lot of the stuff he acquired had been made during it. Here we have a dining table set with the sort of food that was served at the Hellfire Club – Breast of Venus, Devil's Loin – and Dean the butler did these brilliant napkins for me following the instruction in the inventory. We've named them the peniform fold.' Each place setting was adorned with a crisp linen napkin rising up from the side plate like an erect phallus. 'The glasses are from the collection, more phalluses and this set of crockery is hilarious.' Sam reached over the rope and retrieved one of the plates for Max to look at.

'What is it about nuns?' he said.

'Female guests, i.e. prostitutes, were called nuns by the club. Perhaps it's a homage to that, or just that era's fixation with virtuous women beset by marauding rakes.' Sam placed the dish back on the table with care. 'Mind you, it's back now.'

'Is it?'

'There's a huge fiction market for stories of female submission. It seems potty that we live in an era when feminism has triumphed and yet those very same women have an insatiable appetite for stories where the heroine is the pliant foil to a powerful and sadistic man.'

'Really?'

'Absolutely. Ever since women have been able to download books and read them discreetly on e-readers, sales of erotica have increased by thirty percent.'

'Men are reading them, surely.'

'No, it's mostly women and the plots are often versions of *Pride and Prejudice* but with lashings – literally – of sado-masachistic sex.'

'I can't stand Austen,' Max said. 'Let's get back to the Hellfire Club. Weren't they into that far healthier obsession of devil worship?' Sam chuckled and shook her head.

'Not much evidence of that. They mocked the Church and religion, and there were rumours around that time of Black Masses and sacrifices, mostly coming out of France, but Dashwood's lot were more into debauchery and wenching. The next room is about the Beggar's Benison.'

'Again, I know it's rude, but no idea why.' Max rested his shoulder against the gypsum rock wall. He had an extraordinary knack of looking as if he was following every word she said and she found it disarming. His eyes seldom left her face: if he was not looking into her eyes, his gaze would drift no further than her mouth and then back up to engage with her once again. 'Tell me what the Beggar's Benison is,' he said.

'Well, according to folklore, James V was travelling in Scotland in disguise and came to a river which he could not cross, but a beggar girl took pity on him and carried him across the Dreel Burn. He gave her a gold coin for her troubles, and clearly for something else, because the blessing, or benison, that she bestowed on him was: *May your purse na'er be toom, and your horn aye in bloom.*'

Max's eyes twinkled through the half light. He was laughing at her. 'That,' he said, 'is the most ghastly Scottish accent I've ever heard.'

She was within touching distance of him and she pushed the heel of her hand on to his shoulder as a reprimand. Max caught her by the wrist and drew her towards him and as she came closer to his face the light in the room seemed to dim further and a voice behind her said, 'What on earth is going on here?' She turned to see the entrance to the room blocked by BS Moreton, one hand on his hip, the other resting on the head of his stick.

'Hello, BS,' she said. 'I was showing Max round.'

BS stumped into the room, which he seemed to occupy with his bulk. 'That is most irregular,' he said. 'We can't have you bringing every Tom, Dick and Harry up for a private view when you feel like it. What about security?'

Sam was sufficiently confounded that she didn't answer. It was Max who spoke first. 'My fault, I'm afraid,' he said. 'I implored her in a most ingratiating way to bring me up here.' Sam could tell that BS wasn't going to respond to Max's irony.

'Then I suggest you take yourself back down,' he retorted. Max looked at Sam and she nodded her approval of the suggestion. She followed Max back through the exhibition and touched him on the hand before BS caught up with them. 'I'll call,' she said.

'Good luck,' Max answered.

Sam felt less intimidated by BS in the larger room. She had decided she must speak out, but the moment Max had gone, BS launched into her. 'I have to say I am incredibly disappointed in your behaviour,' he said.

'I beg your pardon?'

'I had assumed a professional such as yourself, a woman of your age, would be inured to these salacious images, but I find you up here, alone with another employee, about to engage in goodness knows what sort of profane behaviour.'

Sam wanted to burst out laughing, the suggestion was so ludicrous. 'I have a flat in the building,' she said. 'Why would I bring Max here to seduce him?'

'Good grief!' BS said angrily.

'Max isn't just any old employee, he's a good friend of mine and when I tell you what he's discovered you may well be grateful to him because it proves something beyond a shadow of a doubt about the person who wrote the letters.'

'You had no right to speak to him about those.'

Sam paused to control the frustration that she could feel rising up – she didn't want the interview to end in a slanging match. 'The point is, he spotted the date on the letter that was sent to me, and Maureen could not possibly have franked it in the office at the Hall. She was in Scotland at the time it was franked.'

'Of course she sent them.'

'She could not have sent mine, and the probability of two people being involved is vanishingly small.'

'She would have asked someone in the office to put it in the franking tray after she had gone.'

'Far too risky. She wouldn't do that. The very act would create another witness. If the letters ever became public – and the author of those letters would always have that possibility in mind – it would be a matter of minutes before someone made the connection.'

Sam could see that BS was getting agitated. He had pushed himself away from the cabinets on which he had leaned when he first came in and was now pacing up and down, looking at the tip of his cane as it struck the boards. He turned to face her again and said, 'Maureen is manipulative. Why should we believe she was in Scotland? Have you checked? No, I thought not.'

'But you could, and you should. I have to tell you, BS, that I am pretty angry with you. You put me down on that rota as a guide instead of Maureen.'

'That was Bunty. Bunty does the rota.'

'I don't believe you.'

'It's her writing. Go and look.'

'Under your instruction.'

BS huffed.'Well, that's as may be, but it's for the best.'

'When I spoke to Maureen – '

'You spoke to Maureen?'

'Yes, and she had some quite malicious things to say about me.'

'There you are. I keep telling you, that's what she's like.'

'Oh God,' Sam said, 'this is hopeless.' She saw BS lift his chin a little as if he was winning the argument, however risible his hypothesis. 'Just sort it out, BS. I beg you.' He stared back at her with a cussed look. She took a deep breath. 'Unfortunately, that is a minor problem compared to this one,' and she walked over to her briefcase, pulled out one of the folders she had prepared and handed it to him. He took it from her, balancing the handle of his cane in the crook of his elbow and flicked through the pages, then he reached into the top pocket of his shirt for his spectacles and began to read. After a few moments he let the file flop closed again. 'I haven't got time to go through this,' he said casually. 'I have a mountain of work waiting for me in the office.' He raised his stick and pointed around the room. 'It's finished,' he said. 'The exhibition is complete, and you've done an excellent job, my dear. You don't need anything else, do you?' He smiled blandly at her.

'I do.'

'Why?'

Sam refused to be provoked. 'This exhibition needs prints. It needs the authentic prints that were part of this collection and which you have failed to find. Mass printing is at the heart of the sexual revolution in the eighteenth century. Without it the Church might have been able to keep its stranglehold on spiritual conformity and the concept of people controlling their behaviour with their own consciences might never have developed. How would the west have discovered the different sexual values of people from distant lands if they couldn't read about the exploits of sailors and explorers of these different cultures? But for me the single most important thing on that list is the painting of the ninth earl.'

'It's here,' BS said sarcastically, pointing at the Thomas Lawrence painting on the wall above him of the corpulent earl in his later years.

'You know I'm not talking about that one. I mean the one of him when he was young – the one that aped the Hogarth painting of Francis Dashwood. Crispin Sebastian Falkenstein, dressed in the humble clothes of a friar, kneeling at an altar on which is spread a naked woman, a candlestick in the shape of a phallus, the mask of Priapus and a book of erotic writing in place of the Bible.'

'Blasphemy.'

'Precisely, and at the very heart of this whole exhibition – the break with the Church as the custodian of moral correctness. Even now, in our modern society, a painting that rouses some disgust.'

'And so it should. It is heresy.'

'No, BS. It's missing.'

'Oh, this is all very tedious,' he said. 'I am bored with this whole issue. In fact a less equitable man than me might start to feel decidedly testy.' He patted the file gently against his thigh.

'Well, I'm sorry you feel like that, but I thought it only right to warn you.'

'Warn me?'

'I am honour bound to notify the trustees. They and the earl will be getting a copy of this list on Monday. You have the weekend to sort it out.'

BS stared down at her and in his fury he seemed to swell in size or perhaps, she thought, he was straightening up his body in order to attack. For what seemed like minutes but was probably only a few seconds they stared at one another until finally BS looked away.

'I have never been able to understand the mind of a woman,' he said quietly. Clearly he had succeeded in controlling himself once again. 'Have I not gone out of my way to make you feel at home here? To show you round, to help you whenever you needed my guidance and my expertise? I have been the philosopher Theon to your Hypatia, allowing you to rise up and take the plaudits at the Museum of Alexandria.'

Sam frowned, trying to recollect to whom he referred, then she remembered. 'What a colourful and pointless metaphor,' she said.

BS swept on regardless: 'Like Theon, I have had to swallow my pride. I have been archivist to His Lorship for nearly two decades now, solely responsible for this invaluable collection. Have you asked yourself how hard it was for me to hand it all over to someone else, an outsider and a woman at that? Of course you haven't. I have had to come to terms with your complete lack of sensitivity, but the thing I can't understand is what I have done to make you behave like this towards me. It is vindictive, spiteful behaviour – the sort of behaviour I have seen before in overambitious women who are intimidated by the world of men, who know they are inferior and overcompensate with viciousness.'

Sam opened her mouth to parry his words but he raised his hand to stop her and added, 'You do what you think is right, but let me warn you, if you hand this over to the earl, you are the one who will look a fool, not I,' and with that he tucked the file under his arm and walked past her to the exit without looking back.

## - 24 -

BS Moreton made his way along the formal gravel path until it dropped down towards the River Lugg which ran along the bottom of the valley to his left. At a turn in the river below, his journey continued straight towards a shoulder of hill where he rounded a group of ancient oaks which roared in the wind over his head. He turned his face into the gale and felt the first drops of rain strike his forehead. Planting his stick into the ground, he stared out across the valley, rocked by the storm as it blew and veered around him. A patch of sky glared beneath the clouds and dazzled him before it was pulled back up into a boiling sky, the clouds indigo and black like a bruise. He wanted to shout at the approaching storm with all his might, 'blow winds and crack your cheeks.' He saw himself as King Lear, blundering across the heath. He wanted to call down 'oak-cleaving thunderbolts' to 'singe his white hair'. Eventually the desire to voice his rage became too much and using the modulations of Laurence Olivier he yelled over the gale, 'I am a man more sinned against than sinning!'

He was snapped out of his performance by the sound of a foot slipping a short distance on gravel, and turning, he saw two visitors approaching down the path. They had not seen him because they were crouched together underneath an umbrella with which they tussled as the wind bounced and buffeted it, and he hoped they had not heard him either. His outburst had been for the ears of his maker and no one else. He turned to make his way back to his car and as he drew level with them, they tilted the umbrella to see who was passing. Instantly the wind caught the brolly from below, swerved the canopy up and inside out, spinning the two elderly ladies round before it left their grasp completely and leapt away from them in huge hops and jumped down the embankment into the trees below. Exposed and shocked they continued to spin and came to rest facing BS, but instead of bewailing their predicament they were laughing and panting and leaning on one another.

'There's a nasty storm coming, ladies,' BS said, his voice raised over a sudden slam of wind which seemed to pluck his words away. 'You should get back inside.' The elder of the two ladies raised an acknowledging hand before they lowered their heads into the wind and continued on their way. BS stared after them. 'Bloody women,' he muttered.

He made his way back along the path towards his car and clambered in as the rain worsened. Manoeuvring his stick into the footwell of the passenger side, he glanced down with a shudder at the file on the seat and rested his head back. The rain hit the windscreen like handfuls of grain and the wind pounded and rocked the car. He wondered where those stupid old women were now. Slipping and slithering through the torrent, no doubt. Served them right.

He was fed up to the back teeth with women. His Lear analogy could hardly be more apt; he had shown nothing but kindness to Maureen Hindle and Sam Westbrook, and they had both turned on him. He had helped Maureen at her time of greatest need, had nurtured her failing confidence throughout one whole winter to set her back on her feet, and she had repaid him with a two-year campaign of spikes and rumour to bring him down. And Sam was no better. He could not imagine how he could have been more helpful. He had done everything in his power to encourage her to produce an excellent exhibition, with great humility he had taken a back seat and let her accept the plaudits, but instead of appreciating his sacrifice or thanking him for his help, she too had turned on him. What was wrong with these women? Why did they twist every good intention of his into something base? What had he ever done to them?

He knew he had caught Sam off guard when he went up to the sealed chamber and found her with Max Black, who had scuttled off at such speed. Clearly something had been going on between them. It was totally inappropriate behaviour in a place of work, but instead of showing any remorse, she had attacked him. Initially he thought the problem was just this damned Maureen Hindle issue – Sam had got some notion that she shouldn't have been suspended. As if it was any of her business! BS thought he had parried most of her observations rather effectively, making several good points, but Sam didn't seem convinced.

Then, to his astonishment, she had presented him with that list as long as your arm of things she wanted for the exhibition. He had spun round in disbelief, pointing his stick at the cabinets of artefacts. The exhibition was complete bar a few light bulbs that were still missing, so why should she need anything else? It was preposterous. And when she said she was going to hand the same report over to the earl and the trustees at the beginning of next week he nearly lost it completely. Thank the Lord he didn't, he had used every ounce of his self-control and fired at her with both barrels. He was glad he had told her in no uncertain terms his opinion of her. When she first arrived he had to admit he thought she was rather special, but he had made a terrible error of judgement. She was like all the other members of her sex, ruthless and spiteful. What on earth was she accusing him of? Bowdlerising the collection?

It was an egregious accusation. Over the years he might have filleted out some of the material, but not out of any prudish need to remove anything he considered offensive or improper. Heaven knows, the whole collection was improper – there would be nothing left if he had embarked on expurgating it. He had been the archivist of the collection for nearly two decades, space was limited, and he regarded part of his job to be on the look-out for duplications and to deal with those in ways he regarded as fitting, but there was absolutely no need whatsoever to justify his actions to Sam ruddy Westbrook.

He looked down again at the folder on the seat and pushed it open with a weary hand. Rummaging in the breast pocket of his shirt for his reading glasses, he ran his eye down the first page of the list before turning to the following page. It did seem rather a lot, he was surprised to see. He was sure some of the books were still back in his study at home. He heaved a heavy sigh and looked out through the car window. Perhaps his best course of action would be to gather as much as he could before Monday so that when the list plopped on to the earl's desk he could reassure His Lordship that most of it had actually turned up and that Sam Westbrook was one of those shrill, pushy women who made mountains out of molehills. The thought of making a fool out of Sam Westbrook cheered him.

He was feeling calmer and, as if in concord, the storm seemed to be moving away towards the Black Mountains, leaving behind a steady drizzle of rain. BS turned on the windscreen wipers and pulled himself forward with the steering wheel to wipe the inside of the screen with the sleeve of his jacket. The tweed squeaked on the glass and left a smear of water droplets and lint.

'Oh blow!' he muttered, slipping back into the seat and pushing his spectacles up his nose to enable him to read the symbols on the air conditioning panel. The car was only a few months old and BS was unfamiliar with several of the more complicated modes in the vehicle. He hated modes. The word itself summed up everything fatuous about modern technology. However, he persevered and several modes into the menu the fans fired up and blasted damp air into his face. He sank back in his seat and closed his eyes, letting the row and clatter mollify his thoughts. The breeze, still redolent with the artificial scent of a new car, felt like a balm for the tense and contracted muscles of his face which gradually started to relax.

After a few minutes he stirred himself. The windscreen was beginning to clear and he put the car into gear and drove back across the estate towards the Hall. The afternoon was late and he couldn't face spending the final hour at his desk – he would surprise Patricia. She had seemed rather down since his illness, worried about him going back to work so soon afterwards. It would cheer her up if he showed a willingness to follow her advice by getting home early. It would also give him a chance to have a good hunt for some of the things on Sam Westbrook's list. Patricia would help. They would sort this out together, side by side, contra mundum, against the world. Once again he thought of his Lear analogy with Patricia in the role of Cordelia, loyal and honest compared to the other two harridans who had betrayed him and undermined his authority.

'Patricia, my love?' he called. He shut the front door behind him, dropped his keys on to the brass plate on the hall table and made his way up the corridor into the kitchen. 'Patricia? Are you here, pet?' He gazed around the empty room then leant on his stick to peer into the conservatory beyond. Where could she be? He felt disappointed and piqued that she wasn't home to appreciate the effort he had made on her behalf. He pulled his coat off and dropped it on the kitchen table, glanced one more time towards the conservatory to make sure she wasn't fossicking around somewhere at the bottom of the garden and started back towards the office they shared at the front of the house – although most of the desk space was taken up with BS's belongings.

He put Sam's list on his desk, turned on the lamp and sat down heavily. He drew the file towards him and opened it. Books – he would start by digging out some of the books that needed to be returned. Pushed himself up on to his feet once more, he began to work along the bookshelves which covered the wall on the left-hand side of the door. He ran a finger along the spines to force himself to concentrate on the titles as he knew he had a habit of losing focus and scanning them without taking them in. By the time he had completed the shelf at eye-level, his neck was beginning to ache from holding his head on one side, so he straightened up and turned to look out of the window into the drive in the forlorn hope that Patricia would drive in and come and help him. The stormy day was hastening the approach of dusk, and from the lighted room in which he stood, the front garden looked dark and gloomy. Wherever could she be?

He returned to his desk and began to go through one of the many piles of papers and books stacked up along the back of it. He let out an involuntary 'Oh!' when he spotted the earl's crest on the front of one of the volumes, but it was from the indigo library, not one of the titles on Sam's list. Again he peered into the darkening evening and sighed. He wondered what they were having for supper – perhaps there was something cooking slowly in the Aga.

He made his back down to the kitchen and lifted the door of the bottom oven open with the toe of his shoe. To his dismay there was no immediate smell of food. Gripping the sturdy rail at the front of the Aga, he lowered himself down to peer inside. It was empty. He pulled himself up again and clanked the door shut with his foot. It really was very difficult to settle down if you were waiting for someone to come home. He began to feel aggrieved – it was selfish of Patricia not to leave a note or some indication of when she would be home. By the time he heard her key in the front door he was feeling extremely disagreeable.

'Where have you been?' he said as she pushed past him into the kitchen with a handful of carrier bags.

'Shopping.'

'You don't go shopping on a Friday.'

'Don't I? How would you know, BS? You're never here on Friday afternoon.'

'You go shopping with Jane on Wednesdays.'

'Not when I've got the whole family here for the weekend.'

'The whole family?'

'Our anniversary. Don't pretend you've forgotten.' Patricia stopped her task of unloading the bags and turned to face him. She was frowning. 'Whatever's the matter BS?'

'I came home early and you weren't home.'

Patricia shrugged her shoulders. 'I had to get a few extra things, that's all.'

'There's nothing in the oven.'

'I've got supper here,' and she waved a hand over the bags. 'It's not much, but I've got so much cooking to do for the weekend.'

It was almost as if she was trying to provoke him.

'I simply don't understand you, Patricia. You pester and scold me about my working hours, and the one day – the one single day

– I come home early – solely to please you I might add – you're not here.'

'It's not yet seven o'clock, BS. How was I supposed to know you were coming home early?'

BS ignored her question and continued: 'I have had a most extraordinarily stressful day, a mountain of work is sitting on my desk at the Hall, every hour in my working life is precious, you'd be hard put to find someone over there as dedicated as me, but I set all that aside – all of it – and hurried home. And what happens? I spend hours plodding around an empty house all on my own. I had no idea where you had gone or when you might be back. It really is exceptionally selfish behaviour.' He stared down at Patricia who returned his gaze, but the tiny movements of her head had increased and her face was beginning to colour.

'Selfish? You call me selfish?' She pulled her bag off her shoulder with an angry yank and thumped it down on top of the shopping. 'How dare you BS! Day after day, night after night, I "plod", as you so quaintly put it, around this house waiting for you. Month after month, year after year, I've waited for you to spend more time here. And do you know what? I've been waiting now for nearly twenty years.' She spun away from him and thumped a couple of packets out of the bags and on to the kitchen table before turning on him again. 'I didn't want to move down here when you retired. I had friends up in Manchester – I didn't want to uproot and leave everything, I didn't want to say goodbye to everyone I knew, friendships I'd built up over the years. But I did it because you promised that you'd be around a lot more than when you were running that blasted school. I didn't want to live in that horrible dank cottage on the estate. I wanted to be near people, live in that nice flat that Sam Westbrook has, where you probably spend a great deal more time nowadays than you should.'

'What?'

'Oh, don't play the innocent with me, BS. "Wives are the last to know" – isn't that what the letter said?'

'Not the ruddy letters again,' BS groaned. 'What's the matter with everyone today? The world has gone mad.'

'Yes, those ruddy letters again. Well, I did know. All through your Svengali rule of that staff room at the Cathedral School I knew exactly what was going on: late-night calls, no one on the other end if I answered, a shower the moment you got in from work, an expensive fountain pen you'd "found" in one of the classrooms, a mawkish poem on a bookmark. I have Candida Cochrane's mother to thank for the end of that reign.'

'That was years ago. We dealt with all that. That's history.'

'That was, and you promised it had all stopped when we came here. But it hadn't, had it? I thought if I did a few days' guiding at the Hall I could keep an eye on things, that you wouldn't have the audacity to carry on under my nose, but clearly I was wrong. So I stopped torturing myself and gave up working at the Hall with the only group of friends I had managed to make down here, so that I didn't have to watch you flirting and sniffing around Donna Falkender. Then the letters started to arrive, to make sure I wasn't able to turn a blind eye.'

'No, Patricia. No. I've got to the bottom of all that. I know who was writing those hideous, venomous letters. It was Maureen Hindle – I've had her sacked; she's disturbed, sick – there's something very wrong with her. Everything she put in those letters was a pack of lies. She had it in for me, goodness knows why.'

The strangest expression fluttered across Patricia's face and caused her to pause momentarily, but then she leaned towards him and her neck stretched out like a chicken about to peck. 'I don't believe you. I thought when those letters started that you would have the good sense to stop fooling around, to stop preening and strutting and schmoozing around every single bit of skirt that crossed the threshold. But no. Wrong again. A new one turns up. Sam Westbrook, and you're seen in town having lunch, driving around the estate together, and I know it's starting all over again. And then, hallelujah, you're taken ill – and finally, I think to myself, finally the old goat has been put out to pasture. But I was wrong. Back you go, days after leaving hospital, and here I am, stuck in a house I hate, on my own.'

BS reached out for the back of a kitchen chair to steady himself. He was aware that one of the spotlights in the ceiling was buzzing and it would probably blow in the next few days. Patricia had turned her back on him and was finishing the unpacking. She began to put some of the things away in the cupboards, slamming each door and drawer in turn. He didn't know what to do next. He badly wanted to sit down, but felt rooted to the spot.

When she had finished, she turned to look at him again. 'Nothing to say BS? That's a first.'

It was true, he didn't know what to say, but her question broke the spell of inactivity, and he pulled the chair away from the table and sat down, stretching his leg out to relieve the pain in his knee. He looked up at her as she stood in front of the kitchen window, her arms folded across her chest, her chin still tipped upwards a little, her expression still defiant. He felt overwhelmingly sorry for himself and let his lower lip soften to show his wife that her words had hurt him very much. He leant forward, rested his elbow on his other knee and bowed his head into his hand to give the impression that he was cowed, beaten. When he looked up again, he saw it had worked – Patricia had dropped her hands to her sides and her shoulders had relaxed.

In a quiet voice BS said, 'I came home early because I badly need your help, but you probably don't feel very much like helping me.' He looked down and waited, knowing his wife could seldom resist this approach. One of the reasons he felt such affection for her was that she always put him and his needs before her own and took a direct application for help such as this to mean that he valued her practical mind and his life was hopeless without it. As the minutes passed he worried that perhaps things had come to a very poor pass indeed, but eventually he heard her sigh and he slowly raised his eyes and looked up from under his brow with a doting and bashful gaze intended to be irresistible. It worked. Patricia came slowly forward, took hold of a chair and sat down opposite him giving another sigh as she settled.

BS reached out across the table and grasped her hands in his huge paws. Her fingers felt icy. He rubbed his thumbs rhythmically up her wrists and stared across at her with fervent concentration. Eventually the earnestness of his gaze pulled her eyes up until she looked into his. This was his moment. With careful modulation he said, 'Please will you help me? I think I may be in a spot of trouble.'

This caught her interest and she frowned. 'Trouble?'

'I have a list, in the office here, of a few things that I can't actually find.'

'What sort of things?'

'Sam Westbrook ...' He felt her fingers twist as if to escape from his grasp and saw her lips thin. 'No, no, wait. I promise you, I absolutely promise you, God is my witness, I have no interest in her. I've seen a very unpleasant side to that woman over the last few days. If it gives you any comfort at all, I am certain she has her eyes on someone else at work: a pleasant fellow – divorced, I believe.' He paused again, her hands stilled and he relaxed his grip on them a little. 'The problem is,' he continued in a quiet voice, 'she has produced a list of things, little things like books and prints, which she thinks used to be upstairs at the Hall in the sealed chamber, and which don't seem to be there now, and I need your help, Patricia. I desperately need you to help me find them because I know I've brought some things home over the years, and I know I'm disorganised and careless, but if I can't find at least some of the things, she's going to His Lordship and ...' He felt his throat begin to tighten, it was sore and he swallowed hard to clear it, and something warm plopped on to the back of his hand followed by another and another, and he looked down and realised tears were falling not from Patricia's eyes, but from his. He stared at her in horror, as if she had found him participating in a shameful act, and to underline this she glanced away, probably repelled by his disgrace. Feeling that his nose was about to run and compound his shame, he released her hands and plunged into the pocket of his jacket for his handkerchief.

Patricia took the opportunity to lean back in her chair. She folded her arms and he sensed her watching him once more as he blew his nose with clarion power, dashed the handkerchief across each eye, folded it until he had a dry patch on the top, and blotted and smoothed the whiskers under his nose and around his mouth. 'Dear me,' he said. 'How extraordinary. I don't know what came over me.'

He gave her a wan smile which she returned, and she began to shake her head – not the small, familiar tremor which he knew well, but a slow side-to-side motion of disbelief. 'What?' BS said.

'Why are you shaking your head in that way?'

'Oh BS. Whatever do you mean?'

'What do you mean?'

'It's all gone. I can't help you. You must know, it's all gone.'

'No. Most of it's here, I'm sure of it.'

'You're fooling yourself.'

BS felt a great pull and drop in the centre of his stomach and his throat tightened again. 'I know I filleted a few things out, a few duplicates.'

'You sold them.'

'No, not really. I found good homes for them. I found people who really appreciated them, who understood their importance, their provenance, their beauty. It wasn't any of the really valuable things – only some books, a few prints … You have to do that with collections, otherwise you would just get snowed under with more and more stuff. I had to marshall the good stuff, throw out the chaff.'

'You didn't throw it out, BS. You sold it to that man in the High Street.'

'I did not!' BS yelled. He was on his feet. He thumped his fist down on the table and glared across at Patricia, who cringed away from him like a slug showered in salt. 'Goddamnit woman, if you won't help me, I'll ruddy well do it myself,' and pushing back his chair, which screeched on the flagstones as he passed, he thumped up the corridor to the office and slammed the door behind him.

Half an hour later he heard the sound of his wife making her way upstairs to bed. He opened the door of his office. 'Patricia?' She turned and looked down on him, her hand on the banister, her expression unreadable. 'I'm sorry, pet. I shouldn't have lost control like that.' BS believed that an unconditional apology was best and should be returned by an unconditional acceptance of the apology.

'It wasn't control you lost, it was pretence,' Patricia said. 'The pretence that you are a civilised man.'

# - 25 -

The ugly exchange on Friday night gave BS Moreton the perfect excuse for not presenting his wife with an anniversary gift. He hoped his taciturn silence implied that she didn't deserve to have one. He had, of course, failed to purchase anything on the days he surprised her by saying he was shopping when in fact he had been visiting Sam Westbrook to discuss the problem of the anonymous letters. For months he had been dreading this weekend, the tsunami of family due to arrive on Saturday, but when he woke on Saturday morning in a bed already vacated by his wife, he couldn't have wished harder for their arrival. He knew that the chaos and distraction of sons, daughters-in-law, grandchildren and a badly behaved dog would throw a shield around him.

He had always admired Patricia's ability to cover up any show of ill will towards him in public, but her performance throughout the weekend astonished him. She seemed cheerful and relaxed, if a bit tired by the end of Sunday. She played with the grandchildren, remarked when she served dessert that she had cooked his favourite sticky toffee puddings as a treat, and seemed delighted to be celebrating forty glorious years of marriage. She even managed to sit beside him, pointing things out and remarking on them as they watched a compilation of videos and old photos that David had put together for them, occasionally pushing him playfully on the shoulder when he appeared on the screen with a particularly outrageous haircut or style of clothing. In private, she cut him dead.

He had the occasional stab at searching through papers on his desk and a few more shelves of books in the office, but only as an excuse to shut himself away from the relentless noise and chatter in the rest of the house. The badly behaved dog joined him whenever he disappeared to the study and behaved well, as if to prove to the master of the house that it was years of baiting and teasing by the children that made her chew trainers and piddle on the carpets. If she could just be left in peace, she seemed to say, she could be an undemanding companion.

BS failed to find anything on Sam's list, but he put aside a few small objects from the Hall which he had brought home several years ago to show Patricia: a small Meissen figurine; an emerald, diamond and platinum bracelet by Garrards; a neoclassical mourning brooch with a charming image of a nymph holding aloft a lantern. They didn't belong in the Dywenydd Collection, but he thought it might be expedient in the circumstances to get them back to the Hall.

Then another thought struck him and he unlocked the bottom drawer of his desk. A wooden box filled the drawer. There was a handle on each end, and using the front one, BS struggled to get the box at the right angle to enable him to pull it forward and up out of the drawer. It was heavy and ungainly. Once he had manhandled it on to the top of his desk, he opened up the lid and looked down on the Golden Hand of Jerusalem. It was not the original of course – he would never have kept an item as valuable as that in the house – but rather the giltware replica that had been made when the Cellini was sold at the beginning of the nineteenth century. He lifted it out from its bed of tissue paper using both hands. It was heavy, solid silver dipped in gold, and the silver fingernails had blackened in storage, unlike the rest of the hand where the gold glowed with an amber lustre undiminished by age. The pearls around the wrist were produced by Mikimoto, the very first cultured pearls to come on to the market. The earl had them brought over from Tokyo before their fame boomed across Europe. They were flawless, huge, lustrous – probably far more beautiful than the natural pearls that would have adorned the Cellini. A number of years ago the earl, concerned that the hand was vulnerable hanging in the saloon, had commissioned the second replica which was at the Hall today. It was exchanged in the closed season, and the few people involved in the deceit were sworn to secrecy. BS had been given the task of bearing this beautiful object to the vaults up in London, but he was so fascinated by it that he didn't want to miss the opportunity of studying it before it was locked away from view. The badly behaved dog padded over to him and rested her head on his knee. BS looked down into her eyes and said; 'Yes. It is a beautiful thing, isn't it?' and the dog banged the floor with her tail. He now wondered if he had kept the treasure here for rather too long.

Later in the afternoon, as a reward for her companionship during these difficult days, BS took the dog for a walk around the village and found it an enjoyable sensation to have the company of a living creature without the compulsion to make conversation. The pleasure was compromised somewhat when the dog defecated on the bank at the side of the playing fields. BS looked around and saw a mother pushing a child on a swing a few hundreds yards from where he stood. As she pushed, she watched to see what he was going to do. He nodded agreeably at her and, making sure she could see, he began to pull a black plastic bag out of a bone-shaped dispenser which was clipped to the handle of the lead. The dog had become skittish after her success, and he had to give the lead an irritable tug to calm her down. Turning his back towards the mother and child, he gathered up a handful of leaves and grass a few inches from the pile. He placed these carefully over the faeces, then dropped a stone into the bag and moved away, swinging it from his hand – the badge of the responsible dog owner.

Buoyed by his successful deception, he set off again to circle around the field and back towards his house. He needed time to think, time to review the accusations Patricia had laid at his feet. It was true that the second-hand bookshop had taken some of the titles off him for a small consideration and put him in touch with a Swiss fellow who was interested in prints. It was all so long ago now, but BS began to realise that he probably shouldn't have taken a finder's fee for the material. He was worried that his actions could be misconstrued if presented to the earl and the trustees in the wrong light, although he knew in his heart that his intentions had always been honourable. He was paid for a service, albeit handsomely, but nothing more. However, he was also confident that there could be no record of any of this as the bookshop had closed a couple of years earlier. It was perfectly possible that these things had simply gone missing, as so many treasures had done over the centuries, for entirely innocent reasons. He felt secure in his own mind that he would be able to explain all this if the question arose, but was certain his length of service and loyalty to Duntisbourne would encourage the trustees to be lenient even if they came to the conclusion that he was guilty of gross inefficiency. He knew the earl loathed publicity of any kind, and if it all went horribly wrong and he had to face the possibility of some kind of retribution, it would be a mild rebuke and little more.

The families left on Monday morning and, in order to avoid another scene with Patricia when they had the house to themselves once more, he contrived to leave for the Hall while their guests were all enjoying a late breakfast. He went round the table, shaking his sons by the hand, kissing the upturned cheeks of their wives and patting the grandchildren on their heads before climbing into his car. The dog, who had followed him to the front door, must have jumped on to the chair in the office and from there to his desk, because he saw her silhouette against the window as he drove away, and he raised a hand to wish her farewell feeling a small squeeze of regret that she would not be there when he returned in the evening.

It was nearly lunchtime when he reached Duntisbourne Hall. He regarded it as a peculiarly British phenomenon that the state rooms emptied between the hours of twelve and two o'clock when the nation was feeding.

Noel was manning the door on his own. 'Is Sam here?' BS asked.

'She was upstairs, putting the finishing touches to the exhibition. I think she may have popped off for a spot of lunch though. She often goes back to her flat.'

'Tell her, if she comes back, that I've gone up to have a look.'

'Will do.'

The exhibition of the Dywenydd Collection was complete. Amber lighting from etched glass wall sconces fell on to the original Victorian cabinets. Above them the walls were decorated with paper in the style of William Morris, deep blues and rust colours swirling up to a dark mahogany cornice. A trio of vast leather button-backed sofas formed the three sides of a square in the middle of the room, at their centre a low table set with printed brochures and books from the gift shop covering the history of Duntisbourne Hall and the collections. There was even a half-played game of chess using a set BS knew they sold in the shop. Low lamps in the corners of the room stood on tables draped with antique textiles. BS almost expected to see a humidor or a decanter of whisky and some cut-glass tumblers on a tray. The cabinets had been neatly annotated in gold lettering and he drew open one of the drawers. Beneath the glass lay objects he recognised, many of which he had used from time to time to pique his jaded libido. He had never shared these erotic adventures, but had indulged them in privacy as neatly and cleanly as he could. Any guilt he had felt in the early years soon faded – like a bad smell, breathe it long enough and you stop noticing it. Fascinated, he read the notations and marvelled at the dryness of the script, the complete lack of titillation or lubricity, and realised that Sam's scholarly descriptions robbed them of any erotic power.

He walked slowly on through the exhibition – the tavern room, the Hellfire Cave, the Beggar's Benison with a replica of the ceremonial platter next to the genuine pudenda display trays from the collection. The lighting emanated chiefly from the cabinets themselves, and as he continued his journey through the twists and turns of artificial corridors, the walls of which were packed with display cabinets, he conceded that Sam Westbrook did know her job. She had forsaken most of the SM accoutrements – the Berkley Horse, the Lithuanian Typewriter, the strappados and thumbcuffs. That showed good taste. There was a map of the pony play routes through the estate, but the sulky carts with their elaborate harnesses and whips has been banished into storage in the undercroft along with the swings and other large pieces of erotic furniture. The brass-bound buggery box had a cabinet all of its own, but it was such a wonderful piece of craftsmanship, it deserved a place in the exhibition. Sam had created a gripping visual experience and presented it as a remarkable line of social history through the ages as opposed to a prurient display of man's basest desire for ever-increasing intensities of erotic stimulation.

He heard a noise behind him and turned. It was Sam.

'I would still value your opinion,' she said.

'I'm astonished.' He continued on through the exhibition, aware that she was walking a few paces behind him, monitoring his reaction. When they returned to the gentleman's club she took a seat on one of the sofas. He sat down opposite her and gestured towards the table. 'I see retail are using it as an opportunity to sell.'

'Seemed churlish not to let them.'

'You'll be off soon?'

'I'm packing up the flat now.'

'I do like this room.'

'It could do with some more pictures.'

He looked back sharply and saw that she was not teasing him.

'Have you spoken to the earl?' he said.

'No. But he now has the list.'

'I see.' BS felt a great wave of ennui sweep through him. He was tired, so tired he had an almost irresistible urge to sink back on that comfortable sofa and sleep. The fury he had felt towards Sam seemed to have melted away leaving him feeling bruised, or perhaps he was too exhausted to summon it up again. He didn't have the energy to discuss it any further with her, and he pulled himself forward and rose stiffly to his feet, taking his weight on the arm of the sofa and the stick in his other hand. He started to make his way towards the door when she spoke again.

'I don't suppose you found anything? At home?'

He shook his head.

'Or did anything about reinstating Maureen Hindle?'

Without turning he waved a dismissive hand in her direction and began to make his way painfully down the spiral stairs.

His office was empty and he was glad. The lights and the computer were switched off and he left them that way. The confidence he had experienced walking around the village the day before had waned and he was feeling decidedly dejected. If an audience with the earl or the trustees was imminent, he wanted to get it over with. He wondered if he would lose his job and the thought worried him. This post had defined him for so many years, he couldn't imagine a life without it. He consoled himself with the thought that the same emotion had beset him when he was squeezed out of the Cathedral School, and he had survived that humiliation. What had that girl's mother said outside the court? Yesterday the cockerel, today the feather duster. He proved them wrong – he had proved everyone wrong, rising like a phoenix from the ashes and becoming archivist to The Right Honourable the Earl of Duntisbourne, the dependable public face of the Hall, the man who had the ear of the earl. He would survive this. He was the earl's man.

He stared out of the circular window that looked over the court-yard. He couldn't settle to any work and he didn't know how to fill his time – it all seemed so pointless now. He watched the visitors begin to return, sweeping out from the café in two and threes, then in groups to the left of the Hall. A large group of Chinese tourists came into the courtyard from the opposite end, their guide in front holding a bobbing yellow bird on the end of a stick. He could see the flashes of a dozen cameras firing off from the group. What did these orientals do with all the photographs they took, and why did they point up to the sky when they posed in front of a building? He sat and stared out of the window until the dropping sun tinged the base of the clouds over the lake a soft pink, and then he sat bolt upright as the ringing phone clamoured through the tiny office.

'Moreton? Get over here.'

# - 26 -

Sam was also looking out from her window over the estate. The sun was sinking down behind the Black Mountains and she thought how wild it must be on those lonely escarpments as darkness fell. She had never been a country girl, but she had been a steamy adolescent and had feasted on the writings of the Brontë sisters and Thomas Hardy, and the concept of untamed countryside thrilled her. How lonely she had felt when she first looked out over this landscape all those weeks ago, but how sad she was to be leaving.

Packing had made her hot and she had pushed the sash window open to let in some of the evening air. The sweet voice of a blackbird echoed across the estate, pure and clear, and from the trees on the other side of the Red Lake she heard the echo of another warbling a reply. She thought about the blackbird who sang each spring from the top of a plane tree which was almost level with the window of her flat in London, and she associated the sound with lightening evenings and the coming of summer. How beautiful the estate must be, she thought, when summer comes.

With a sigh she turned back to the room and stared at the boxes and newspapers spread across the table in the dining room. She gathered up her photographs and wrapped each one separately. The daffodils she had bought earlier in the week as tight buds had opened, and with regret she pushed them into the bin in the kitchen, emptied her vase, and wrapped that too. She wanted to be on the road early in the morning – she had no desire to witness the downfall of the archivist of Duntisbourne Hall. She had found BS irritating, pompous, obstructive and difficult, and yet she liked the old boy. He had great charm, he had tremendous brio, and his knowledge of the history of the Hall and the family was astonishing. She hoped that the answer to the mystery of the missing objects was nothing more than inefficiency and sloppiness and not the more sinister theory postulated by Max. Either way, the time had come for BS to move on and let younger blood take up the baton, but she regretted her part in his downfall.

Then she thought about Max. She was leaving in the morning and she hadn't told him. She had thought it would be easier, less complicated, but now she regretted her decision and the most irritating part of it was that even though she had promised to call him, she didn't have his phone number. She assumed she would see him in the Hall, but hadn't – then she had meant to ask Rosemary for it before she departed, but she had left it too late this evening, her mind distracted by the problems with BS. She probably couldn't even find her way to his cottage if she wanted to and besides, that would show a kind of desperation which wasn't the case at all.

She might not feel crazy about him, but she knew she liked him a lot and when they were together, she had that comfortable feeling that he thoroughly liked her too. This was a new experience for her. Historically she had always been attracted to the wrong kind of men, dangerous men, probably – if she were honest with herself – men who needed her help, men she could save, but by definition these were flawed men, insecure men who came to resent their dependence on her and rebel – competitive men who begrudged her success and tried to diminish her achievements. She was a little intimidated by Max – he didn't need her, he seemed happy with his life, secure and confident. She felt no vacuum in Max that needed filling and yet clearly he wanted to start a relationship with her. Someone had once asked her, 'What is the greatest turn-on? A man who says "I need you" or a man who says "I love you"?' Historically for her it had been the former. She found it hard to imagine being with a man who didn't need her but simply wanted to be with her.

There was another deeply attractive quality to Max which she had felt but not defined until the evening she took the call from her daughter when he was here, in the flat, and that was the fact that he was a committed father. No man could ever take the place of her daughter. The men she had dated who had children had all been absentee fathers and they interpreted her commitment to Claire as a criticism of their own parenting; while the ones who had no children found Claire's intervention unacceptable. Max's attitude to that difficult phone call was one of complete understanding – no need to comment, that's just the way children behave. How wonderful it would be to have a man in her life who could listen to her problems with Claire without judging her, knowing that she loved her daughter more than any living soul, but at the same time was occasionally driven mad by her.

And finally he had sent her a powerful but unspoken message – he had quit smoking. She suspected it the last evening he came to the flat and ploughed his way through several bowls of nuts and crisps, but knew it for certain when he came up to the exhibition and stood close to her. She didn't want to ask him, she didn't want to embarrass him, but she found it hard not to be flattered by it.

This was all academic now – she was on her way back to London. The exhibition had been officially handed over to the trustees and she must move on to her next project, move back to her flat, to her well-meaning friends who would ask her to dinner whenever a man in their circle was newly dumped and available. It was all so predictable. Duntisbourne Hall had never been like that. She heard a pheasant clatter out a warning in the distance and went to close the window. It was getting chilly.

It was a beautiful evening as Max made his way along the river walk with Monty who was weaving in and out of the trees to the left-hand side of the path. Since the clocks changed, Max had got into the habit of these evening walks around the estate. It helped to fill in the times when he was in danger of reaching for a cigarette, and it also made him feel closer to Sam. He could see the Jacobean balustrade along the north side of the Hall above the trees to his right and as dusk fell, he liked to imagine that the lighted window he could see glowing yellow against the darkening countryside belonged to her. A song his mother used to sing kept playing in his mind because he was feeling 'starry-eyed and vaguely discontented'. Spring was here, the evenings were lightening, all his senses seemed heightened, he felt fit and well and happy, but he was also melancholy and wistful. He had felt like this before, but not for many years, and as he could never have been described as a romantic, he resolved to enjoy the evening and the walk and not think about it too much.

Monty put up a pheasant which stumbled across the path in front of Max and with a raucous cry flapped up into the air and flew low up the bank, gliding down in a shrubbery at the top. Monty gave chase, ignoring Max's shouts for him to come back, and rushed up the sharp incline on the right towards the Hall. Max struck off the metalled path after him. Monty disappeared into a thicket of dogwood and he could see him spinning around the canes with his nose to the ground. By the time Max reached the thicket he was a bit puffed, but he didn't have that heaving, desperate feeling he usually had after a short sprint. Perhaps his lungs really were recovering from all those years of abuse.

'Monty! Come here,' he said, but Monty pressed deeper into the bushes and the pheasant fired up above his head and flew off towards the Hall. Max saw Monty's spectral shape bomb out of the other side of the shrubbery and he hurried round the bushes and followed after him, enjoying the sense of running without distress. He caught up with Monty in the staff car park because Monty had found Sam.

Sam had just balanced a box on top of the car while she searched her pocket for her car keys, when out of the darkness on the other side of the car park burst the pale shape of a small dog, panting as it ran towards her. Momentarily she leant back against the car, worried it was going to attack her, but as it neared it looked familiar and it rushed up to her wagging and pleased to see her.

'Hello, Monty,' she said. 'Where have you come from?'

She knelt down, caught him by the collar and looked around in the darkness. She thought she could hear someone running and hoped it would be Max. She had never managed to get used to the Cimmerian gloom of the estate after the sun had set: she didn't like being out after dark, she heard noises she couldn't explain, saw shapes shift in the shadows which made her heart miss a beat, felt as if someone was watching her when she locked her car at night and hurried to the foot of the staircase up to her flat.

And there he was, as familiar to her now as if she had known him for years, and yet different from the way he looked the first time she saw him, when they had stood side by side in the saloon looking up at the Golden Hand of Jerusalem. Her earlier doubts about her feelings were overridden by the deep pleasure she felt to see him standing in front of her.

'Stupid dog. He's about as obedient as my daughter,' he said, still panting slightly. 'Goodness, you're packing. When are you off?'

'Tomorrow morning. Early.'

'So soon? Weren't you going to say goodbye?'

'I was, of course I was, but I didn't have your number.' Max gave her a disbelieving look. 'I honestly didn't. I was going to drop you a line when I got back to London, send it to the Hall.'

A fox screamed, out on the estate, a screech on the edge of hysteria. Instinctively Sam released Monty and moved closer to Max. She spun round, staring out into the dark, and pressed herself to him for safety. Turning towards him, she caught his scent, fresh from the outdoor air – that hint of citrus she had smelt on his robe but without the reak of cigarettes to overwhelm it.

'You've given up smoking?' she said quietly.

'Ages ago.'

'Was that for me?'

'Of course.'

The fox shrieked out again and she folded herself into Max's arms. He lifted her chin and kissed her and he smelt wonderful. For several minutes they were lost to one another, but then she felt Max's concentration slipping. He pulled away and looked around him to left and right.

'Bull shit!' he said. 'Where the hell's Monty?' He held her away from him at arm's length, calling over her shoulder, 'Where are you? Here, boy!' Releasing her, he turned and began to walk in a circle, calling. He was now several feet away and he broke into a run in the direction the fox had called. 'Oh Jesus, Sam, I'm so sorry,' he called back to her and she watched him disappear back into the night.

## - 27 -

When Dean showed BS into the smoking room, the earl was standing in front of the fire puffing on a Dunhill International, but he was not alone. At the desk to the side of the fireplace sat Simon Keane, the chief executive, and in front of him lay a file identical to the one Sam had given to BS. Things did not look promising.

Keane was the first to speak. 'We seem to have run up against a problem,' he said. BS didn't like Keane. He was a cold fish, a tall, gangling sort of man with a dark, saturnine complexion and deep-set eyes. 'I understand you have seen this list?' BS nodded his assent. He was aware of the earl watching him. 'Can you shed any light on the whereabouts of anything here?'

'Not at present, but I have spent the weekend gathering up a number of other items that I have been working on – studying, of course. I must confess that this business has caught me rather by surprise as I was unaware, before I had the conversation with Mrs Westbrook before the weekend, that policy at the Hall had changed.'

'Policy?' said Keane.

'Well, I have always been given carte blanche to carry on with my study and research in the best way I see fit, and have enjoyed the privilege of full freedom which, over the years, I can assure you I have never abused. I am sure His Lordship will vouch for this,' BS glanced across at the earl, who did not catch his eye but stared at the tip of his cigarette. 'However, if this policy of trust is now redundant, and the trustees and yourselves feel – probably quite correctly – that an old-style gentleman's agreement in the modern world is not sufficient security, I will of course honour that, but it will take me more than a weekend to track down everything on that list. I will need to check down in the muniments room, up in my office, a few locations around the Hall, and all this will take a considerable amount of time. Oh yes, and I will also need to speak to Laurence Cooke.'

'Laurence Cooke?'

'One of our guides. He takes all the photographs for me.'

'Are you telling me,' Keane said, 'that there are valuable items on this list that are scattered all around the Hall, as well as some of them in your home and some of them in Laurence Cooke's home?'

BS didn't like the tone of his voice. 'They're perfectly safe,' he said, 'I can assure you.'

'And what sort of system do you have in place to keep track of things?'

'System?'

'Yes. Where do you log things out? How do you know who has what?'

'All up here,' BS said and tapped his middle finger on his forehead.

Keane frowned at his playful mime. 'I would have thought, if you know where it all is, a weekend is plenty of time to gather it together. It strikes me as strange that you didn't bring it into the Hall with you this morning, particularly as Sam Westbrook told you she was handing this list to us today.'

'I've had a very busy weekend.'

Keane sniffed, then turned back to the list and appeared to be rereading it. He moved on to the second page, running his finger down as he read, then looked up at BS. He was still frowning. 'You are confident that you know the whereabouts of everything on this list? Twenty-five books, eight of which are first editions? Fifteen engravings? A profane painting by Luke Sullivan in the style of Hogarth? A bronze of Leda and the swan?'

'That's definitely down in the muniments room.'

'Why?'

'I've been researching its provenance.'

'A Meissen figurine?'

'Also in the muniments room.'

Keane removed his reading glasses. 'I understand from Dean that this figurine used to be in the cabinet in the undercroft along with the other pieces of Meissen, but that it disappeared a number of years ago.'

'It didn't disappear. I took it. I was sure Dean knew that. When we opened the private apartments for tours, I felt that she was a bit – how shall I put it – racy for public viewing, so I took her out of the cabinet and down to the muniments room. I'm sure I spoke to Dean about it. I must have, or someone would have thought it had been stolen,' and BS gave a snort to underline the foolishness of the notion.

'So let me get this right. You have had an extremely rare, erotic Meissen figurine hidden down in the muniments room and no one except yourself knew?'

'Not hidden. I hadn't got round to discussing with Lord Duntis-bourne where he would like the figure displayed.'

'The private apartments opened ten years ago. That figurine has been in your possession for ten years.'

'No. Not at all. It's here, in the Hall. I can retrieve it instantly.' Keane sighed and glanced up at the earl, who flicked his ash into the fire with an irritable tap of his finger.

Keane returned to the list and appeared deep in thought. BS

shifted his weight on to his stick to relieve the pressure in his knee. He thought he was parrying the questions rather effectively, but then he saw Keane turn the final page of the file and draw out an envelope from the back of it. He recognised the laid vellum with a jolt, and mild nausea washed up into his chest as an uncomfortable feeling of weightlessness opened in the pit of his stomach. He watched as Keane drew the letter out. 'The problem is,' Keane said without looking up, 'I received a letter this morning which makes an accusation against you ...'

'For pity's sake,' BS interrupted, 'that's another of those poison pen letters, isn't it? You can't possibly take that seriously. Those letters are a pack of lies, aimed at me. We've discussed this, we've talked about this.' He stopped himself for fear it sounded as if he was gabbling, then he raised his left hand, dropped his head and slowed his speech. 'The good news, however, is that I now know who's been writing them.'

'Do you?' said Keane.

'Indeed. By analysing the speech, the content, and the intent of the writer over the many months this scurrilous campaign has lasted, I have managed to identify the perpetrator. It is one of the guides – a woman called Maureen Hindle. I'm dealing with it. I have dealt with it. It's a hoax, a vicious prank. There's no substance to anything that harridan writes.'

'In isolation I was prepared to believe you. Unfortunately, this particular letter ties in with the problem under discussion.'

'How can it?'

'It says that you have sold a number of the items on this list.'

'Sold them? That's an outrageous accusation, completely without foundation. This woman has run a campaign of fraudulent lies against me for months. This is just another one of her mad notions.'

'She's very specific.'

'Completely unsubstantiated accusations. She's making the whole thing up. I can guarantee there's no evidence of any wrong-doing on my part, whatever that virago says.'

'You don't know what she's said. I'm afraid it really is rather damning.'

'Let me see it then.'

'I don't think that'll be necessary. There are some names here.' Keane replaced his reading glasses and returned to the letter. 'A man called Strickland who ran a second-hand bookshop in Shrewsbury, and a contact he made on your behalf – a fellow called Zubriggen from Switzerland. Do either of these names mean anything to you?'

Sweat as sharp as needles pricked BS's armpits and he felt the palms of his hands tingle with a burning sensation. Simon Keane's face swam in front of his eyes as if it was coming in and going out of focus, framed by a sort of blackness that seemed to wash in from the corners of the room as if dusk had suddenly fallen outside, although he knew it was dusk when he arrived. To his left he heard the earl bark something at him and Keane was out of his seat, had him by the elbow, and he felt himself being lowered into a chair. He let go of his stick and it fell to the ground with a clatter as the silver handle dashed against a piece of furniture.

'Dean. Get this man a glass of water,' he heard the earl bellow, and moments later he felt a cool tumbler being pressed into his hand. He sipped at it and the light began to return to the room, his heart thumped with less violence, and he subsided into the back of the chair. Raising his eyes he saw Keane in front of him, kneeling; the earl had come forward too, but remained standing. This nasty turn, although unpleasant, had changed the dynamics in the room. Both men looked perturbed. Keane had an expression which could almost be described as sympathetic and the earl also showed concern, but BS didn't see much compassion in his expression, more a desire to get him out of the private apartments if he was going to be ill.

'Are you all right?' Keane asked. 'Feeling better?'

'Yes, thank you, sir. I'm not very good at standing for any length of time, after my illness.'

'Of course, of course. Thoughtless of me.' Keane sat back on his chair next to him. He seemed indecisive. 'Look, BS,' he said, 'I agree with you, in principle, about anonymous letters, but I have to follow this up. I've already got a number for this man Strickland and we'll have an answer by the end of the day, I'm certain of it. I am sure you would feel impelled to do the same in my position.' BS nodded meekly.

Finally the earl spoke. 'I simply don't understand how you have managed to make such a hash of things,' he said irritably, 'but I've got to tell you, Moreton, if you go on behaving like a damned fool, sooner or later everyone's going to start believing you are a damned fool.'

After he was dismissed, BS asked Dean if he wouldn't mind him sitting in the butler's pantry for a few minutes before leaving. 'You look like you could do with a bit of a stiffener,' Dean said. 'Can I fetch you a whisky?'

'I don't think I'd better. I've got to drive,' BS said. 'I'll just sit here in the quiet for a few minutes, and then I'll be off.'

'I've got to supervise the table,' Dean said. 'Come and find me if you need anything, but use the back stairs.'

BS sat at the table and stared down at the wooden floor. He was still feeling a bit sick, but he didn't think he was going to be sick. He checked the distance to the sink just in case. He could see the top of the wooden lining box that sat in the kitchen sink to protect delicate glasses when they were being washed by hand, the tray of detritus left from the earl's afternoon tea standing beside it. The earl's Labrador down in its kennel gave a howl – it must have heard Dean moving around upstairs and was calling to go out for its evening walk.

BS felt winded. He didn't think for a minute that they would be able to track Strickland down and even if they did, he still thought he would be able to deal with that, although with a heavy heart he was beginning to accept that his post here was in serious jeopardy. The earl wouldn't want a fuss – any interaction with the law would bring the journalists out, and the earl would move heaven and earth to prevent another scandal appearing in the *Daily Mail*. It was those names, Strickland and Zubriggen – they were his apocalypse for another reason. There was only one other person in the world who knew the names of the men he had dealings with, and it wasn't Maureen Hindle.

His gut gave a great lurch. He knew the truth and it tore him like silk. It had been in every line of those terrible letters; but to accept that they had been written by the person who had watched him and known him for forty years flayed him. Half-truths he had told down the years crowded in, a thousand spurious excuses and lies, insignificant at the time, mortified him now. Had he always judged the gravity of his misdemeanours by the severity of the punishment?

Ever since Maureen Hindle left his employ, he had been certain she was writing the letters. He had carried his certainty around with him like a talisman, moulded each piece of new evidence into his conceit, had worn his conviction smooth until it sat comfortably in his consciousness. He didn't want to let it go. He didn't want to accept that his own wife was the moving finger, and having writ, moved on to pile more dishonour and shame on to his head. He shuddered as the rest of the quote flooded back, 'Nor all thy piety nor wit shall lure it back to cancel half a line, nor all thy tears wash out a word of it.'

And why? If she hated him so much, why had she stayed? And if she wanted to stay, why had she done this to him? Then it struck him like an epiphany. What had she said? 'I thought when those letters started that you would have the good sense to stop ...' God almighty, was that her plan? And this final letter to Keane, to get him away from the Hall, and back home, was that to force his hand? Of course, it made complete sense. Why, oh why, couldn't it be Maureen Hindle?

Wearily he pushed himself up on to his feet. He was too tired to work out what to do, too depressed to do anything except go home, ignore it, see if he could live with it. Intense emotions eventually waned. He would attend Mass, confess, and gradually the magic of absolution would soothe him as it had done so many times in the past. He toyed with the idea of challenging Patricia, but felt it would be disingenuous and could lead to another horrible scene. It would be better to pretend he didn't know. And what about Maureen? Was he going to have to crawl on his belly to her? Have her back in the Hall, watching him with those kohl-black eyes? Patricia had always hated Maureen Hindle, suspected him of a liaison – the guide's downfall must have been the climax of her achievement. Perhaps he could leave things as they were on that front. Sam Westbrook was the only person who could prove he had something to do with Maureen's sacking, and she was leaving in the next few days.

Save for a sliver of brilliant sky above the tops of the Black Mountains, it was dark by the time Dean let him out through the undercroft. The air smelt of vegetation, approaching spring, and a single blackbird was calling from a high perch somewhere close by, but none of these signs cheered him. He made his way across the great courtyard, the ferrule of his stick striking the stone flags, the sound echoing around him, and as he approached the dark arch through to the car park, he heard a car door open on the other side. He stopped and listened. He heard footsteps coming in his direction, recognised the click of a female shoe, and from the archway a figure appeared swathed in dark clothing against the chill of the evening, and he knew by the way her arms clutched her coat shut, her shoulders hunched to minimise her height, that it was Maureen Hindle. She stopped several feet away.

'What do you want?' he said aware that his voice echoed around the buildings.

'I want my job back. You did it. Bunty told me you'd been interfering with the rota. You got rid of me, but I don't know what I've ever done to you to make you want to get rid of me.'

'Maureen, Maureen,' he said. Momentarily he allowed himself to see her one last time in the role he had given her, the poison-pen-letter writer. He didn't want to cast her as anything else. 'Oh Maureen,' he said, 'why couldn't it have been you? Why can't it still be you?'

His words seem to galvanise her to the spot. 'What did you say?' she breathed softly, her breath forming a cloud of vapour as it rose eerily in front of her face.

'Why couldn't it be you?'

To his horror she began to stumble towards him, and as she stretched her arms forward, her coat boiled open like the caparison of a medieval horse charging into battle. He braced himself with his stick and tried to fend her off with his free hand, but she was all over him, clinging like ivy, running her hands up and down his body, her face, wet with tears, seeking out his, her hands on his face trying to turn his lips towards hers. He caught a smell like the handkerchief drawer of an old lady – stale perfume, cloying and heavy, mixed with the scent of greasepaint coming off her skin. He was gripped by a sickening sense of doom and with sudden violence he shook her off with a groan, turned and took three paces away from her to face the wall, placed his hand on the rough stone and leant forward to avoid his shoes. His stomach gave a huge lug and he vomited and wretched and spat. He heard a squawk of misery, of disgust, and Maureen sobbing and blundering back towards the arch, the sound of her feet hurrying away, the slam of a door, the high-pitched revving of an engine and grind of a gearbox before the silence of the night closed in and he knew he was alone again. With another groan he pushed himself away from the wall and looked down at the glistening pool at his feet. Is this the final humiliation, he thought – vomiting in the great courtyard of Duntisbourne Hall?

# - 28 -

BS stood facing the wall for a few minutes until he was certain his stomach had disgorged all it could. He swallowed with difficulty, his saliva sour and burning as it crawled down the back of his throat. He longed for a draught of cold water to clean his palate. He fumbled in his pocket for a handkerchief and wiped it around his lips and beard, finally possetting into it a tart mouthful of saliva before pushing the damp fabric back into his pocket with a shudder of disgust.

He heard the clattering cry of a pheasant out on the other side of the arch and turned slowly to make sure that he was alone, that Maureen had indeed gone. He looked over towards the private apartments – the lights from the windows bathed that corner of the courtyard in a sulphur glow. As he watched, a shadow moved away from a window on the first floor and he felt an uncomfortable certainty that it was the earl, and he had witnessed his humiliation. He knew this could not be true, that it was not possible to observe a scene unfold in the darkness from a lighted room.

He heard the sound of a door opening above and footsteps descending the first flight of stairs. Fright gripped him anew – he did not want to see Sam Westbrook. Resting his hand on the wall, he navigated his way back from the archway and round into the shadow of the north wing. He heard her pass, travelling in the opposite direction towards the car park. Her footsteps were careful – she must be carrying a heavy weight, packing up to leave. He looked skyward. The clouds had sped away and uncovered a white moon which seemed to be racing in the opposite direction.

He heaved a breath of worry and frustration. His car was in the car park. He was trapped. How long would she take to pack?

He shivered. The earlier gales had moved on but the night wind, although light, was from the north-east. He could smell frost in the air, icy particles blown down the spine of the Black Mountains. He had to find shelter somewhere to wait things out until he could reach his car. Moving a few more paces along the walls of the old stable yard, he reached the door of the chapel. In the darkness he began to feel along the shaft of each key on the bunch clipped to his belt hook. As he did so he reflected that the earl and Keane could not be overly concerned with the situation. After all, they had let him keep his keys. Eventually his fingers located the quatrefoil head of a large key and, running his hand beneath the door handle, he found the keyhole with a finger, and inserted it. He used both hands to turn it in the hope that he could control the speed of the bolt and minimise the sound, but as the mechanism sprang open, the sound boomed out across the courtyard. He listened until the echo died away, and hearing no other sound he opened the door and let himself in.

The moon was shining through a window high in the wall above his head and by its light he made his way over to the pews on the left-hand side. Being a Protestant chapel, the atmosphere differed from BS's usual place of worship, but nonetheless he hoped he would be comforted to be in the presence of God. He sat down and laid his stick beside him, then shifted forward in his seat so that he could rest his elbows on the pew in front. He looked up at the monstrous sculpture in front of him, the marble rendered translucent by the light of the moon. When Jean-Baptiste Carpeaux, the French sculptor, had accepted the commission, the ninth earl was already morbidly obese and crippled with gout, but he depicted a much younger man in the sculpture, recognisable as the ninth earl only by the weakness of the chin. Everything else about him signified magnificence, intellect, discovery. Entwined around his manly leg was the figure of his second wife, Fanny, her flowing Grecian costume slipping coquettishly from her shoulder. His first wife, the poor, bullied Augusta, was depicted as the loyal wet nurse gazing up at the earl with adoring eyes as she suckled the son she could never give him. The tableau was supported by a commanding angel on either side, one about to trumpet out the fame of the earl, the other poised with quill in hand to write his history. At the foot of the sculpture peered a hideous beast from mythology, signifying envy, who looked up at the earl with begging eyes as his sarcophagus crushed her.

Where was God in this place? BS asked himself. The huge sculpture occupied most of the end wall of the chapel, dwarfing the simple altar table in front. It was impossible to worship even a Protestant God in this chapel when every eye was turned to gaze up at a man who in his own time was known as a philanderer and a pornographer – a man who had plundered the treasures of the Hall and replaced them with erotica. But as he gazed at the depiction, an uncomfortable thought came into his head. Did this travesty embody another truth? When all his secrets were laid bare, would his adoring colleagues regard his image in the same way as he regarded the statue of the ninth earl? Would they remember BS Moreton striding along the corridors of power at the right hand of the Earl of Duntisbourne? Would they remember him as a man of letters, a man of principle, a man of strong moral fibre? Or would they speculate what other secrets lay hidden behind his external persona? He had few illusions about human nature and knew how pleasing the downfall of a great man was to the English psyche.

If God was here with him now instead of this weak-chinned Georgian earl dressed like a Spartan, could he truly confess? He felt he probably could. In the past he had confided many of his misdemeanours in the confessional, but sitting here now, in this cold Protestant chapel in the moonlight, he realised that although he had confessed, he had never truly repented. Was he an adulterer? He didn't think of himself in those terms. Was he a thief? Of course not, the inner voice of habit answered, but as he lifted his eyes up towards the earl he knew his inner voice lied, and another voice filled his head and he said out loud to no one in particular, 'I am so, so sorry.' A film of moisture bathed his eyes and the statue shifted and swam until he blinked and it was still again.

As the hours passed and he became colder and colder and his limbs stiffened, BS thought of his discomfort as a type of penitence. He watched the moonlight travel across the wall of the chapel. He had abandoned the idea of making it to his car and driving home because now that he was here, paying his penance, he thought about his wife, his Judas, and imagined the misery his unexplained absence must be causing. She had been clever writing anonymous letters to herself, and also clever to leave Maureen's name out of them – the only woman who worked for him who didn't get a mention. It had helped him reach the wrong conclusion. He hoped Patricia was lying awake in their bed at home in torment. She must know that her letter had arrived, that he had been called to see the earl. Did she realise that by naming Strickland and Zubriggen she had revealed her hand to him? Perhaps she intended that to be part of his punishment, perhaps she wanted him to know she was betraying him.

He checked his watch. It was a quarter past three in the morning – she must be seriously worried about him by now. He hoped she imagined he had killed himself, that they would find his car parked down in the woods near the river walk, a pipe leading from the exhaust to the car interior – that would serve her right. No, he thought, that wouldn't work nowadays – he had heard that all new cars were fitted with a catalytic converter which eliminated ninety-nine per cent of the carbon monoxide in the exhaust. Besides, Patricia was unlikely to imagine suicide. She knew how strongly he held the Catholic opinion that life was the property of God, only God himself had dominion over life, and to take his own life would mean putting himself higher than God. Perhaps she thought he had found a safe haven with a woman, Sam Westbrook even; that at this very moment, despite his assertions that there was nothing going on between them, she was torturing herself with the thought that her betrayal had pushed him into the welcoming arms of another woman. Maybe she thought he had fled the country. He preferred that idea and played a scene out in his mind of arriving on foot at a quay in Holyhead. He could take a ferry to the Hook of Holland or over to Scandinavia, Gothenburg perhaps – he liked the sound of that.

He had no idea when he had fallen asleep, but he woke with a start, his pulse thumping in his ears, a brilliant light shining into his face. For a split-second he thought it was a torch, Pugh shining it down on him as he slept on a makeshift bed of cassocks, but the moment he rolled his head to one side he realised it was the light of the setting moon burning down on him from the windows on the opposite side of the chapel. It must be nearly dawn. He knew the time had come for him to make his way home.

Stiff and tired he exited the chapel and locked the door behind him. He heard a door shut in the distance, over towards the south wing; someone over in the private apartments was up early. Hugging the wall, he made his way towards the staff car park as stealthily as he could, pulling the car door shut instead of slamming it. He drove out and round the longer road to avoid having to pass in front of the Hall. The edge of the Black Mountains were sharp against the lightening sky, the surface of the lake dappled in patches by the breeze. He was chilled to the core and hungry too. He hoped Patricia would let him eat before they trawled through their respective confessions, but somehow he doubted it, so he decided to stop on his way home and have a bit of breakfast.

He took the road out towards Llandrindod Wells until he came upon an out-of-town superstore. The empty car park disorientated him – he couldn't make a decision about where to park and drove around in a large circle, peering from left to right, finally settling on a bay some distance from the entrance to the store. Dawn had broken and with it came a freshened breeze which rolled a soft plastic bag across the car park in front of him until it lifted it up and whipped it away at speed towards the trolley stand. The landscaped trees were full of birdsong and he could hear the occasional drone of a car on the adjacent A-road.

Once inside, the smell of coffee drew him through the empty shop towards the café and it wasn't until he peered into the display cabinets that he realised it wasn't a proper café at all, but one of those coffee house outlets. No bacon and egg breakfast for him here, he thought with a heavy heart. He scanned the menu boards on the wall watched by a sulky girl with bad skin and a pronounced overbite. Wordlessly she fetched his coffee and slouched impatiently behind the display as he tried to choose a cake. Hooking his stick over his arm, he carried his pauce breakfast away to a table at the back of the room. The coffee invigorated him, but the cake was swathed in sickly butter icing, and after taking a couple of mouthfuls he felt the queasiness return so he pushed the plate to the side and sat back. The sulky girl was picking the skin at the edge of her nail. She must have sensed he was looking at her because she stared back insolently before disappearing through a door behind the counter. He felt profoundly lonely sitting in that brightly lit shop devoid of customers, and he felt sorry. Yes, he thought, that's how I feel – extremely sorry for myself.

When he eventually rounded the corner and drove into his street, he thought he spotted a speed camera van parked ahead and checked his speedometer to make sure it hadn't crept up over thirty miles an hour, but as he neared his house, he realised it was a police car. He saw a neighbour dallying around his dustbin and watching the car as he drove towards his house, another standing at a window on the opposite side of the road with a cup of coffee in her hand. An unpleasant sensation began to grow in his belly, a flutter of anxiety, a growing unease. Were they here for him? Surely not. His interview with Keane and the earl had not been pleasant, but he hadn't got the impression that they were putting the matter into the hands of the police. That was not the way the earl did things. When it came to light a few years ago that the gatemen had been running a cash scam they all got the sack, but the earl never pressed any charges. What on earth had Strickland told them last night?

He swung his car into the drive. Another police vehicle was parked near his front door, and a constable was coming out of his house carrying a large bag, which he stowed in the back of the police van. The sound of his arrival had brought a second man to the front door and he now approached BS's car and opened the driver's door for him.

'Mr Moreton?' he said. BS nodded mutely. 'I am Detective Constable Cragg.' The officer held a warrant card out towards BS. The photograph showed a man in his twenties, slim-faced and sporting a moustache, and bore no resemblance to the heavyset man who held the door. 'Could I ask you, sir, to turn off your engine and come inside?'

'Do you mind telling me exactly what's going on?' BS said.

'Come inside please, sir.'

As he approached the house, he saw Patricia's pale face staring out of the office window. It disappeared and she was at the front door before he reached it. She was still in her dressing gown, her hair greasy and flattened down one side, her face grey with worry. He wondered how long the police had been here, how long she had been keeping her vigil at the window. An unexpected wave of sympathy for her swept through him with such vigour he felt his eyes moisten again. She looked so undignified in her night things, so unprepared, so vulnerable, that the fury he had felt towards her for putting him in this terrible situation waned. She came towards him a little unsteadily and caught hold of his arm. 'Just a minute, pet,' he said, releasing his arm from her grip so that he could remove his overcoat. He was aware that DC Cragg was waiting at the open door for him to greet his wife, and he was impressed by his sensitivity.

'They're taking things out of your office,' Patricia whispered. 'They've got a search warrant. Why are they searching our house, BS?'

BS had been prepared for her to lash out at him the moment he entered the house for subjecting her to a long night of worry, he had intended parrying her with a blast of accusations for betraying him, but her question astonished him. He leant towards her and said quietly, 'You, of all people, should know the answer to that.' Her hand flew up to cover her mouth. She really hadn't known he would guess she wrote the letters.

When Patricia heard DC Cragg say the words 'Bartholomew Moreton, I am arresting you on suspicion of theft ...' she began to cry in a way so undignified that anyone would think it was she who was about to be taken down to the station, not him, and his irritation diluted his own shock. She wailed, she pulled at one of the constables as he came down the stairs and headed for the front door with another bag. She pushed past him and spread herself across the open door to prevent him from leaving. The young officer turned to his superior for guidance, but BS kept his poise and admonished her several times until she calmed down. He then led her through to the kitchen and sat her down before turning to ask DC Cragg how long he thought they were going to be. He assured him there had been a mistake which he would be able to clear up swiftly and suggested to Patricia that now she had calmed down it would be a good idea if she popped upstairs and put some clothes on. He even offered to make tea for DC Cragg and the constables, but they refused the offer.

Once out in the street with the officers he talked at them with cheerful banter, ignoring the confused look on the Detective Constable's face. He even laughed agreeably for the neighbours to see, hoping they would assume he was helping the police with some crime that had been committed at the Hall – which, of course, he was. He felt confident that he wouldn't face a custodial sentence, not at his age, not on a first offence, but Patricia's frantic behaviour, the fear in her eyes, the clutching at his sleeve as he left the house, told him she thought otherwise. Her plan had backfired horribly and although he knew it was a base thought, her pain and distress was a fitting punishment for her betrayal and it gave him exquisite pleasure.

# - 29 -

Max arrived at the lake just after three and found the key underneath the life jackets. He was glad the owner didn't want to meet him on his arrival. Before letting himself into the log cabin he strolled on to the veranda and gazed out across the water. In the distance he could make out the ridge of another lodge behind the island to his left, but apart from that there were no signs of human habitation. A tern, neat and angular, plopped on to the surface of the water in front of him, making a shoal of small fry dimple the surface. The sun pierced the water and Max could see the fish gliding through the forest of weed anchored in the gravel. He took a deep breath and smiled to himself. He had made an excellent choice.

He let himself in. The building was constructed of pine, which scented the air inside. He didn't really know Sam's taste, but he was sure she would not be disappointed. Two burgundy sofas were drawn up next to the log burner off the kitchen, the Welsh dresser was stocked with books. He opened a door into the bedroom and felt a tremor of excitement when he saw the crisp sheets on the double bed. He sat down on the edge and looked out of the window across the lake again. He couldn't believe his luck. He had chosen it because it was called Monty's Retreat, and it was perfect.

Monty. He was still in the car. Max went round to the front of the lodge. Monty stared out at him.

'Sorry, old chap' he said, clipping the lead on to the dog's collar. Monty bounded out, raised his leg against a clump of grass and rushed off towards the thick undergrowth until the lead reached the end of the reel. 'Smell rabbits, eh?' Max said, coaxing the dog back round towards the lake. Monty rushed ahead down the steps to the lower pontoon and barked at the ducks bobbing in the water. They ignored him. Max tied the lead to the railings and left Monty pacing up and down the pontoon while he unpacked the car.

He went into the bathroom and began to lay out the contents of his soap bag. Then he paused. It seemed inappropriately intimate to put his toothbrush and shaving equipment in a shared bathroom. Shared – he spun round – there was one loo, and it was in here, the only bathroom. Always a problem early on in a relationship when it is important to imagine your goddess devoid of human frailty and function. He caught sight of himself in the mirror over the basin and smiled, turning sideway to inspect his stomach and sucking it in to counteract the extra pounds he had gained since he quit smoking. However many years had it been since he last felt like this? He finished unpacking his soap bag and marked his territory, leaving the table to the side of the basin free for Sam's toiletries.

His next job was filling the fridge. He had brought smoked salmon, cheese and bread. He had found four lobster tails in Waitrose which cost a fortune, and he planned to cook these for Sam on the open barbecue and serve them with lemon and mayonnaise for dinner with the bread, followed by strawberries and clotted cream and a bottle of pink champagne. He worried that pink champagne was trashy, and put a bottle of sauvignon into the fridge as well. The pink champagne could come out with the strawberries – that seemed more sophisticated. He uncorked a bottle of red wine too to let it breathe, in case Sam wanted some with her cheese. He had no appetite at all at the moment and recognised this feeling as excitement, so to calm his nerves poured himself a glass of beer and went out on to the veranda to watch the lake. A pyramid of gnats, backlit by the sun, tumbled over the reeds.

It had been an extraordinary few months, the Hall bubbling with speculation and gossip. It seemed inconceivable that poor old BS would get a custodial sentence, but it was rumoured that the insurance value of the stuff missing was reaching the million pound mark, cunning old fox. This could just be gross exaggeration, but if it was true, Max thought, the poor old boy really would go down. How would he cope with jail? he wondered. Max was sure he would spend his sentence in some sort of open prison but that's not where he would start. He was still going to have to face the humiliation and loss of control that comes to any prisoner, however gentlemanly his crime.

He checked his watch. It was four thirty, an hour and a half before Sam was due to arrive. He set aside his worries about the archivist and instead focused on the coming weekend. He still couldn't believe his luck. Here he was, on a still June afternoon, looking out over the flat calm of the lake which was occasionally disturbed by a grebe surfacing or the lazy roll of a fish just below the surface. She had said yes. He had said, 'I've taken a lodge, on a lake. It's going to be lovely weather this weekend. Why don't you come?' And she had said yes.

A dreadful thought struck him. Had he assumed too much? Would she peer into the double bedroom, then open the door of the other room and be horrified that the bed in there wasn't made up for her? Ridiculous. Of course she wouldn't. They had, after all, shared a chaste kiss. He shot Monty a disagreeable look. By the time Max had returned with Monty that night they were both muddy and exhausted and the moment had passed. Although he was furious with him, he couldn't bring himself to physically punish his dog, but his retribution was that he didn't trust him off the lead any more, particularly out here where he could hear wildlife scurrying and scratching, plopping and flapping all around the lodge. Sam had, however, agreed to meet again. Max had found a symposium to attend in London and they had lunched together. It was clear to both of them that they were getting close. They spoke regularly on the phone in the evenings and some of the conversation invariably involved flirting. She wasn't an innocent young thing. She knew what a weekend away together in a lodge entailed. And she had said yes. He must relax. The beer was helping him to relax.

'Come on, Monty,' he said, 'let's recce,' and, without bothering to lock up, he set off along the path through the woods with Monty heaving ahead on the end of the lead as if he was pulling a tractor tyre behind him. Rabbits hopped off the path and into the undergrowth, but Monty missed them – he was peering into the bushes on the other side of the track. Max walked on until he saw another lodge hidden among the trees across the lake but he didn't want to meet anyone else, he turned round and headed back, planning to get the barbecue lit early so that it was at a perfect cooking temperature by seven that evening. He checked his phone to make sure he hadn't missed a call from Sam, and carried an armful of logs round from the front of the house as he passed.

The barbecue pleased him. It was a half oil drum, rusted and buckled, serviceable and unpretentious. He tied Monty up again on a long leash and built a pyramid of charcoal over rolled-up newspaper. Once the paper was burning, he stacked pine logs on to the pyramid and stepped back as the resinous smoke billowed up and out over the lake. The logs spat and crackled. He poured himself another beer and checked his watch. Less than an hour now. She'd already be on her way.

Monty was trying to squeeze himself between the steps down to the pontoon, his chest flat on the ground, front legs splayed, haunches raised. He barked and shot out backwards, stumbling down the steps. Max guessed there was a duck underneath the pontoon. He checked his watch again – twelve minutes had passed. This was a beautiful place to be, but did time really have to pass so slowly? He checked the barbecue again, stirred the logs around with a leather glove he had found next to the wood burner, and went into the kitchen to fetch another beer. He wished he hadn't quit smoking. He would love to have a cigarette now – he could hear the crackle it would make as he inhaled, see himself blowing out a perfect plume of smoke into the evening sky. He watched the ducks spooning their beaks along the surface of the lake and remembered a story his father had told him about the war when he was surgeon out in the Middle East: he had thought a tent in the desert was full of ducks, could hear their watery nibbling, but when he looked in, it was full of soldiers with their broken jaws wired, pumping their cheeks to push puréed food through their clenched teeth.

Stop! Now! Why must his imagination end up careening along some path of distress and despair, today of all days, when Sam Westbrook – beautiful, cultured, unattainable Sam Westbrook – was at this very minute driving from London across to the Cotswolds to meet him here, at Monty's Retreat? An evening stillness had calmed the lake, and he must calm down too or this was going to be a catastrophe.

His mobile phone rang. It was in the kitchen. He put his beer down, it spilled. He bounded up the steps into the lodge, tripping on the top step – it was higher than the others – and in the split-second it took him to raise the phone to his ear, he saw that the caller was Sam.

'Darling,' he said, 'I'll come and open the gate. It's the single gate, second in the lane. I won't be a minute,' and breathlessly, the phone still clamped to his ear, he ran down the steps, sashayed around Monty who was barking and jumping up, and was in the lane and running through the woods to the gate.

'Max!' her voice said.

'Yes, it's me.'

'Max, listen, please.' He stopped in the middle of the lane. A rabbit loped off in front of him. She was whispering – not actually whispering, but her voice was soft and sounded strange.

'What's the matter?' he said. He felt alarmed, something was wrong. Had she wrapped her little Mazda round an oil tanker?

'Max, I'm so, so sorry.' Cold concrete poured into his lower gut.

'Are you all right?'

'Yes, yes, I'm fine. But Claire ...'

'Claire?'

'My daughter ...'

'Of course, I'm sorry.'

'She's arrived.'

'From New York?'

'Yes. From New York. She's left her husband. She's here now.'

'You're still in London?'

'Of course. She turned up a few hours ago. I couldn't get to the phone any earlier, she's in such a state.' In the distance he could hear Monty barking. 'I'm really, really sorry. I so wanted ...' Max knew he should say something, but he couldn't imagine what. 'You do understand, don't you?'

He realised he had turned and was heading back towards the lodge and Monty. He remembered Charlotte when her heart was broken, when all she wanted was to curl up at home with her dad and feel sorry for herself, and all that was expected of him was to be there. Of course he understood, but it didn't make it any easier. The smell of the wood-smoke came through the stillness of the evening and he knew he couldn't manage all four lobster tails himself. Perhaps Monty would like a couple of them. He wasn't sure about the food, but he knew he could manage the red wine, and the sauvignon, and the pink champagne all on his own.

'Of course I understand,' he said. 'I've been there myself. Nothing's more important than family.'

# Acknowledgements

The creation of the world of Duntisbourne Hall would not have been possible without both the direct and indirect help and influence of the friends and colleagues with whom I work in one of the major stately homes of England, but I owe a far greater debt to my husband Chris, who has shown infinite patience throughout the plotting of this story and glittering imagination in the creation of many of the more ridiculous ideas in this book. I would also like to thank Adrian Lewis who created the Welsh mottos for the Earls of Duntisbourne, Chief Inspector Mick Vance for making sure that the arrest scene wasn't solely sourced from television drama and Margaret Histed, my excellent editor. And I must thank other members of the family who have individually contributed to the project: my son Sam, who wrote the music for the original website about the Hall; my other son Ben who read several earlier drafts and has given me invaluable advice about the craft of writing; and my daughter Katie, whose faith in my ability to succeed has never wavered.

www.lpfergusson.com